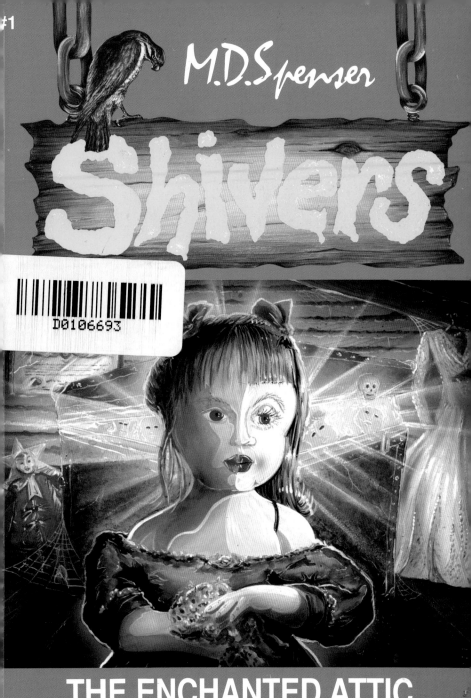

#1

M.D.Spenser

Shivers

THE ENCHANTED ATTIC

DO YOU ENJOY BEING FRIGHTENED?

WOULD YOU RATHER HAVE
NIGHTMARES
INSTEAD OF SWEET DREAMS?

ARE YOU HAPPY ONLY WHEN
SHAKING WITH FEAR?

CONGRATULATIONS ! ! ! !

YOU'VE MADE A WISE CHOICE.

THIS BOOK IS THE DOORWAY
TO ALL THAT MAY FRIGHTEN YOU.

GET READY FOR

COLD, CLAMMY SHIVERS
RUNNING UP AND DOWN YOUR SPINE!

NOW, OPEN THE DOOR—
IF YOU DARE ! ! ! !

Shivers

THE ENCHANTED ATTIC

M. D. Spenser

Paradise Press, Inc.

Plantation, Florida

To Jaime and Jennifer

Copyright © 1996 by M.D. Spenser. All rights reserved.

Published by Paradise Press, Inc. by arrangement with River Publishing, Inc. All right, title and interest to the "SHIVERS" logo and design are owned by River Publishing, Inc. No portion of the "SHIVERS" logo and design may be reproduced in part or whole without prior written permission from River Publishing, Inc. An application for a registered trademark of the "SHIVERS" logo and design is pending with the Federal Patent and Trademark office.

ISBN 1-57657-045-2

EXCLUSIVE DISTRIBUTION BY PARADISE PRESS, INC.

Cover Design by George Paturzo
Cover Illustration by Eddie Roseboom

Printed in the U.S.A.
30572

<u>Chapter One</u>

Nicole pulled the covers up to her nose. Only her eyes peeped out, big and round and frightened.

She did not like this house at all.

It was her first night here. Forget about the bed being lumpy. That she could live with. But this house came with strange noises.

There seemed to be a scurrying sound coming from her ceiling. Maybe it was rats, she thought, and shivered. Beneath her, the floorboards creaked, even when no one walked on them. The wind rattled her windowpanes. Outside, the trees moaned in the breeze.

There's nothing wrong, Nicole told herself. These noises don't mean a thing. It's just me being a scaredy-cat again. As usual.

Nicole was 11, and she didn't much like new things. They made her uncomfortable. She loved to read, but she read the same books over and over. She loved music, but she listened to the same songs again and again. In fact, one of the things that had made her saddest about moving was having to leave behind her favorite radio station.

She liked familiar things. Here, in a new house in a new state, nothing was familiar.

Nicole closed her eyes and tried to sleep. She might as well have tried to fly to the moon. The rats, or whatever it was, scratched in the ceiling. The windows rattled. The trees moaned.

She opened her eyes again. The moon was full. The shadows of tree limbs danced crazily on the wall. Nicole pulled the blankets even closer to her nose.

It was her father's fault that she couldn't sleep, she thought to herself. He was the reason they'd had to move. They'd had a nice, familiar house in Virginia. It didn't scratch and creak — or if it did have noises, she knew what they were, and they didn't bother her.

But then her father had announced he was taking a job at a newspaper in Boston. He said it with a big smile on his face, as if it was good news. Sure. Uprooting the whole family, and making everybody leave behind their best friends and favorite radio stations was good news.

All for some dumb job. At a bigger newspaper.

Like that really mattered to the rest of the family.

And then, with an even bigger smile, he had announced he'd bought a house way off in the woods that was a hundred and fifty years old. The way he grinned, you would have thought he'd just won the lottery or something.

Nicole sure didn't feel that way. She was not fond of the woods, to put it mildly. And she had liked the house in Virginia, which was new. It had nice white countertops and a microwave and wall-to-wall carpeting and faucets that worked.

When you turned on the faucets in this house, you got hot and cold running rust.

She thought sadly of that morning, when the whole family, all four of them, had pulled into the new house. They had driven for what seemed like an hour and a half over a bumpy dirt road through a forest. There sure weren't going to be a lot of neighbors, Nicole thought. Not a lot of other kids to play with, either.

Nicole realized she'd probably get stuck playing with her little sister, Casey, a lot, which was not an attractive prospect. Casey was OK, but she was pretty tricky for a seven year old. She liked to torment Nicole — by pinching her, or refusing to leave her room, or grabbing one of her toys.

Then when Nicole yelled at her, Casey would cry. Their parents would barge in and yell at Nicole every time, even though Casey had started it.

And Casey would slink off with a smirk on her face, thinking how clever she had been.

· It drove Nicole crazy. Her mother and father never understood.

"You're older, so we expect more of you," her mother would say.

Great. That was a lot of help.

After jouncing along the dirt road forever, in and out of potholes, their father turned the car off onto an even smaller road. Actually, calling it a road was generous, Nicole though. It was really two ruts in the dirt with grass growing in the middle.

"Oh, Daddy, this is going to be neat!" said Casey. That was just like her. Thinking stupid stuff was neat, and trying to kiss up to Dad. This wasn't going to be neat at all, Nicole though. Not even a little bit.

"Don't you think it's going to be neat," Casey said to Nicole.

"No," said Nicole. She crossed her arms, pouted, and stared out the window, with her back to her little sister.

"That's no way to approach a new experience," their father said from the front seat. "This is going to be fun."

"Nicole," their mother said, "I am *not* going to have you pouting all over the house. Now shape up. You're old enough for us to expect more from you. Look at the way Casey is approaching it. Now get that look off your face."

Casey had done it again. She'd made herself look good and gotten Nicole in trouble with her parents.

Nicole snuck a peek over her shoulder at Casey. She was sitting there with that little smirk of triumph on her face. Nicole felt madder than ever.

People always said Casey and Nicole looked alike, but Nicole didn't think so. They both had blond hair, true, but Casey's was shorter and lighter. Nicole wore hers in a long sandy blond braid. And Nicole wore glasses, maybe because she read so much. And even if they did look alike, she thought, they sure were different inside.

Their father turned the car into a little driveway.

"Ta-da!" he said.

The house loomed in a dark clearing shadowed

on all sides by tall trees. It had all kinds of spires and turrets. The roof went in about eighteen different directions. Windows stuck out of it weirdly.

The porch was uneven, tilting and curving. A wooden porch swing rocked back and forth with no one in it. Probably the wind.

Behind the house on one side stood a ramshackle shed. Behind it on the other side, gravestones stuck out of the ground at crazy angles.

For a moment, everyone sat in the car staring up at the house.

"Cool!" said Casey.

Nicole scowled at Casey. Their mother shot Nicole a look.

Now, lying in her bed, Nicole's mood remained as dark as ever. She was as mad as she could be. And more than that, she had to admit, she was scared. This house made so many different noises she couldn't tell them apart. They just blended into one big symphony of the weird.

Nicole realized there was no way she was going to sleep. At least not alone.

Until a couple of years ago, whenever she got scared she had taken her blanket and pillow into her parents' room and slept on the floor. But she had given that up. And, now that she was eleven, she was determined not to start again. Especially since she was so mad at them.

Besides, they slept downstairs at the back of the house. That would be a long walk through a dark, unfamiliar house.

Nicole got out of bed and crept down the hall. She wanted to see if Casey was awake.

The floorboards squeaked. She stopped. She thought she heard scuffling noises in the ceiling again, noises that reminded her of a hamster trying to scratch its way of its cage.

She took a deep breath, ignored the noises, and walked toward Casey's room.

The door was open. Casey lay on her back, bathed in the moonlight. Her arms were splayed wide. Her head was tilted back at an odd angle. She was snoring a little, seven-year-old snore.

Fat lot of help she was, Nicole thought.

She returned to her room, got into bed, and pulled the covers up over her head. She had to stop being a scaredy-cat, she told herself. Her parents were right. She was old enough to expect more from herself.

She closed her eyes, determined to will herself

to sleep.

With the covers over her head, she analyzed each noise. The one in the ceiling was the rats — or, more probably, mice, she decided. The rattling was the window panes in the breeze. The moaning noise was tree trunks swaying in the wind.

And that creaking was ... was ... something she didn't recognize.

She listened more closely.

Creak.

Silence.

Nicole held her breath.

Creak.

Silence.

Creak.

Silence.

Creak.

The noise was getting nearer. Each creak was a little louder than the one before.

Nicole opened her eyes wide under the covers.

Creak.

Silence.

Creak!

Nearer and nearer.

Creak!

8

Nicole's heart leapt into her throat. For now she had no doubt that someone — or some*thing* — was actually in her room. And coming closer every moment.

Chapter Two

Nicole sat bolt upright and clutched the blanket to her chest.

The moon had gone behind a cloud. Her room was dark.

Creak!

She strained her eyes trying to see.

Creak!

Then she heard a voice. It spoke her name.

"Nicole? Are you awake?"

It was Casey.

"You jerk," Nicole hissed. "You scared me half to death. Why didn't you say something?"

"I just did," Casey said. "And I'm going to tell Mom you called me a jerk."

"What are you doing here?"

"I got scared," Casey said. "I thought I heard something in my room."

"That was me, you bonehead."

"What were you doing in my room?" Casey asked.

"I got scared, too," Nicole said. "This house is weird. Too many noises. Now get in bed with me. And don't tell Mom I called you a bonehead. Sorry, cross my heart and hope to die, and if you tell I'll make you cry."

Casey climbed into the bed. Cuddled together, the two sisters slept peacefully the rest of the night.

*   *   *

The old house didn't seem so spooky the next morning. The day was bright. A shaft of sunlight poured into the center of the clearing.

It was December. Despite the sunlight, the air was cold — and it was even colder inside the house than it was outside. Dad was clanking around in the basement trying to find the heat.

He had said the house was a "fixer-upper." To Nicole, that meant it was a broken-downer. She longed for the white countertops and working faucets and drinkable water of the house they'd left behind. No way was she going to brush her teeth with rust. And she longed, too, for heat that actually worked.

11

This house had been unoccupied for a while, Dad said. But he claimed it had a fascinating past. Some interesting people had lived in it, from before the Civil War onward, he said.

"You're going to love it, Nicole," he said. "You know how much you like history."

"Dad," Nicole replied. "I like history in books. I prefer not to live in it."

Casey announced she was going outside to explore. Nicole wasn't much of an explorer, but she went outside, too. In the morning light, she could see that the gray paint was peeling off the sides of the old house. The porch was missing some boards. The roof was missing some shingles.

The house gave Nicole a spooky feeling. She shivered, and wrapped her arms around herself to keep warm.

Casey said she was going to explore down the road a little.

"Keep walking for about three days," Nicole said, "and you might get to a neighbor's house."

Nicole went back inside. For the first time, she began to really look around the house. The day before, she'd been too busy hauling her suitcases up to her room, unpacking, and hanging clothes in the closet.

12

Her mother always insisted that Nicole unpack right way. As if there was some incredible urgency. As if they weren't going to be living in this creepy old house for the rest of their lives.

Which, by the way were ruined. All because of her father's stupid job.

A layer of dust covered everything in the house. The floors, the counter-tops, even the toilet seats. As Nicole walked through the house, she left clean footprints on the dusty wooden floors.

The kitchen was sunny enough. A wood stove was connected to the chimney by a black pipe. Nicole's mother was scrubbing out the sinks, which had been full of spider webs. She didn't look as happy as she had the day before. She was scrubbing madly, and looking very red in the face.

Nicole wanted to tell her mother that it sounded as if there were mice in the ceiling. But she took one look at her mother's face and decided now was not the time.

She went out the back door of the kitchen and found herself in an enormous study. The room was very dark. Thick red velvet curtains shaded the windows, blocking out the light.

A huge dark mahogany desk dominated the

room. The walls were lined with bookshelves, also made of dark wood. They stretched from floor to ceiling. A ladder leaned against them to allow someone to reach books that would otherwise be too high.

And every shelf was filled with books. There were hundreds of them — maybe thousands.

Nicole's heart beat a little faster. Maybe this wouldn't be such a bad place to live, after all. She loved books. Let her little sister skip off down the road on her grand adventures. Nicole preferred to sit inside and read. That was her kind of adventure — exciting, yet safe.

She moved closer to examine the books. Most were bound in leather, with gold lettering. Here and there, strands of cobweb clung to the covers. Nicole brushed them away.

She read some of the titles. There were novels by famous writers — Charles Dickens and George Eliot and Mark Twain. Many others were by people whose names she did not recognize.

She moved to another shelf, and found books about the ancient Greeks and Romans. Nearby were atlases, with maps of all parts of the world.

Nicole's eyes moved upward. Above her head, she saw a row of books about the Civil War. Now, that interested her.

She had read about Harriet Tubman, an escaped slave who then helped other slaves flee to the north. And her father had told her that they had an ancestor who had fought for the Union. He had been captured by the Confederates, and taken to the prison camp in Andersonville, Georgia, where he died.

Nicole moved the ladder and climbed up to the Civil War shelf. She reached for a book called *Great Battles in the War Between the States.*

It wouldn't come off the shelf. It was stuck fast.

Boy, Nicole thought, this book has been here a long time. She grabbed it and tugged harder.

The book still would not come loose.

Nicole pulled a little harder — but carefully, too. She didn't want the book to jerk loose all of a sudden, sending her sprawling backwards off the ladder.

Slowly, the book started to come out.

But then, with a start, Nicole realized that it wasn't just the book that was coming loose. It was a whole section of the bookshelf. Not to mention a whole section of the wall.

She kept pulling. Slowly, with an awful creaking noise, the top half of the bookshelf swung away.

Behind it, Nicole saw a tunnel. It was dark as night in there, and it smelled of mildew.

Where it led, Nicole had no idea. But she was not about to find out. She thought she heard coming from the tunnel the faint sounds of scuffling feet.

Those mice again, probably, she thought.

But, just for a moment, she could have sworn she heard a sound of voices. They sounded muffled, as if coming from under a blanket or inside a box.

She swung the bookshelf back into place as fast as she could. When it was closed, she leaned against it, panting with fear, her heart beating in her throat.

Get a grip, she told herself. Mice don't talk. Therefore, there had not been any voices. There could not have been. It was just her imagination.

But as she leaned there catching her breath, with her head pressed against the bookshelf, her heart almost stopped.

There they were again. Voices.

Chapter Three

Slowly, Nicole climbed down the ladder. Her knees were shaking. Her stomach felt queasy. Her heart had started beating again — fast.

She took three deep breaths. That didn't work, so she took three more.

Calm down, she told herself. The first thing to realize was that there were no voices. None. Period.

There could not have been. Mice don't talk. And the house was definitely not haunted. Because there's no such thing as haunted houses.

It was her imagination. Her parents always told her she had an over-active imagination. Boy, were they ever right about that!

She collected herself, took one more deep breath and walked out of the room.

Her mother was still scrubbing the sinks in the kitchen. Her face was redder than ever. Beads of sweat were running down her forehead. Under her breath, she was muttering words that Nicole assumed she was not supposed to hear.

Nicole could see that this was still not the time to tell her about mice. Especially mice with voices.

Besides, Nicole wasn't so sure what she wanted to tell her parents right now. She wanted the mice exterminated. But it might be fun to have a secret passageway her parents knew nothing about. She would keep that to herself for a while.

Clearly, this passageway had to be explored. Clearly, this was an adventure waiting to happen.

Clearly, this was a job for Casey.

*   *   *

Casey was nowhere to be found.

Nicole walked completely around the house. There was no sign of her sister.

If her sister were smart, Nicole thought, she would play within sight of the house rather than wander off into the forest where she was likely to get eaten by bears or whatever else lived here.

Well, that was her business, Nicole decided. She would stay near the house and have an adventure that was safe. An adventure that wasn't, well, adventurous.

She had decided that she had imagined the voices. And she knew why.

Too many books.

Her father always told her that books stimulated her imagination. Apparently so. Nicole decided she would read fewer books from now on. A lot fewer.

Rather than follow Casey down the road and into the bears' den or the hornets' nest or whatever other trouble she had gotten into, Nicole decided to have a look around the clearing.

She looked up at the house, with its crazy roof and weird windows. Whoever built this house was strange, she thought. Demented, even.

She looked around the clearing, and her eyes fell upon the graveyard. It was the family graveyard, no doubt. Who else would be buried here, so far from civilization?

Maybe even the weirdo who built this house was buried there.

Nicole wondered what his gravestone would say. Maybe, "Here lies Joe Shmoe, 1742-1805. Boy, he was a weird one."

She walked over to have a look.

She was a timid person, but she had always enjoyed graveyards. When she was younger, her father used to drive her to a graveyard in Virginia every Sunday so they could feed the ducks.

Of course, that was a very different sort of graveyard. That one was spread over acres of rolling hills covered with neatly mowed grass. The graves were all decorated with silk flowers. In springtime, the blossoming trees made it one of the prettiest places around.

Here there were no silk flowers. There was no neatly mowed grass, only an overgrowth of weeds. There weren't hundreds of gravestones, only twenty or thirty.

And they weren't even straight. They stuck up from the ground at odd angles, one leaning to the left, another to the right.

A couple had fallen over and seemed to be sinking into the ground. The older ones had moss growing on them. The names and dates were hard to read.

Nicole felt excited. Graveyards were like history books, in a way. They were about real people. It was fun to read the markers and try to guess what you could about the people buried underneath.

You could see if the husband or the wife lived longer. She had seen one set of graves where a woman had outlived her first husband, remarried, and had herself buried with one husband on either side of her.

Nicole kneeled down and brushed the weeds away from one of the stones.

"James Fowler, 1899-1918," the marker read. "His memory will be with us always."

He died when he was only nineteen, Nicole thought. Probably some kind of illness. Doctors weren't too skillful in the old days.

She looked at another stone.

"William Fowler, 1849-1865," it said. "His memory will be with us always."

This family wasn't too original in thinking up epitaphs, Nicole thought to herself. And family members seemed to have a habit of dying young.

Suddenly, a cloud blotted out the sun. The clearing was plunged into shadow. The trees, their branches black and bare, seemed to lean in toward the clearing.

Nicole felt nervous.

Out of the corner of her eye, she saw an area of gravestones smaller than the rest. These must be the graves of children — not sixteen-year-olds or nineteen-year-olds, like William and James.

Little children.

She felt afraid. Fear gripped her heart like a cold hand.

Where was Casey? Why wasn't she back yet? She'd been gone for hours.

Nicole leapt to her feet and ran toward the road.

"Casey!" she yelled. "Casey!"

She sprinted down the road, nearly tripping in the rutted tire tracks, feeling desperately that something was wrong.

"Casey! Casey!"

There was no reply.

<u>Chapter Four</u>

Nicole panicked.

She didn't know whether to keep running down the road looking for her sister or stay close to home so she wouldn't get lost herself.

Even in her fear, it struck her as odd that, already, the idea of staying near that weird old house had become comforting. But she didn't want to lose her way in the woods.

Getting lost in the suburbs was one thing. You could always ask a policeman or a store clerk for help.

But who was she supposed to ask for help if she got lost here? The local moose?

She stopped running. She peered down the road. There was no sign of her sister. She turned and looked back. She couldn't see the house any more. It had disappeared behind the trees.

She stood for a moment, panting. She knew in her gut that something was wrong. Something bad had happened to her sister. Casey was just seven years old, and she must have been gone two hours by now. That wasn't right.

But Nicole decided she wouldn't help anything by getting lost herself. She had to go get her parents, who were undoubtedly blissfully unaware that one of their children was in trouble.

Nicole began to trudge back up the road toward the house.

Then she heard someone yelling.

"Hey! Wait up!"

It was Casey. She was coming up the road, shouting and waving, and pointing at something in her hand. She had dirt on her knees, mud on her hands, and a smile on her face.

"Look what I found," she said breathlessly when she caught up. She held out her hand. "This really cool bug."

OK, Nicole thought, sometimes my gut lies. There was nothing wrong with Casey. Except her brain.

After the really cool bug, Casey showed Nicole two really cool snails and about 15 really cool rocks.

"Great," said Nicole. "Really cool."

Nicole said it in a tired and sarcastic voice, but

Casey didn't get it. She puffed out her chest proudly and explained that she had found a stream. From the looks of her, she had explored it thoroughly. Right up to her elbows.

Nicole rolled her eyes, embarrassed by having been so worried, and a little mad about it, too. Then she remembered that she had more important things to do than to be mad.

She told Casey about the secret passageway.

"Cool!" Casey said. "I'll explore it!"

You know, Nicole said to herself, sometimes people with damaged brains come in handy.

Chapter Five

Casey climbed the ladder first. Nicole stayed on the floor, giving instructions.

"Pull on that book," she said. "No, that thick one over there."

Casey pulled. Nothing happened.

She pulled harder. Still nothing.

No matter how hard she pulled, the bookcase would not swing open.

"Nicole," she said. "You lied, just to get me to come back in the house."

"I did not!" Nicole said angrily. From the tone of her voice, Casey knew she meant it.

Casey could be very determined when she wanted to be. Now was one of those times. A look of total concentration took over her face. She grabbed the book with both hands, leaned back as far as she could, and yanked.

"Stop!" Nicole hissed as loud as she could

without attracting her parents' attention. "If the wall comes open, you'll fall backward off the ladder, hit your head, and my whole day will be ruined. What, are you stupid?"

This remark made Casey mad. Her eyebrows came down over her eyes. Her bottom lip stuck out. Even up on the ladder, she tried to hunch her shoulders and cross her arms. She got so involved in acting mad she let go of the ladder and almost fell off.

She stomped down the ladder and announced she was going to tell their mother. But she only walked three steps away, and there she stood with her back to Nicole and her arms crossed.

It was obvious she was mad. But it was equally obvious she didn't really want to go tell their mother and ruin their secret.

She had been excited when Nicole told her about the passageway. She had been more excited still about the idea of keeping it as their secret place.

Before coming into the house, the two girls had retrieved the flashlight from the glove compartment of the car. They shut the car door as quietly as they could. It didn't close all the way. The dome light was still on inside the car, and Nicole got the door shut all the way by whacking it with her butt.

They wanted to get into the study without attracting their parents' attention so they would be free to explore the secret passage way.

They crept stealthily across the yard.

Nicole, by far the taller, peered in through a window. Their mother was still cleaning the kitchen. Going in that way certainly wouldn't work.

Nicole signaled that they should go around the back of the house. She bent over at the waist so she wouldn't be seen through the windows.

Casey bent over, too, even though there was no need. She wouldn't be seen through the windows even if she walked on stilts, Nicole thought.

There was a door on the far side of the house. Nicole hoped it would get them into the house near the other end of the study.

There was no way of knowing, however. The door had no windows. And no one in the family had used that door yet — which meant that probably no one had used it in the last 20 years, or however long it was that the house had been unoccupied.

Gently, quietly, Nicole turned the knob.

The door wouldn't open. It was rusted shut or something.

Casey put her shoulder against it and pushed.

The door was stuck fast.

Nicole put her shoulder against it and pushed. The door groaned a little under her weight, but would not give.

Then both girls put their shoulders against the door, grit their teeth, and, on the count of three, pushed with all their might — and the door flew open and the two of them flew into the house and landed in a heap.

From under the floor came a loud voice.

"What the heck's going on up there?"

It was their father, still clanking around in the basement trying to figure out how to work the heat or the water or whatever.

"Uh, nothing, Daddy!" Nicole called out.

The girls found themselves in the middle of what looked like a coat room. An ancient coat rack stood in the corner. On one of its metal arms hung an old, faded army hat. Moths had eaten holes in the cloth.

As they looked, the hat disintegrated, falling off the rack and fluttering to the ground.

Casey gasped and turned white. She grabbed Nicole's arm.

At first, Nicole said nothing. She simply stared

at the hat, now nothing more than dusty bits of cloth in a pile on the floor.

Finally, she caught her breath.

"Vibrations," she said, slowly. "I think it was a very old hat and was just ready to fall apart. When we burst in through the door, that was all it needed."

That answer seemed to satisfy Casey.

"I *like* this house," she said.

Nicole rolled her eyes. This house, roller coasters — Casey liked everything dangerous and un-settling and stupid.

Including, luckily, dark passageways.

The girls scrambled to their feet and looked around.

Nicole pointed through an open doorway. There was study, with its wall-to-floor bookcases.

Casting a last glance at the tattered hat on the floor, the girls had headed into the study, with Casey leaving muddy footprints all the way.

But now Casey was mad — arms crossed, back hunched, eyebrows scrunched down over her eyes — refusing to talk to Nicole.

Nicole walked over to her. She apologized for calling her stupid and promised to lend her one of her Barbies if she would get over being mad.

An apology was all Casey had needed. That, and a bribe. She brightened up at once.

"OK," she said. "But I have to have the Barbie for a whole hour."

"Deal," Nicole said. They spit into their palms and mushed their hands together to seal their agreement. Their parents would have been grossed out if they had seen the secret handshake — which was one of the reasons Nicole and Casey liked it so much.

Now Nicole climbed the ladder to see if she could get the wall to swing open, since Casey had not been strong enough.

She tugged on the book. Nothing happened.

She began to wonder if she had imagined the secret door. Was she confusing fiction with reality? Boy, she really *was* reading too much. Maybe she had come in, taken a great book off the shelf, and gotten so involved she thought it was real.

No. That couldn't be so.

Could it?

She grabbed the book firmly, and pulled harder.

Nothing.

She pulled harder still, grunting with effort as she yanked.

31

Slowly, with a heavy creaking noise, the top half of the bookshelf swung open.

Nicole climbed down the ladder.

"Your turn," she said.

Casey climbed up.

Nicole handed her up the flashlight. Casey shined it into the passageway.

"Cool!" she said. "This is really neat! Wait 'til you see what's in here."

Chapter Six

"What?" Nicole asked. "What is it?"

"Oh, cool!" Casey repeated, shining the flashlight into the passageway.

Nicole craned her neck. She stood on tiptoes. She tried jumping. But she could not see into the tunnel.

"What!" she demanded, exasperated.

"Cobwebs!" Casey said. "Cool!"

Great, Nicole thought. Cobwebs. I have a sister who is fascinated by cobwebs.

"Anything *else*?" Nicole asked.

"Nope," said Casey. "Just a lot of cobwebs."

Nicole looked up and saw Casey's feet disappearing into the passageway. There was nothing to do but follow her.

"Wait!" Nicole said. She heard a little quaver in her voice, and she realized she sounded almost scared that her little sister was leaving her behind.

33

How embarrassing.

She clambered up the ladder and peered into the passageway. All she saw was total blackness. There was no sign of Casey — nothing but utter darkness.

Her sister had disappeared. Vanished.

Nicole heard a scuffling noise. She caught her breath in a way that sounded like a hiccup.

Where was Casey? Why couldn't she see her?

"Casey!" she called, louder than she meant to. This time there was a big quaver in her voice as it echoed through the passageway. "Casey!"

The scuffling noise continued.

Nicole saw a glow far down the passageway. It wavered and moved.

Half-frozen, she tried to make out what it was. Then she saw the outline of a body sideways in the passageway, on its hands and knees.

Suddenly a beam of light stabbed her in the eyes.

Then she heard Casey's voice.

"Yes?"

Nicole closed her eyes and turned away.

"Get that light out of my eyes, you little brat," she said.

"Sorry," said Casey. She was enjoying this adventure too much to be offended, even when she was called a brat.

"Look," she said. She shined the flashlight around the edges of the passageway.

Nicole had never seen so many cobwebs. She'd never seen even half that many.

They hung from the ceiling like strips of gauze. The passageway looked as if it were filled with a thick, gray fog.

In the center of the cobwebs was a hole, where Casey had torn through as she crawled.

"You coming?" Casey asked. "This is fun."

She shined the light up at her own face. She was grinning, but the strange angle of the light gave her face an evil glow. So many cobwebs clung to her head that her blond hair looked gray and stringy. Strands stuck to her cheeks. She seemed not to be crawling through cobwebs, but swimming through them.

"I'm coming, I'm coming," Nicole complained.

She placed her fingertips slowly on the floor of the passageway, as if she could somehow avoid touching the cobwebs if she was very careful. The idea was ridiculous — like trying to step into a swimming pool slowly so you wouldn't get wet.

Suddenly, it occurred to Nicole that *something* must have made all these cobwebs. And that could only be one thing.

"Casey," she called, her voice a little shaky. "Do you see any spiders?"

Casey shined the flashlight all around. The beam of light illuminated the low ceiling, the walls, the floor.

"Not yet," she called happily. "Maybe soon."

Gingerly, Nicole put one knee into the passageway. Casey was getting impatient.

"Come *on*," she said. "You're a scaredy-cat."

This was so obviously true that it made Nicole angry.

"I am not!" she said. Her words echoed emptily through the eerie tunnel.

Silently, she told herself this was no time to let her sister get the best of her. Everyone can change, she thought. And if she was going to stop being a scaredy-cat, now would be a good time. A true test of her resolve, that was for sure.

She gritted her teeth and scrambled down the passageway after her sister. Cobwebs clung to her hands and her arms and her face. Some whipped across her eyes, and dangled from her lashes.

This stinks, Nicole thought to herself. I should never have told my dumb sister about this place at all.

Just as she caught up to Casey, the cobwebs stopped. The air was clear. Nicole moved her arm around in front of her face. She felt nothing. The cobwebs were gone.

She looked up. The ceiling, which had been so low they were forced to crawl, was suddenly of normal height. Casey was already standing up, shining the flashlight all around.

"Here, give me that," Nicole said. She grabbed the flashlight out of Casey's hands.

"Hey!" Casey said. "I'm going to tell."

"Go right ahead," Nicole said, knowing full well she wouldn't. She couldn't see Casey very well, but she imagined she was pouting into the darkness.

Nicole looked around. The opening through which they had climbed into the passageway was a square of light in the distance.

She shined the light in a different direction. It shone on a wall with paint peeling and splinters showing.

She turned around. Behind her was another wall, draped with a decaying American flag.

She moved the beam of light slowly across the flag. The stripes, so faded you could hardly tell the colors, ran up and down. Moths had eaten holes in the cloth. At the top were the stars, dirty white in a faded field of blue. Nicole could not count the stars in the darkness. But there were a lot fewer than fifty, that much was certain.

She directed the beam of light toward the middle of the flag. There, in the center, was a gaping hole, almost as if a cannonball had torn through it.

Near the hole spread a large, dark, rust-colored blotch. Surely, this flag had been carried on a battlefield. And, just as surely, that large, dark stain was blood.

Chapter Seven

Nicole shivered.

Suddenly, she felt very cold. Who would build a secret passageway, and why? Whose blood was on that flag?

What kind of house was this?

She wrapped her arms around herself for warmth. Her mind wandered to battlefields about which she had read. She thought of muskets fired and flag bearers falling, mortally wounded.

She felt around her the spirits of people long since dead. She felt it so strongly it seemed as if she could almost see them, hear them, even touch them.

Suddenly, a voice brought her back to the present.

"So, it's a flag," Casey said. "Are we going to explore, or what?"

With the sound of Casey's voice, the spirits seemed to go away. Nicole didn't feel so cold any more.

Whoa, Nicole thought, I *have* been reading too much.

She looked around. On her right was the small square of light from the entrance to the passageway. Behind her, she knew, was a wall. On her left hung the bloody flag.

She shined the light in front of her.

A staircase rose before them and disappeared into the gloomy darkness.

"If we're going to explore," Nicole said, "I guess we go up the stairs."

She was still humiliated by having been called a scaredy-cat by her little sister — and even more humiliated by actually having *been* a scaredy cat. She was determined to change. It was time to grow up, time to show Casey who was older.

She clenched her jaw and started up the stairs, shining the flashlight in front of her.

"Wait!" Casey said. "I can't see where I'm going."

Ah ha! Nicole thought with a secret little smile. This time, her sister had the quaver in her voice.

They climbed the staircase side by side. The stairs creaked and groaned with each step. Some of the boards looked rotten. Others were not nailed down. When you stepped on one side, the other side lifted up.

Nicole shined the light on each step, and the girls examined it carefully, before slowly testing it with their weight. They had no wish to crash down a floor and a half, or however far it was into the basement.

They also had no wish to attract their parents' attention.

Nicole shined the light toward the top of the staircase, but she couldn't see where it ended. Slowly, step by step, they creaked their way up the staircase.

It was long, and very narrow. The walls pressed close on either side. They climbed with their shoulders touching.

The higher they got, the more the walls pressed in on them. The opening through which the stairs climbed grew narrower and narrower.

Casey tripped on a nail that was sticking out. She fell forward with a little cry, and caught herself with her hands.

Finally, they reached the top. In front of them stood a massive, heavy door. It was made of thick boards that went from ceiling to floor. Two rough-hewn beams were nailed across it from side to side, one near the top, the other near the bottom.

Whoever built this door had wanted it to be extremely strong. The girls had seen no other door like it anywhere else in the house. Someone had certainly wanted to keep people away from whatever lay beyond.

On the right-hand side was a square doorknob fashioned from black metal. Beneath the knob was a black metal plate pierced by a long keyhole.

Nicole tried the knob. It would not turn. The door was locked.

Chapter Eight

There seemed nothing to do but turn around. This particular adventure was at an end. Whatever lay behind the massive wooden door would remain unexplored.

Or so it seemed.

Casey was not ready to concede defeat. She got that determined look on her face again.

"I know how to open a lock," she announced.

"Oh, really?" said Nicole. "How?"

"With a barrette," Casey replied. "Dad did it one time at our old house when I locked the door 'cause I was mad."

Nicole rolled her eyes.

"I think this door is a little different than the one to your room in Virginia," she said.

But Casey paid no attention. She plucked a barrette from her hair, bent it open, and inserted the flat metal end into the big keyhole.

"Casey," Nicole said in an exasperated tone. "This is *not* going to work."

Casey made no reply other than to say, "Shine the light this way, so I can see what I'm doing."

Nicole did so. And as she did, she could see determination reflected in Casey's eyes. She was squinting in concentration. Her lips were pursed. Her jaw was set. If there was a way to open a cast iron lock with a little girl's barrette, Casey would find it.

Suddenly she stopped.

Nicole froze, as well. She had heard the noise, too.

Both girls held their breath and pressed their ears close to the thick wooden door.

For long seconds they held their breath, straining to hear. The noise came again. It was a scritching noise, sounding again like a hamster trying to scratch its way out of its cage.

"Rats," Nicole breathed softly. "Maybe mice. I heard them the other night."

Casey resumed her work on the lock. Nicole resumed breathing.

Then the girls heard another noise that made their blood run cold.

Voices.

At least it sounded like voices, though they were so far away and faint it was hard to tell. The voices — if that indeed is what they were — were too soft to make out the words.

They sounded muffled, as if they were made by very little people stuffed under a very big blanket so the noise could barely get through.

Again, the girls held their breath and pressed their ears to the door. Whatever the muffled noise was, it was definitely coming from behind the door. The scritching noise and the noise like voices alternated — first one, then the other.

All of this made Casey more determined than ever to open the door. She started picking at the huge metal lock with renewed energy.

Nicole wasn't sure now that she wanted to open the door at all. In fact, she felt like leaving. Right away. Her body almost started to leave before her head came to a decision.

But her head won out. She was *not* going to be afraid any more. If her seven-year-old sister wanted to find out what was behind that door, she most definitely was not going to leave.

Besides, there was no real danger, she reminded herself. Casey would never get the door unlocked, anyway.

The voices started again. Or did they?

Nicole had just convinced herself that it was just the old boards of the house creaking when, suddenly, from far off in the distance, she heard another noise.

This was definitely a voice. It was not coming from beyond the door.

It was coming from behind them.

And it was calling her name.

<u>Chapter Nine</u>

Everything closed in on Nicole. The walls, the voices, the fear, everything.

She crouched at the top of the narrow staircase like a frightened rabbit, not sure which way to run. She was totally in the dark, but for the narrow beam of the flashlight which quivered now as her hand shook in fright.

Voices were murmuring in front of them, beyond the door. Another voice could be heard behind them, in the direction from which they had come. There was no escape, no way out.

The voice behind them grew a little louder.

"Nicole!" it called.

Whose voice was it and how did it know her name?

And a little louder ...

"Nicole!"

Nicole clutched Casey's arm.

"Don't move," she breathed. She squeezed her sister's arm so tight it hurt.

"Nicole!" the voice yelled. "Casey! Where are you? It's time for lunch!"

Casey spoke to Nicole very slowly and deliberately, as if she were speaking to a three year old.

"If you would please let go of my arm," she said, "that happens to be our Mom."

* * *

The kitchen looked practically like new. Well, not quite like new — that would take white Formica counter tops, fresh cabinets, new sinks and even a new floor.

Mom always said she loved hardwood floors, but this one was a bunch of splinters. Not something you'd want to walk on barefoot.

Still, the kitchen was spick-and-span. Actually, it looked good, considering how old it was. There were no more cobwebs in the sinks. The walls had been cleaned. The counters had been scrubbed. Even the splinters on the floor looked clean.

Sunlight streamed in through the windows, which were now so clean you could hardly see they were there. The whole place looked a lot brighter — and a lot less sinister — than it had when Nicole had first seen it. It looked almost fit for ordinary human beings to live in.

The girls arrived in the kitchen quite out of breath and looking very strange — and not very much like ordinary human beings.

Casey's hands and feet were still muddy from exploring the stream, but that wasn't unusual.

What was unusual was the dust on their faces, and the huge number of cobwebs hanging from their hair and clinging to their clothes.

For a moment, the two girls just stood there panting, their faces full of spider webs, their eyes as round as saucers.

And for a moment, from across the kitchen, their parents stood looking at them with their mouths open — and *their* eyes as round as saucers.

No one said a word. The two grown-ups and the two children just stood staring at each other.

Finally, their father spoke.

"Been playing, have you?" he asked.

"Uh, yeah," said Nicole. "Playing. Right."

"Playing where?" their mother demanded. "Look at you!"

Nicole wondered how she could look at herself without a mirror, but she decided this would not be a good time to ask. Besides, she could look at Casey, and that gave her a pretty good idea of how she looked herself. Ridiculous.

Nicole looked at her sister, who was wide-eyed and covered with dirt and cobwebs, and she felt herself start to smile. Suddenly, relief swept over her. She had been incredibly tense from having braved the passageway and the cobwebs and the narrow stairs and wondering about the voices, which were probably boards creaking.

Now she was safe. She could breath again.

And her sister looked absurd.

The corners of Nicole's mouth turned up more and more, and she started to laugh. She covered her mouth with her hand, and tried not to look at Casey.

But a second later she heard Casey start to laugh, and she couldn't hold it in any longer. She burst out laughing, and Casey burst out laughing, too.

Their mother burst out yelling.

"I don't see what so funny about being dirty," she said. "I want both of you to take a shower before you eat lunch. And get out of my nice, clean kitchen. Now!"

The two girls turned and ran from the kitchen almost doubled over, with tears of laughter streaming down their cheeks.

Chapter Ten

Over the next several days, life settled into a regular routine.

It wasn't regular in the way life in Virginia had been regular. There, everything had been familiar — the wait at the bus stop, the route the bus took to school, their teachers, even the family's Saturday evening trip to the drive-through ice cream shop.

Here, everything was unfamiliar. No school bus was coming this far off the beaten track just to pick up the two of them, so one of their parents had to drive them to school every day.

That seemed to mean no more throwing spitballs at the other passengers.

And on the ride home, they had to listen to all those boring, parent-type of questions about what they had done in school that day. I mean, Nicole thought, I've just lived through the whole school day. Why would I want to live through it again by talking about it? I went to class. What did you think I did in school?

She thought that, but of course she never said it.

Instead, she said, "Nothing," and tried to look as bored as she possibly could.

In Virginia, Nicole and Casey had gone to different schools. Casey had been in second grade at the Robert E. Lee Elementary School. Nicole had been in sixth grade, in her first year at the John C. Calhoun Middle School. That was a big school, with a thousand students — much bigger than the elementary school. Nicole had just been getting used to it when their father decided it would be a great time to uproot the family and move.

All for some stupid job.

I mean, Nicole thought, he already works for a newspaper. What's the difference?

But their father had said the Boston Globe was a bigger and better newspaper than the one he already worked at, and it had a better reputation.

"It's the *Globe*!" he said, as if that meant something to her. It didn't.

Here in Massachusetts, the girls would have to join classes in the middle of the school year. They would attend the same school, which ran all the way from kindergarten through eighth grade.

The day after the excursion up the secret passageway, the whole family had driven to see their new school, the Abraham Lincoln Elementary School. The girls could see it was different as soon as they drove into the parking lot.

The school in Virginia had been new and fresh-looking, and one story tall. This was an old, five-story brick building. Ivy clung to the walls. It looked as if someone had to lean out the windows and clip it, or else the leaves would have covered the glass, preventing anyone from seeing out..

They stopped first at the office of the principal. He was a funny-looking man with thick hair and a huge black mustache. He reminded Nicole of a comedian she had seen on TV. The principal shook their hands, boomed out, "Welcome to Lincoln," and laughed heartily.

Nicole couldn't see what the heck was so funny.

Then the entire family trooped off to Casey's new classroom. The teacher introduced Casey to the class. Casey was smiling ear to ear. She was so eager to begin that she almost tripped over herself getting to her seat.

Nicole's parents took her to her new home-room on the third floor.

The teacher, whose name was Mrs. Chestnut, had enormous front teeth, like a horse. She said she was absolutely delighted to have Nicole in her class.

Nicole didn't see how she could be delighted, since they'd never even met before.

But, instead of mentioning that, she went into her polite routine where she pinched up her face and looked serious. She spoke in sentences only one or two words long, and nodded her head each time she spoke.

"Nicole," she said, and bobbed her head.

"Thank you ..."

"Eleven ..."

"Yes ..."

"Thank you."

*   *   *

The days in the new house started to become the same as each other. Gradually, daily life developed an order, a rhythm.

The girls woke up at 6:30, when it was still dark outside. They put on five times as many clothes as they had worn in Virginia. They ate breakfast. The weather had turned sharply colder, Casey's stream had frozen, the snow had come, and every morning the girls waded out through knee-deep drifts and freezing cold, went off to school, then came home and did a ton of homework.

Life became predictable again.

Nicole noticed that even the noises of the strange old house became familiar. She recognized the creaking of the boards and the rattling of the windows and the moaning of the trees.

And as the noises became familiar, they became comforting. They were turning into old friends. Instead of keeping her awake, they helped her fall asleep. She thought that now she would have a tough time sleeping if the noises suddenly stopped, and she was forced to listen to the silence.

The scritching noise in the ceiling annoyed her now and then. But she realized there had been no voices. Boards must have been groaning in the wind, and that was what they had heard. She and Casey had only thought it was voices because the passageway was so dark and weird and filled with cobwebs. Besides, the top of the stairs was such a narrow space that there probably wasn't much air in there, and the lack of oxygen had probably affected their thinking.

Once, Nicole mentioned to her mother that she'd heard mice in the attic. Her mother sighed and said she would try to remember to get some mouse-traps and put them up there. The way she said it made Nicole think that her mother would not be remembering any time soon.

That didn't matter. Nicole was at peace with the mice. If they didn't bother her, she wouldn't bother them. She shrugged and turned away.

Her father popped his head out from behind the newspaper.

"You know, it's funny," he said. "From the outside, it looks as though there ought to be an attic. But I have gone over every square inch of the house, and there's absolutely no way to get to where the attic ought to be."

He scrunched up his forehead the way he did when he was working on a crossword puzzle.

" I can't figure it out," he said. "There may be mice in the ceiling. Probably are, in fact. But the really peculiar thing is — " he scrunched his forehead up even more — "this house doesn't *have* an attic."

Chapter Eleven

Nicole knew, of course, that there *was* an attic. There had to be. Why else would there be a door? Surely something lay behind it.

But why would someone take such pains to hide the only way into the attic? Why barricade it with such a thick, heavy door?

These questions and others ran through Nicole's mind when her father declared so positively that there was no attic.

But, overall, she thought of the attic less and less often. Mrs. Chestnut, with the horsy teeth, was not only delighted to have Nicole in her class, she was also delighted to assign humongous amounts of homework.

And considering that Nicole was joining the class in the middle of the year, and so was already behind everyone else in the class, there seemed no end to the school work.

Besides, why think about the attic? There was no way to get into it. A person would need dynamite to get that door open. She didn't need to be fixated on a place she couldn't get into.

She avoided discussing the attic with Casey. She didn't want to have to go back up that dark passageway while Casey got all determined again and tried to pick the big metal lock with the end of a barrette. And if Casey wanted to go back up there, Nicole would have to go, too, to prove she wasn't chicken.

She'd already proved that once, and once was quite enough, thank you.

Casey, however, seemed to have forgotten about the attic. She was busy telling stories every afternoon about how great she was doing in school, and how many friends she had made, and how much the teacher liked her.

Besides, to her, one adventure was as good as another. She had probably had more fun looking for bugs in the stream than going up the cobweb-filled passageway — though she'd enjoyed that pretty much, too.

Just don't mention it, Nicole told herself. Let Casey move on to other adventures.

And so Nicole tried to put the attic out of her

mind.

*   *   *

Then one night something happened that made that impossible.

Nicole was lying on her back staring at the ceiling and trying to go to sleep.

Mentally, she went over all the things she was supposed to have done that day.

Math homework? Check.

Writing assignment? Check.

Geography research? Yup.

Permission slip signed for the field trip? Yup.

Book bag packed? Done.

Nasty note slipped under Casey's door? Check.

She took a deep breath, sighed, and closed her eyes. To help herself fall asleep, she counted the noises of the house, making sure all her old, familiar friends were there.

The creaking of the floors? She listened. There it was.

The rattling of the window panes? She heard it.

60

The moaning of the trees? Yes. It sounded like music to her now.

Then she heard another noise. She caught her breath and listened.

I'm dreaming, she thought. I've already fallen asleep and I'm dreaming. This could not be happening.

From above the ceiling, sweet and mournful and so unhappy it made you want to cry, came the sad, sad sound of someone playing the cello.

Chapter Twelve

So mournful and melancholy was the melody that Nicole wanted to weep.

Someone was playing the cello solo — all alone, with no orchestra. The sound was rich and full. The music rose and fell so sorrowfully it broke her heart. The high notes ached with anguish. Then the tune dropped low with despair.

It was music fit for a funeral.

Nicole turned as pale as her sheets. She sat up and pulled them to her chest. She scooted back on her bed into a corner where one wall met another, and tried to force herself to breathe.

For a terrifying second, her lungs refused to work. Try as she might, she could not breath in, could not get air into her chest.

Someone, or something, was in the house. Nicole trembled with fear. Her eyes bulged. The hair on the back of her neck stood up.

The sound of the cello rose into a wail, vibrating with loss and sorrow.

Nicole felt a tear run down her cheek.

This, she knew, was the music of death.

*   *   *

Nicole felt her way through the next few days as if she were moving though a thick fog. She was so preoccupied she was almost unable to see her surroundings.

In the morning, she dressed in clothes that didn't match. At breakfast, she ate her cereal so absent-mindedly she missed the bowl with her spoon.

At school, she couldn't concentrate on what the teacher was saying. On the ride home, she didn't hear when her mother asked questions.

"Mike, I'm worried about her," her mother said to her father one evening when Nicole had happened to be passing by the kitchen door.

"She's just having a little trouble adjusting to the move," her father replied. "It's to be expected. Leave her alone and she'll be fine."

But the truth was that Nicole was worried about herself.

The morning after hearing the cello, she had awoken huddled in the corner into which she had crawled in fear.

She had not felt well since. Her stomach hurt. Her head ached.

And her ears throbbed with the melancholy music. She couldn't get it out of her head. She heard it when she dressed. She heard it when she ate breakfast. She heard it in class.

Wherever she went, the deep, rich notes pulsed through her brain and made her sad and afraid.

She knew she had to do something. She would not last long like this. She'd have a nervous breakdown, or become the first eleven-year-old in history to get an ulcer.

But there was no way she could tell her parents. They would never believe her. She'd never be able to convince them that mice were playing cellos in an attic that was not there.

Especially since they had not heard the noise for themselves. And Nicole knew they had not.

The next morning, she had asked Casey if she'd heard anything unusual in the night. Casey had said no.

If Casey hadn't heard it, her parents hadn't

heard it. Casey slept on the second floor, like Nicole. Their parents slept on the first floor, even further away from the attic.

There was another way Nicole knew her parents had not heard the music. They had not run from the house screaming in fright, their hair standing on end. They had not piled into the car, leaving all their belongings behind, and zoomed down the road, leaving this strange old house for good.

Which they most certainly would have done had they heard eerie midnight music coming from a place that wasn't there.

So Nicole was on her own.

But she had to do something. She could not go on living this way.

As far as she could figure, there were only two things she could do — and both were impossible.

The first was to flee — to run away and get as far from whatever unearthly thing was making the noise as possible.

She couldn't do that, because her family wouldn't come with her. They'd have her committed.

The second was to confront whatever was in the attic — face it down, and make *it* scared instead of her.

But she couldn't do that, either, because there was no way to get in there.

She thought about it long and hard, as her stomach tied itself in knots and her homework piled up undone.

She decided in the end that Option Two was less impossible than Option One. She couldn't run from whatever was terrifying her. She had to face it down.

Maybe the essence of not being a scaredy-cat was not having any choice.

If she really put her mind to it, she thought, she could find a way. She knew she was smart. She just had to get as determined as Casey.

She needed to get into the attic.

Chapter Thirteen

The deep and mournful music echoed through Nicole's soul as she explored the study.

She had not heard it again since the night, a week ago, when it had scared her into the corner. But the tune had burned itself into her brain. She could not get rid of it. Her heart felt heavy in her chest from the sadness of the melody.

She had decided to enter the attic alone — if she could find a way in. There was no reason to get Casey involved. This was serious business. Nicole considered how she herself had already been affected — her stomach trouble, her poor performance at school, her worried parents.

Casey was doing well in school, even if she did brag about it too much. There was no need to ruin that. No need to scare a little kid.

Besides being scary, this might actually be dangerous. Casey was fine for exploring dark passageways where you might find spiders or slimy things. But since there was the possibility of running into ghosts — and this was the first time Nicole had allowed herself to think of that possibility — this was no job for a seven-year-old.

Nicole had sat in her room for hours trying to think of a way to get into the attic. No good ideas had come to her.

She finally decided that investigating and thinking might be more useful than just sitting and thinking.

She had begun her investigation in the study, for obvious reasons. The entrance to the passageway was hidden here. Whoever's study this had been, so many years ago, must have had the passageway built here for a reason. Maybe he or she had left behind some clues about how to get into the attic.

Nicole stood in the middle of the gloomy room, looking it over from top to bottom. The thick red velvet curtains blocked so much light that it took a minute for her eyes to adjust to the darkness.

She scanned the thousands of leather-bound volumes lining the bookshelves from floor to ceiling. She looked at the ladder leaning against one of the bookshelves, and at the huge dark wooden desk that dominated the room.

Her first thought was that maybe there was another passageway. Perhaps it led into the attic by a different route, and maybe the door at the top of those stairs had been left unlocked.

She tugged on one book after another. Each slipped out from its space on the shelf, sending a cloud of dust up her nose and making her want to sneeze.

She wiped her nose on her sleeve. This was no time to go off in search of a tissue. She was determined. Nothing was going to stop her, least of all a runny nose.

After trying books on each of the lower shelves, she tried those that were higher. She moved the ladder from one bookshelf to another, trying books on all four sides of the great, gloomy room.

But all the books she tried turned out to be, in fact, real books. She could find no secret passage way other than the one she and her sister had already explored.

Nicole paused. It was time for a little more thought and a little less investigation. She wiped her forehead with one sleeve and her nose with the other.

Again she looked around the room, more closely this time.

An enormous painting hung on the wall behind the desk, a painting so huge that it was surprising she had not noticed it before. Perhaps she had missed it because it was so dark and gloomy that it blended in with the rest of the room.

It was a portrait of an elderly man. He had a thick head of white hair and a drooping white mustache. He wore a dark suit, accented by a gold watch chain which dangled across his stomach. He wore wire-rimmed spectacles — and behind them, his eyes seemed to be angry, ferocious and sad all at once.

He seemed to be looking straight at Nicole.

She walked slowly across the room.

By some trick of the painter, the old man's eyes seemed to follow her as she walked.

She stepped closer. She saw now that the portrait had been painted in this very room. The man was standing in front of the great dark wooden desk. Behind him were the ceiling-to-floor bookshelves, lined with leather-bound volumes.

Maybe *that* was why the painting had blended into the room, Nicole thought. Because it was, itself, a picture of the very same room.

Suddenly it struck her. What a fiendishly clever way to hide something — behind a painting so big you couldn't fail to notice it, except that you did.

Maybe something was behind it, she thought — the entrance to a passageway, or a vault full of old papers, or perhaps even pictures of the people who used to live in this house.

Nicole stepped closer. The man in the painting glared at her. Slowly, she reached out and touched a corner of the great gold frame that surrounded the painting.

Her heart beating fast, she grasped the frame and inched it out away from the wall. Holding her breath, she bent her head close to the wall and peered behind the painting.

There was nothing there.

Chapter Fourteen

Nicole sighed. Another dead end.

But she wasn't about to give up. Her eyes scanned the dark room, probing every crevice and corner. If she was to understand about the attic, surely there would be something in the study to help.

She gazed upward. From the ceiling hung a circular metal chandelier, with places for eight candles.

That was no help.

She stood at the desk and swung her eyes in a circle. The bookcases she had already covered. But — what about the fireplace?

That was another part of the room she hadn't notice before, though she had walked right by it. It was huge, and made of dark stones, some of them blackened by stray tongues of flame.

Nicole peered inside. Ashes lay in a heap on the bottom, the remnants of a fire started who knew how many years ago.

One by one, Nicole tried to loosen the great stones. Perhaps there would be a secret compartment behind one of them. Or she would move one of the stones and elsewhere in the room a doorway would swing open. Or someone would suddenly start playing the cello.

In this house, anything seemed possible.

But all the stones were stuck fast. The fireplace seemed to be nothing but a fireplace.

Nicole paused for a minute, squatting on the hearth. The ashes reminded her that other people had used this cold dark study, years and years ago. Fires lit here had probably warmed the hands of the sad and angry man who glared down at her now from the portrait on the wall.

Maybe this room had not always been so gloomy.

With another sigh, Nicole got to her feet. She turned slowly around. Something in the room would help her. If only she thought hard enough and looked carefully enough, she would find something, however small.

Or however huge.

Suddenly it hit her.

"The desk!" she cried aloud, slapping herself

on the forehead. "How could I be so dumb?"

With her heart racing, she walked behind the desk. She knew from the painting that this desk had belong to the man in the portrait. Maybe he had been the master of the house. And where else would someone keep records other than in his desk?

Nicole sat behind the desk. It was so large that it made her feel very small.

The desk had seven drawers — three on each side, going from the desktop down to the floor, and a wide, shallow one in the middle, above her legs.

Nicole reached for the top left-hand drawer and pulled.

It was locked.

She tried the one below it. It was locked also.

The one beneath that was locked, as well.

She tried the drawers on the right. All locked.

With both hands, she tried the drawer in the center, above her legs. With a creak, it slid open. A moth flew out, and Nicole jerked back, startled.

The moth flew by her head and fluttered lazily around the room, landing on a bookshelf, then on the chandelier. From there, it fluttered down to the top of the desk, in front of Nicole, opened and closed its wings three times, and keeled over on its side, dead.

Nicole stared at it for a moment. It seemed somehow a bad sign. That moth must have waited a long time for its one last chance to fly, she thought. She hoped it had been worth the wait.

Then she turned her attention back to the open drawer. She had more important things to worry about than a dead moth.

She looked inside. Three quill pens were lined up on one side, their feathers all facing the same way. On the other side was a neat stack of plain paper. The person who used this desk certainly liked things organized, Nicole thought.

She picked up the stack of paper and flipped through it. Not a single sheet was written upon. Every one was blank.

Nicole opened the drawer wider. There was nothing else in it. Just three quill pens and a stack of writing paper. Nothing at all to explain the mystery of the attic.

She had hit yet another dead end.

She slammed her fist on the desktop in frustration. She had been so sure the desk would offer up a clue. But there wasn't a darned thing.

Suddenly she remembered a desk her father had had at work. You locked all the drawers just by locking the middle one. If that drawer was closed, all the others were locked. If it was open, the others would open, too.

With the middle drawer still open above her legs, she tried the top left-hand drawer. It slid open.

Inside were some glass inkwells, caked black with dried-up ink.

She tried the drawer beneath it, and opened the large book she found inside. It contained hand-written notations of business transactions — horses bought, salary received, payments made.

Nicole tried the bottom drawer.

In it she found another large book. She opened it, and on the first page, which was yellow with age, she found the handwritten title: "Fowler Family History, 1751 to the present."

She turned the page and began reading:

"The first Fowler to settle in Massachusetts was Josiah Fowler, a gentleman farmer who moved to this area from the colony of Virginia in 1851."

The handwritten history identified Josiah Fowler's parents, his wife, and his children, his aunts and his uncles, where he was born, why he had moved, and in what year his parents had sailed from England to the New World.

With a sigh, Nicole closed the book, sending a puff of dust billowing into the air. She liked reading about history, but only if it was the history of interesting people. Who Josiah Fowler's parents were, and in what year they came here from England, interested her not at all.

Nicole was about to replace the book in the drawer when a dull gleam caught her eye.

In the bottom of the drawer, beneath where the book had been, shone a huge golden key. It was long, with key parts sticking off one end. At the other end, an old black ribbon was tied through the key's ring-like handle.

Nicole placed the book gently on top of the desk. With trembling fingers she reached for the key. The cello music played inside her head, rising and falling and sounding sorrowful.

Nicole's heart stopped beating for a moment. Then it hammered like mad in her throat.

She closed her fingers around the key and brought it to her face for a closer look. She felt terribly afraid. She realized now that, determined as she was, she had almost hoped that her search of the office would fail. Then she could have told herself there was nothing she could do.

77

But her search had succeeded.

For, as she gazed at the key gleaming now dully in her hand, Nicole knew one thing, beyond any doubt.

This was the key to the attic.

Chapter Fifteen

That night the music began again.

The cello wailed its sorrowful song. The music began softly, but grew louder and louder until Nicole was certain other people in the house must be hearing it, too.

But no one stirred. Maybe she had gone crazy, she thought. Surely, losing your mind would feel something like this — hearing things no one else heard, being terrified of things no one else would even believe existed.

Nicole crept to the head of her bed, scrunched herself into the corner, and cried.

But this time she cried more in anger than in sorrow. Whoever, whatever, was playing that music *knew* she had found the key to the attic, and was trying to scare her off.

That made her mad. Whatever it was didn't realize that it was dealing with the new Nicole, not the scaredy-cat of days gone by.

She pulled her knees to her chest, wrapped her

arms around them, and tried to sleep sitting up, with her back wedged into the corner.

Then she heard another noise. This was not a solo any longer. Mingled now with the cello was the rolling rhythm of a drum.

It was being played military-style: Brrrat-tat-tat! Brrrat-tat-tat! Brrrat, brrrat, brrrat-tat-tat! It sounded like the drumming she had heard when she had seen soldiers march in parades.

The drummer was not keeping time with the cello player. Each was playing his own music, with no attention to the other. The mournful moan of the cello continued, slow and soulful, punctuated by the sharp and rapid Brrrat-tat-tat! of the drum.

The strange, disconnected music echoed louder and louder in Nicole's ears until she thought her head would burst.

And still no one else in the family stirred.

Nicole hugged her knees and cried herself to sleep.

*   *   *

The big gold key gleamed in the glare of the flashlight.

"Point it at the keyhole, dummy, not the key," Nicole hissed.

Casey did as she was told. Nicole slid the key into the lock and gave it a turn.

The lock clicked. The door started to slide open.

Nicole had had second thoughts about not exposing her sister to danger. After all, she decided, Casey was very mature, considering she was only seven. And what were sisters for, if not to support each other in times of need?

Besides, Casey was the one who had been so determined to open the door in the first place, working the lock with the clasp of her barrette. If she wanted to find out what was in there, who was Nicole to deprive her of that experience?

Together, the girls leaned on the thick wooden door. It yielded to their weight and creaked open.

Beyond it, they saw — nothing.

The attic was completely cloaked in darkness. There seemed to be no windows, nor even any cracks in the wall to let in the slightest ray of light.

Casey shone the flashlight into the room. The beam bored a tunnel in the blackness.

Stepping carefully, the girls entered the room. Their footsteps echoed in the silence. The air was musty, as if no one had been in the room for years.

Casey moved the beam of light slowly around the room. Something hanging from the wall caught their eyes. Casey let the light linger on it.

It was an old wedding dress, white with frills at the neck.

Just beyond the dress, on a pair of wooden pegs that stuck out from the wall, an ancient musket was mounted.

Beyond that, they saw what appeared to be a window, covered by thick blankets that were nailed to the frame so tightly that not a speck of light leaked through.

And beyond that, in the flashlight's beam, a sword gleamed sharp and dangerous. Beyond that, a framed document. Looking closer, Nicole saw that it was a college degree, from Harvard, dated June 15, 1891. It bore the name Henry Fowler.

The girls paused. Casey shone the light toward the middle of the room, sweeping the beam across the floor from side to side.

The floor, wooden and dusty, lay empty. There was no sign of any cello player, no hint of any midnight drummer.

Suddenly the beam of light happened upon a large object in the middle of the floor. The girls approached for a closer look.

It was an old trunk, almost as high as Casey's waist. It was made of wood, and bound with leather straps. It looked like the kind of trunk you saw in pirate movies, or maybe strapped to a stagecoach in old westerns.

Nicole reached down to open it.

But she could not. Casey moved the light, and they saw that the trunk was sealed fast with a huge padlock.

Chapter Sixteen

Nicole rummaged through the drawers of the big wooden desk, searching for the key to the padlock. Casey, meanwhile, looked underneath the desk.

"Maybe somebody dropped it on the floor," she said.

Nicole ignored her. She looked first in the bottom left-hand drawer, where she had found the key to the attic. She lifted up the Fowler Family History, sending another small cloud of dust billowing, and looked under it.

Nothing.

But surely the key would be here, in this desk, where the other key had been hidden. Why would someone keep keys in different places?

She realized that, the last time she was here, she had only looked in the drawers on the left-hand side. She had found the key to the attic before she had even opened the three drawers on the right side of the desk.

She opened the top right-hand drawer now. She found papers, yellowed with age, some so brittle they cracked and crumbled in her hands.

But no key.

In the second drawer, she found more papers but no key. And in the third drawer, the same.

Another dead end.

Nicole put her elbows on the desk, dropped her head into her hands, and closed her eyes to think.

Casey spoke up.

"If we had, like, a really long pole that we could pry with," she said, "maybe we could, you know, like pry the lock open until it broke."

Nicole looked up. A smile spread over her face. She jumped up.

"Casey, you're brilliant!" she exclaimed. "Come with me!"

And she grabbed Casey by the hand and pulled her toward the side door to the house, the one through which they had tumbled on the day they had first explored the passageway together.

* * *

The two girls stood outside the ramshackle shed that leaned crazily behind the house on the side opposite where the family graveyard lay.

"There has got to be a crowbar in there," Nicole said.

But the door to the shed was locked. Everything around here was locked, thought Nicole. Whatever you try to do, you run into one lock after another.

Still, it didn't look as if getting into the shed should be a problem. It was old and rickety and practically falling apart on its own.

Nicole found a board that was loose. She swung it to one side. There was a narrow gap where the board had been. But it was too narrow to squeeze through, especially if you didn't want to get pierced by a rusty nail or two.

She saw a window with some of the panes broken out. But she could not open it.

She walked around to look at the front door again. The lock looked solid. Then she looked at the hinges that fastened the door to the shed. There were two of them, one about eye level, the other at about the level of her knees.

Both looked like they were coming loose.

She dug behind the upper hinge with her fingers. The nails holding the hinge in place slid easily out of the rotten wood. The hinge pulled away from the wall.

Then she tried the lower one. It, too, came loose.

"Help me," Nicole said, grabbing the side of the door that would have stayed closed if the hinges had still been in place.

Together, she and Casey worked the door open, lifting and pulling and grunting, using the padlock as a hinge.

Suddenly, from inside the dim light of the shed came a great whirring of wings. Nicole looked up and saw a swarm of shapes rise up in the gloom and fly toward the door.

"Look out!" she screamed. "Bats!"

The swarm was headed right for their faces. The girls hurled themselves to the ground, wrapping their arms around their heads for protection.

The bats flew out the door in a thick cloud, passing so close to the girls that they could feel the air from the beating of the wings.

Nicole lay on the ground gasping. Casey opened one eye and looked at the departing swarm.

"Nicole," she said. "I think it was birds."

Nicole opened her eyes.

The birds darted and swooped and flew off through the trees and into the gray, cloud-filled sky.

Nicole let out a deep sigh.

They had obviously frightened some barn swallows when they had opened the door of the shed. And the barn swallows had obviously frightened them in return.

The girls got to their feet and explored the shed.

A little light leaked in through the broken windows. Once their eyes adjusted to the darkness, the girls could make out objects leaning against the walls.

There was a shovel. Nicole's mind wandered to the tombstones just across the way. She wondered how many graves this shovel had dug.

They saw a rake, and a long-handled pick. A sledgehammer lay on the floor, next to some metal wedges used to split logs in two for firewood. A two-man saw hung in the corner, a wooden handle attached to each end.

Nicole kept looking. She stepped deeper into the shed. Her toe clanked against something hard.

She reached down and found what she had

been looking for.

A crowbar.

"Come on," she said to her sister. "Let's go!"

Chapter Seventeen

Nicole stuck the end of the crowbar through the loop of the padlock. Casey held the flashlight.

Nicole braced herself against the trunk with one foot, took a deep breath, and yanked back on the crowbar.

The lock popped open.

Nicole and Casey knelt down in front of the trunk.

"Maybe it's treasure," Casey whispered.

Nicole didn't know what to think. Slowly, she lifted the lid. It rocked back on its hinges.

Nicole didn't know what she had expected, but it wasn't this.

The trunk was filled with dolls. Dozens of them.

Nicole and Casey gasped.

The dolls were beautiful. There was a bride and a farmer and one who looked like a schoolteacher and another dressed as a sailor.

Their clothes were perfect miniatures of real clothes, down to the last detail. The stitches were tiny. The shoes had miniature laces.

Nicole picked up the bride and examined her while Casey held the flashlight. Nicole was fascinated. The doll looked so lifelike, down to her fingernails and her eyelashes. She even had fine lines under her eyes, and a mark on her right cheek that looked like a small scar.

"Cool!" Casey said.

The girls were so entranced by the dolls that they played with them for an hour, forgetting the danger they had felt before.

Sometimes Nicole felt she was a little old to play with dolls. She never discussed dolls at school any more. But she liked plays — she had acted in several of them — and she loved to stage plays with her dolls, as if she were a movie director. Plus, it was something she still liked to do with Casey, and that made it fun, too.

Casey put the flashlight on the floor, shining it toward the trunk. It lit up an area of the floor and the trunk in a way that made it look like a stage.

The bride was marrying the sailor. The

schoolteacher was the bride's mother; the farmer was her father. For other guests, they rummaged through the trunk and brought out, among other dolls, a soldier carrying a musket in the crook of his arm, and some sort of scholar wearing the cap and gown of a college graduation.

Eventually, they heard their mother calling them and, leaving the wedding party at the altar, they scrambled down the narrow staircase as quickly as they could while keeping reasonably quiet.

I'm getting over my fears, Nicole thought. At least this time, I recognized my mother's voice and didn't get freaked out.

*   *   *

But her fears returned soon enough.

That evening, as Nicole snuggled into bed, smiling at the memory of playing with the new dolls, the cello music began again, — low, mournful, unspeakably sad. And louder than ever, much louder. It did not sound muffled, as it had on previous nights.

Then the drum started banging out its own separate beat: Brrrat-tat-tat! Brrrat-tat-tat! Brrrat! Brrrat! Brrrat-tat-tat!

Nicole did not want to hear. She had been inside the attic now and she knew there was nothing up there that could be playing any music. She shoved her head under her pillow.

But the pillow did not block out the noise. A flute joined in, playing yet another different melody. And there was a scuffling over Nicole's head from where the attic must be.

Suddenly, Nicole heard another noise in the hall — right outside her room. It was a slow shuffling sound, as if something were dragging its feet along the hallway.

Nicole whipped the pillow off her head and sat up to listen.

The cello music grew louder, the drumming grew sharper, the scuffling in the ceiling grew more distinct, and the shuffling sound in the hallway grew nearer and nearer and nearer.

Nicole's eyes were wide with fear. She couldn't breathe. She stared in horror at the door to her room.

As she watched, the doorknob slowly started to turn.

She opened her mouth to scream, but no sound came out.

93

The door started to open — and in walked Casey, her favorite yellow blanket draped over her arm, her slippers shuffling along the floor.

Nicole let out a long breath. She could breathe again.

Then she looked at Casey's face. It was white with fear.

"I heard music," Casey said. "From the attic."

Nicole didn't know whether to be relieved or frightened. On the one hand, at least she knew she wasn't crazy. She wasn't the only one hearing the music.

On the other hand, there really *was* music. And it was coming from the attic, where there was absolutely nothing that was capable of making music.

At least nothing she could see.

Chapter Eighteen

By the next morning, Casey had forgotten about the attic. Either that, or she was pretending she'd forgotten.

It was Sunday. The sky was gray and dark, but it was unseasonably warm. Outside, the snow had melted, creating small rivers beside the dirt road that lead to their house. The fields were filled with mud.

After breakfast, Nicole said, simply, "Come on." She assumed they were both going to explore the attic once more.

But Casey decided to explore outside instead.

Nicole wasn't sure whether Casey was just too scared to go into the attic, or whether she was really attracted by all the new streams outside. Either explanation seemed possible. Casey certainly did enjoy examining streams for any signs of life — or any signs of mud, and there was plenty of that.

And her mind might really have been on the

school play the next night. Casey, of course, was going to be the star. She said it was going to be the most important night of her life.

But she *had* seemed awfully frightened the night before.

Well, let her go outside, Nicole thought. I'm going up to the attic. I'm not afraid.

She had second thoughts, though, when she pulled the bookcase open and shone the flashlight down the dark passageway. It occurred to her that this would be the first time she had been along the passageway and up the stairs by herself.

She took a deep breath and crawled in. Many of the cobwebs were gone, cleared out by the previous two trips she and Casey had made through the passageway. Still, it was dark and silent and eerie in there.

She turned the corner, stood up, and started up the narrow staircase, the beam of light shining in front of her so she could avoid the steps that looked dangerous. At the top of the stairs, she shined the light on the keyhole and inserted the key.

She had locked the door when they had left the day before. She didn't know why. Something had told her that it ought to be locked. Maybe it had been locked before for a reason.

The key turned, and she opened the door. As she pushed on it, she heard something scraping along the floor, being pushed across the floorboards by the opening of the door.

She slipped into the attic and shone her light at the base of the door. Lying on the floor was schoolteacher doll.

Nicole knew she had left it leaning against the trunk, in the center of the room. The schoolteacher had been beaming with pride at her daughter, the bride.

How did the doll get over to the doorway? Who had moved it?

Nicole knew no one could have gone into the attic. She'd had the key the whole time. She had slept with it under her pillow.

Fearfully, she stepped further into the attic, looking left and right as if she expected something to jump out at her.

She walked to the trunk. It was still in the center of the room. The top was still closed, as she and Casey had left it, when it was the backdrop to their stage show.

But none of the dolls was nearby! The bride, the groom, the wedding party — all were gone.

Nicole felt the hair on the back of her neck lift up.

There was only one possible explanation — ghosts. Nothing else could go through a locked door. This was the first she had ever heard of ghosts playing with dolls, but that didn't make her any happier about the possibility of meeting them.

Every instinct she had told her to flee, to save herself, to get out while she still could.

But she wanted to investigate just a little more. She shined the light around the room. Against one wall, she saw an object. She stepped closer to look. It was the bride.

Nicole's heart almost stopped. The doll was in a totally different position than she'd been in before. Yesterday, she had been standing, looking straight ahead, with her hands at her sides.

Now she stood with her arms folded, looking back over one shoulder. But the most amazing thing was — *the expression on her face was different.*

Where before there had been a radiant smile there was now an angry frown. Eyes that had glowed with pride glowered now in a scowl.

Nicole ran for the door, slammed it shut, and locked it behind her.

*　　*　　*

Back in the study, Nicole composed herself and tried to gather her thoughts.

The answer to whatever was going on in the attic lay here, in this room — probably in the desk. Whoever had built the attic and locked it and then hid the key had known what was going on. There was a reason for all this.

She walked to the desk, resolutely opened the bottom left-hand drawer, and pulled out the book. She knew now that books had not caused her imagination to be over-active. Whatever was going on in the attic was real. And she thought perhaps this book, far from misleading her, could tell her what it was.

She opened it, turned to the first page, and read again the handwritten title: "Fowler Family History, 1751 to the present."

She turned the yellowed pages carefully.

She skipped that parts about Josiah Fowler, his parents, his wife, children and aunts and uncles. She was good at that. She had once read "Gone With the Wind," all 1,000-plus pages of it, in two weeks. Her father had been stunned. He just couldn't believe it.

What he didn't realize was that Nicole was skimming over the boring parts — long battlefield scenes and the like — and reading carefully again when the book returned to the business of discussing Rhett and Scarlett.

She read like that now, skipping every other paragraph, and reading the beginning of the next to see if it interested her. It was a little harder here, because the Fowler Family History was handwritten, in an old style with lots of curlicues, so it was a little hard to read.

She skipped the parts about coming to America and moving from Virginia to Massachusetts, and about who had married whom on what particular day.

She scanned several pages like that, standing at the desk, her eyes moving swiftly from the top to the bottom of each handwritten sheet.

Suddenly, one particular sentence caught her eye. The words almost jumped off the page at her. She bit her lip and slowly sank into the chair.

It was time to sit down, to stop skimming and start some careful reading.

"There is, I believe, a curse on the Fowler family," she read, "although whether the curse is on the family or on the house in which I sit, I cannot say for sure."

Chapter Nineteen

Nicole scarcely breathed as she read the words. They were written by Josiah Fowler's son, Franklin Fowler, who had been born in 1851, the year his father had moved into this house.

"When my brother died, I thought it was nothing but a cruel twist of fate," she read. "And cruel it was indeed. He was only 16 years old, just two years older than I was myself, when his life was so brutally cut short.

"William was a drummer for his regiment in the Civil War until, finally, he became the flag-bearer. He took such pride in it. Other members of his regiment told me afterward that he carried the Union flag into every battle as if he would rather die than see it touch the ground. He survived them all, including the terrible battle at Gettysburg, waving the flag of his country proudly above the smoke and the gunfire.

"He was shot through the heart April 9, 1865,

just hours before Lee surrendered at Appomattox, ending the war.

"His whole life was before him. Just one more day and he would have been free to come back and inherit this house — the very house in which I now sit writing these sorrowful words. Instead of becoming master of this house, William was buried behind it. And I, only 14 years old, had to toss the first clod of dirt onto his coffin."

Nicole thought back to the old and crooked gravestones she had seen behind the house. She remembered — "William Fowler, 1849-1865. His memory will be with us always."

She read on:

"Of course his death was tragic. And the timing was so very hard for me to accept. I thought then — I had no reason to think otherwise — that it was just horrible luck, grim fate. Some poor soul has to be the last to die in every war.

"But I know now it was more than that.

"My wife, Karen — my beautiful, beautiful wife — had waited so long for a daughter. Three sons she had, and no little girl to call her own.

"She died May 1, 1875, the day our daughter was born. She had her little girl, but never got to hold her even once. Forever after, I had to remember Lenore's birthday as the day I lost my wife.

"And my children — the same. Lenore was killed on her wedding day, just minutes before the happiest event of her life was to take place. A wheel broke loose from the carriage in which she was riding to the church, the carriage toppled, and she was trampled by her horse, which had taken a fright."

Nicole read, spellbound. She did not recall seeing either Karen Fowler's grave, or Lenore's, but she had only looked at a few of them.

She read on.

Franklin's son John, a musician, had died in 1890, the day before he was to give his first public recital in Boston. Henry, another son, had died the morning he was to graduate from college. Whitaker, the third son, died in 1915, the day before he was to realize his life-long dream and be sworn in as a United States Senator. He left a wife and four children.

And there was more:

"My grandson James died in Germany on Nov. 10, 1918 — the day before the armistice was signed ending the First World War," Franklin Fowler wrote. "It was then I knew that the curse had been passed to a new generation.

103

"Yet it seemed my lot to live on and on and on — my fate to suffer the grief of all the deaths in the family. My wife was dead. All four of my children were dead. And now I was to lose my grandchildren, too? It was too much to bear."

Nicole looked up at the portrait on the wall of the old man with the thick white hair and drooping mustache. This had to be Franklin. She understood now why his eyes looked sad and angry all at once.

She continued reading.

"After James died, I traveled to Salem. I knew of a witch there, a woman descended from one of the witches who had escaped burning at the stake in the days of the witch trials.

"I went to see her. I asked what could be done. She pursed her lips and studied me. 'Fate cannot be avoided,' she said. 'If that is your family's lot in life, nothing can be done to change it.'

" 'But I cannot stand to lose them!' I cried. 'There must be some way you can help!'

"Again she pursed her lips, narrowed her eyes, and studied me closely.

" 'There is one thing I could do,' she said. 'I cannot remove the curse. Members of the Fowler family will still die before their time. But perhaps I can alter the curse just a little so that, in a way, the members of your family will remain with you always.'

" 'Do it!' I begged. 'Whatever it is, please do it!'

" 'All right,' she said. 'But I must warn you there may be consequences that none of us can foresee. Spells are best not tampered with, and the dead prefer to sleep undisturbed.' "

Chapter Twenty

Nicole jumped out of the chair and headed for the attic. Suddenly, everything seemed to make sense.

There were pages and pages of the history left to read, but she had to check on something first, to see if she was right, to see if she was really starting to understand what was going on.

She scrambled up the ladder and scooted along the passageway on all fours as fast as she could. She bounded up the dark staircase, not caring which ones were dangerous, the beam of the flashlight zigzagging in front of her. At the top, she jammed the key into the lock and shoved the door open with her shoulder.

She ran to the middle of the room, flung open the lid of the trunk, and shone the light inside.

There were perhaps two dozen dolls piled up inside.

Nicole took a deep breath to calm herself, and began to sort through them. One by one, she placed them on the floor outside the trunk, handling each one more tenderly than she had ever handled any dolls of her own.

Because, if she was right, these were more than just dolls. Much more.

The bride ... that would be Lenore, who had died in the accident on the way to her wedding. The scholar in the graduation cap and gown ... that must be Henry, who had died the morning of his college graduation.

These must be the ghosts of those who had lived in this house and died before their time. The witch in Salem must have transformed their spirits into dolls, so the old man could take them out and see them again and not feel so lonely and deserted and filled with grief.

His children and grandchildren were still dead, as the witch had said they would be. And yet in a way they were still here, too, still in the house.

Nicole removed some more of the dolls, or whatever they were.

Then she saw what she had been looking for. She picked it up gently and examined it in the beam of her flashlight.

It was a doll in the image of a young man. His

black hair was parted in the middle. He wore gold-rimmed spectacles and a serious expression. He was dressed in a white shirt, bow tie, and a black formal jacket with tails.

He was seated in a chair. Against his left shoulder rested a cello.

Nicole sighed, and her whole body seemed to relax. At least now she knew what she was dealing with.

This, surely, was John Fowler, the musician who had died the day before he was to give his first big concert in Boston. He was the one who had been making the mournful music that had disturbed her sleep and made her weep.

Nicole didn't know what she was supposed to do now. But at least now there were some things she *did* know.

No ghosts had been playing with the dolls, putting them in different parts of the attic. No mouse had been playing the cello. The dolls somehow came to life themselves and played music and moved around and did who knew what else.

And there was something else Nicole now knew. She wasn't crazy. This stuff — the music, the scuffling noises, the dolls moving into different positions — had really been happening. It hadn't been her imagination, or too many books, or just plain insanity.

It was real. Scary things were happening, but losing her mind wasn't one of them.

Her body relaxed so much she felt like collapsing. She hadn't realized how tense she had been. But now the tension was gone, and her legs felt rubbery.

She was about to leave the attic, and perhaps even take a nap, when something in the trunk caught her eye.

Lying face-down was a doll smaller than many of the others, with bright, shoulder-length golden-blond hair. It looked like a child.

Nicole gently picked it up and turned it over.

Then she screamed.

It was Casey.

Chapter Twenty-One

Nicole ran from the attic, slamming the door behind her.

That doll could only mean one thing. The curse was on the house, not the family.

Now it had struck Casey. There could be no other explanation. Casey's big moment was supposed to come tomorrow. She was going to star in the school play. Now that would never happen.

Unless there was still time to save her.

Hoping against hope, Nicole half ran, half tumbled down the stairs. Tears streamed down her face. She ran out of the house and looked around wildly.

"Casey!" she yelled.

There was no reply. Black clouds billowed in, throwing the house and the clearing into shadow.

Nicole stood frozen. Then she ran to the cemetery. She ignored the adult graves and sprinted to the smaller stones under which the children were buried. She ran from one stone to another, read the name, then moved on again.

It started to rain.

Nicole ran to another grave, and another, until she came to one that made her blood run cold.

"Casey Fowler," the stone read. "1914 - 1921. Her memory will be with us always."

It was too late. Everything fit. This girl was named Casey; so was her sister. This girl was seven years old; so was her sister. The dates were wrong, but history had surely repeated itself.

Casey was dead. Nicole sank to her knees. The wind kicked up, and the rain slanted to the ground and turned to sleet. Nicole's hair was wet and matted, and it stuck to the back of her neck.

She didn't care. All she knew was that her little sister — her beautiful, smart, funny little sister — had died. Nicole regretted every unkind word she had ever said to Casey, every trick she had ever played on her, every time she had ever called her a name.

She could not live without her. There was nothing left for her, no reason to go on.

She knelt among the gravestones, weeping, her head bowed, her clothes soaked through, the sleet forming icicles in her hair.

Suddenly, she heard a voice behind her.

Nicole turned. It was Casey.

"What the heck are you doing out here?" Casey asked. "Have you lost your mind?"

"Casey!" Nicole shouted. "You stupid jerk! I love you!"

Chapter Twenty-Two

       Nicole sneezed all the way through Casey's play.

       She had taken a hot bath that night to try to get some warmth back into her bones, but she had caught cold anyway. She was scolded by her mother, who wanted to know what in the world she had been doing outside in weather like that.

       "Playing," Nicole said weakly, but her mother didn't find that answer very convincing.

       Each time Nicole sneezed during the play, her teacher, Mrs. Chestnut with the horsy teeth, glared over at her disapprovingly. She didn't seem so delighted by Nicole any more.

       But Casey didn't mind the sneezing. She was the star of the show, which was all she cared about.

       Nicole looked at her father. He was looking up at the stage, beaming with pride.

       Nicole scowled at him and sneezed. What did

he care that Casey had almost died?

Of course, he didn't realize it. Then again, he didn't realize much, Nicole thought. He still thought moving to an old house in Massachusetts had been a terrific idea. What the heck did he know?

Nicole had to admit, when she thought about it, that Casey really *hadn't* almost died. In fact, nothing had happened to her at all.

"*I'm* the one who almost died, out there in the rain and sleet," she thought to herself bitterly. "And he doesn't even care, grinning up at the stage like that."

The whole thing with Casey had been a mistake. Nicole realized now that she had put two and two together and come up with five.

There had been a doll that looked similar to Casey — startlingly similar. And there had been a grave for someone with the same first name, and the same age. But the different last name and the wrong dates of birth and death should have been a tip-off.

It had all been nothing but a horrible, horrible coincidence.

*   *   *

Casey carried the flashlight as she and Nicole

114

entered the attic.

The music had woken them in the night again, after they had come home from the play, and kept them awake all night. They knew something had to be done. They couldn't go on like this, scared and sleepless.

They walked to the trunk, the beam of the flashlight cutting a tunnel of light through the darkness.

The trunk was empty.

Nor were there any dolls on the floor nearby.

Suddenly, they heard a noise behind them. They turned, Casey swung the beam around, and they saw the scholar standing frozen against the wall, his hands in front of his face. His cap had been knocked askew, and he had a bruise on his face, as if he had been in a fight.

But the most amazing thing was he wasn't the size of a doll any more. He still looked like a doll, and he wasn't moving.

But he was the size of a full-grown man!

Nicole and Casey gasped.

Then they heard a voice screaming from another side of the room

"Why don't you let the dead rest in peace!"

yelled a woman's voice.

The girls swung around again, and the beam of light settled on the woman who looked like a farmer's wife. She was full-sized, too — and frozen in place with a yell on her lips and her finger pointed straight at Casey and Nicole.

From off to their right came a man's voice: "We hate you!"

Casey screamed.

"Nicole," she cried. "Something's trying to grab me!"

The flashlight clattered to the floor. Nicole dived to pick it up. She shone the light on Casey, who was caught in the grip of the cello player — who was now frozen in place, motionless, an angry grimace on his face. Casey was kicking furiously, trying to wriggle free.

"Nicole, help!" she yelled. "They're going to kill us!"

Nicole heard a swish of air right above her head. She turned, and shone the light on a doll she had not seen before, a man frozen in place with a sword in his hand.

"Nicole, help me!" Casey yelled.

Suddenly, in her terror, it dawned on Nicole

that she never saw the dolls move. They couldn't move in the light! They could only move in darkness!

She had to get to the window and tear the blankets off it. But the flashlight wasn't enough. She had to let the sun into the room.

She ran, but she couldn't remember which wall the window was on.

"Please!" Casey screamed.

Nicole shone the light on the wall, but saw only the wedding dress and the musket. Then she whirled around to shine the light behind her so she could freeze anyone who was about to attack her.

She sidled along the wall, groping for the window.

Finally, she found it. She grabbed the blanket with one hand and tried to yank it away. It was nailed tightly to the window frame. It wouldn't come loose.

"Nicole! He's choking me!" Casey yelled.

In desperation, Nicole dropped the flashlight and grabbed the blanket with both hands and pulled with all her might.

Something grabbed her from behind and tried to pull her away from the window. Whatever it was wrapped its arms around her waist and tugged. Nicole could hear angry gasps in her ear and feel its hot

117

breath on her neck.

Suddenly, the blanket gave way and ripped from the window. Casey and whatever was pulling her from behind tumbled back onto the floor. Sunlight streamed into the attic, slanting in through the window and lighting the particles of dust that floated in the air.

Nicole stood up and looked around. Behind her on the floor, motionless, lay a man in a suit. The one who was elected senator had been trying to pull her away from the window. In the middle of the floor, Casey was in the grasp of the cello player, who now looked like a large statue.

His hands were still clamped around Casey's throat.

Nicole walked over and, using all her strength, pried the hands apart.

Casey wriggled free and bent over, gasping and catching her breath.

"You all right?" Nicole asked.

"Yeah," Casey said. "I am now. Thanks to you."

Arm in arm, the girls walked slowly toward the door. All around, life-sized dolls lay in strange positions. Some had been fighting with each other. Others had been ready to leap on the girls. In the corner, a soldier was kneeling down, aiming a rifle.

Fortunately, he had never gotten the chance to fire.

The girls walked out the door, and locked it firmly behind them.

Chapter Twenty-Three

Nicole and Casey slept together again that night. It wasn't so much that they were scared. After what they had been through, each just wanted to make sure the other was there. It had been a close call.

When they awoke, the whole house seemed sunnier. They knew they were safe. There would be no more scritching in the night, no more cello playing, no more drumming.

If the dolls only came to life in total darkness, they would never come to life again. Nicole and Casey knew that, no matter how cloudy or moonless the night, there was always some light, even if only the teeniest bit. It was never really totally pitch black. The attic would never be totally dark again.

The way Nicole figured it, old Franklin Fowler had gotten tired of looking at his relatives as lifeless dolls. And he had figured out, perhaps by accident, that they came to life in total darkness.

Then, perhaps, he had built the attic, and nailed the blanket over the window, so they could come to life. Maybe he even visited them, blew out his candle, and talked to them.

Why he locked them in the trunk was impossible to say. Maybe they had fought one another, as even living family members of the same generation will do from time to time. Or maybe, angry at not being left undisturbed in death, they had attacked the old man the way they had attacked the sisters.

Well, they could rest undisturbed now. Nicole would never nail the blanket over the window, that was for sure. There would always be at least a little smidgen of light filtering in through the window.

All these things were still going through Nicole's mind that morning at breakfast. The kitchen seemed sunny, bright, and comfortable. Their mother was bustling about making their lunches. Their father was reading the newspaper.

"Dad," Nicole said. "If I should ever die, like, before my time?"

Her father's face peered quizzically from around the newspaper. He had one eyebrow up and the other down, the way he always did when he was baffled by something she was saying.

"If that should ever happen," Nicole said, "could you, like, just bury me and leave me alone? I mean, it would be okay to grieve and all, but don't try to bring me back to life or anything, okay? Just bury me, accept it, and move on."

Her mother had paused with a knife full of peanut butter half-way between the jar and the bread. Her father's face looked more befuddled than ever.

"Why, Nicole," he murmured. "I do believe that's one of the strangest things you've ever said."

TUESDAY'S CHILD

a memoir

REVIEWS

"...A magnificent guide for readers unfamiliar with Ghana and its culture.... Her love of people and their individual idiosyncrasies is consistent throughout. From [her] no-nonsense Nana, who wonders why anyone would try to combine love with marriage, to her supportive and sharp-minded father, to her junk-food- craving mother, who alternates between western notions and small-town tribal ideas, the characters are memorable."

~Publishers Weekly [2010 Amazon Breakthrough Novel Contest]

"...the memories are fond, and never does the writing become fraught or melodramatic. Instead of sinking into sadness...a wonderful companion piece to My First Coup D'Etat, a memoir by John Dramani Mahama."

~Ayesha Harruna Attah, Author of Harmattan Rain

"Mary Ashun's Tuesday's Child is a lively and lyrical memoir...a refreshing alternative to the dominant discourses that circulate in the Global North of austere African childhoods, Mary's narrative is full of love, abundance, the rich potential of cross-cultural friendships, and a fascinating family not soon forgotten.

~ Cheryl Cowdy, Assistant Professor, York University

Kente Publishing
P.O Box AH1350
Achimota,Ghana

All Photos courtesy of Mary Ashun

Layout and Cover design by E.K Bitherman

Printed in Canada

ISBN-13:978-1481195096
ISBN-10:1481195093

Author's Note

This non-fiction work has taken liberties with names and places but all memories are
mostly my own. Many thanks to all those who helped solidify some of those memories by
recounting their perspectives of incidents that have been modified to allow the privacy of
some individuals to be maintained. All Rights Reserved. Any questions? Please write to
kentepublishing@gmail.com. My website also has links that readers might find interesting
(www.maryashun.com) and I can be reached at asabeaashun@gmail.com

Tuesday's Child

A memoir

MARY ASHUN

<<>>

Monday's child is fair of face

Tuesday's child is full of grace.

Wednesday's child is full of woe.

Thursday's child has far to go.

Friday's child is loving and giving.

Saturday's child works hard for a living.

But the child who is born on the Sabbath Day

Is bonny and blithe and good and gay.

First recorded in A. E. Bray's Traditions of Devonshire
(Volume II, pp. 287–288) 1838, England

TABLE OF CONTENTS

Part 1

Mmere Dane

Time Changes

PROLOGUE:

"A Person who has children does not die"
~ A proverb from Nigeria

TUESDAY Nov 5, 1968, Ghana

The red and yellow taxi sped into the tiny alcove at the entrance to the Korle-Bu Teaching Hospital, spewing toxic smoke from an exhaust that was so loud it announced its presence long before the car was visible. It was 2:35 a.m. and the hospital was swathed in darkness, with the few orderlies and nurses holding lanterns or candles up to light whatever needed to be lit. A rickety hospital gurney, flying at top speed down a corridor, met a tall, slim *Hausa* orderly and literally knocked the man over. Its inept driver was another orderly, who was stocky and bore a tribal cut on his left cheek. He lumbered down the corridor, struggling to hold onto the wayward gurney. Half way down the hallway the gurney got stuck in a large crack on the floor where an errant tile, laid down *circa* 1950, had finally decided to give up the ghost after eighteen years of scant maintenance. It would seem that the orderly had received instructions to bring this gurney down because of the screaming

woman being helped out of the taxi with legs open wide and pain contorting her features.

No telephone call had announced her arrival. Two years after Kwame Nkrumah, the architect of Ghanaian independence, was deposed by a military coup, it was unlikely that telephone lines were in operation, or that if a call had been placed, anyone would care enough to answer it. The pregnant woman was just over five feet tall with a bouffant hairstyle, large eyes and, save for the protrusion of an oncoming baby, a slight build. Helping her out of the taxi were two people: a very short woman, wizened and yet firm, with a strong jaw and piercing dark eyes, wearing traditional cloth and fake leather slippers and a tall man in his thirties with thick black hair and large glasses that made him look every inch the academic. He looked nervous, like an unwilling participant; the tiny old woman was leading the way.

"Can't anyone see we need a doctor?" she shouted through the darkness.

No one answered her, so she continued pulling the pregnant woman and the man towards the stocky orderly who was failing to dislodge the gurney from the cracked floor. She gently released her hold on the pregnant woman who then leaned heavily on the man. The old woman rushed towards the orderly, yanked his hands away from the gurney and, with all the force of her small frame, struggled to dislodge the gurney from the cracked floor.

"So is no one going to help me? The fact that Nkrumah has been deposed doesn't mean we can't use common sense to help people!"

"Please Madam, I was trying to help but…"

"But what? Since you people kicked out the white people, everything has gone downhill. Are you one of the people who pulled down Nkrumah's statue in Accra after the coup? Or are you one of those who admired him?"

The orderly did not respond. The old woman sucked in her teeth with a *tschew* sound as she kept tugging and pulling the crooked gurney in pitch-black darkness while muttering to herself.

"This Ghana of ours, when are we going to be truly free eh? We have the Volta Lake but we can't make enough electricity. We have gold but somehow, it cannot be sold to build proper hospitals. We have diamonds and yet our paved roads end just outside the capital city of Accra. And then some stupid people decide that the best way to move forward is to kick out the people who at least knew what they were doing!"

Two things then happened all at once. The gurney came loose, flinging the old woman against the cement wall just as a wail emanated from the pregnant woman. Suddenly, lanterns appeared as nurses seemed to spring into action.

"Look at you people—can't you see that she is the one who needs the help? She's having a baby and if you don't hurry up, her husband will also faint from anxiety!"

The old woman was looking angrily at the hospital workers who

had rushed to her aid. She pointed them in the direction of the pregnant woman and her husband as she struggled to get back on her feet. They wheeled the pregnant woman along the corridor, taking care to avoid the potholes in the floor as well as the nervous husband. The pregnant woman whimpered. The man consoled. The old woman glared.

By 3:30 a.m. everyone was tired, especially the pregnant woman. A doctor had come into the birthing ward to assess her and declared her to be well on the way to delivery of a healthy baby. The husband was pacing up and down the darkened hallway; anyone passing him as he paced could hear him muttering a prayer. The old woman was inside the room holding the pregnant woman's hand. Every so often she'd bend towards the pregnant woman and say something softly…it almost sounded like a song.

"Yeh me ho nsenkyerene, Na ensi mi yie, Na ma tanfo ehu…"

At 4:30 a.m. as the sun began its ascent into the Ghanaian sky and the cocks were beginning to let out their morning welcome, the contractions were now just one minute apart. The wails had increased in number and intensity and the prayers coming from the hallway continued abated. There were now two nurses and a doctor in the room. And of course, the old woman.

"Push, push, push," they all seemed to be saying.

The pregnant woman did as she was told.

4:45 a.m. arrived. The old woman moved towards the single window in the room, standing with her back to the action, muttering under her breath; every so often, she'd turn to look at the heaving woman. She moved closer as the doctor announced that the head was crowning.

At 4:55 a.m. a baby's wail pierced the crisp morning air. There were claps everywhere as all those present rejoiced in the new birth. Or maybe they rejoiced at the sunlight streaming through the single window, allowing everyone to do their jobs without the help of a candle or a lantern. The old woman kept shouting,

"Halleluyah! Praise the Lord! Halleluyah, he is good!"

The husband dashed in from the hallway, jubilant. The doctor held up the screaming baby, mucky from the ordeal, as one of the nurses enveloped it in a thick white towel.

"Congratulations Mr. and Mrs. Apea, you have a baby girl," announced the doctor.

"Correction. *We* have a baby girl," said the old woman.

Everyone laughed heartily, as if they had never been worried at all. A flurry of activity ensued as the doctor gave orders to the nurses. The lady in the bed looked exhausted but relieved. The baby was being measured and prodded at a wooden table by the window while the old lady looked on. After a few minutes, the doctor left and returned with some papers on a clipboard.

"Mr. Apea, I'm going to have to confirm some details in order to register the new baby. Let's start with the name."

"Mary Abena Asabea Apea," the father responded without hesitation.

"Uhm.... father's name we have on record: Emmanuel Apea. Profession: Chemistry Teacher at Achimota School. Hometown: Asamankese in the Eastern Region. An address?"

"P.O Box AH1245, Achimota," Mr. Apea replied.

The doctor made a few scribbles on the clipboard.

"And Mr. Apea, can you please confirm your wife's details for me?"
"Yes of course. Her name is Emma Apea. She is also a teacher by profession, currently at Anumle Middle School and her hometown is Asamankese also."
"Thank you," acknowledged the doctor. He continued his scribbling for a minute more and turned around when he heard one of the nurses call to him.
"Doctor, we are done. Would you like to take another look?"
"Why, what is wrong?" said the old woman springing into action from her perch at the corner of the room.
The doctor ignored her as he poked and prodded the little baby. Mr. Apea left his wife's side and moved across the room to the old woman, imploring her with his eyes and his words.
"Nana, you know they just say these things as they check the baby over, so please don't be worried. We've prayed long and hard and look, Emma is doing well so I'm sure there's no cause for alarm."
"But…but…ah well…are you sure?" Nana bleated out.
Mr. Apea smiled a very re-assuring smile. Even Nana couldn't afford to be worried as she basked in the glow of Emmanuel's confidence that everything would be all right with this first-born child.

I loved this story of how I was born because, somehow, all three family members present at the birth—Nana, Mummy and Daddy —managed to tell the story differently. This version just recounted is Mummy's and I guess I should take her word for it since after all, she was the one giving birth. Daddy claims that he fell asleep at home after dropping Mummy off at the hospital, and that he

knew I'd been born only because one of his friends, who was a doctor at the hospital called to congratulate him; he'd thought the birthing process was a few days long, so it'd be okay to take a nap while Mummy negotiated labour all by herself! For me however, Nana's tale—given her larger than life personality—always seemed to have a ring of truth to it. In her version, she alone delivered the baby. And when I came out, I shocked everyone by uttering my first word.

And of course I said, 'Nana'.

1

*"They will turn around and eat you up.
Then what?"*

1968-74, Ghana

Dad was a teacher in Achimota School, named for the suburb
where we lived on the outskirts of Accra on Outlaws Hill. He spent
his days mixing chemicals in the lab, causing mini-explosions that
excited his students, and at night for no charge, he tutored students
who were falling behind. In those days, teaching at the prestigious
Achimota School was an honour. It was the first government
funded school that educated Ghanaian boys and girls together.
The Gold Coast—as Ghana was then called—was governed by Sir
Gordon Guggisberg, who wanted to set up a school to train those
who were born 'but to rule, through service given' according to the
school song.
Several African leaders—some famous, many infamous—have
been educated at this institution: the first president of Ghana and
architect of independence Kwame Nkrumah, presidential

candidate Edward Akuffo Addo, two-time president Jerry John Rawlings, late president John Evans Atta Mills, and former president Kofi Busia; as well as Robert Mugabe, president of Zimbabwe, Dauda Jawara, the first president of Gambia, authors Ayi Kwei Armah and Cyprian Ekwensi, and Ekow Spio-Garbrah, former Ambassador to the United States.

Part of Dad's joy at teaching in Achimota was the fact that he was an alumnus. His father, Nenye Adu, took great pride in the fact that his son had won a scholarship to attend the prestigious school. A cash-poor but politically powerful landowner, Nenye had managed to make himself a chief of the village of *Anum*. along with that position came many wives and many children. Dad's mother Asabea was the only wedded wife; the others were really chieftaincy concubines who together produced babies at the rate of about three a year, as was their royal duty; as a result, Dad had many brothers and sisters he hardly knew. No child from the village had ever attended Achimota School, so for the very special occasion of his departure for school, Dad was given all the earnings from his father's cocoa production for the month, to buy a pair of shoes—his first real pair, at the age of fifteen. All students at Achimota had to wear the same shoes—they were part of the uniform—and they came to be known as 'Achimota sandals'.

Dad finished Achimota School, went on to the University of Ghana, and completed his teacher-training course at Cape Coast as well as the required practice teaching. He was thrilled when he was offered a teaching job at Achimota because it came with a bungalow; Number 14, right at the corner of the main entrance to the school, minutes from the school post office and the swimming

pool, and just three doors from the Headmaster's Residence. This was where I began life.

<<>>

Mum and I stayed in the hospital for two days after my birth. Although visitors were not allowed to stay all the time, my ubiquitous grandmother Nana, found a way to be there around the clock until we were discharged. She smuggled food in even though the nurses forbade mummy from eating certain foods until she'd recovered. Nana carried me up and down the hallways, praying for me, singing to me and telling me what was going on in the hospital that day. When we were finally discharged and got home to Number 14, Nana never left my side even though Mummy was on maternity leave and was perfectly capable of handling a new baby. Nana bathed me several times a day, rubbed shea butter all over my body, put a huge glob of it on the soft membranous portion of my head, all the while blowing into my face several times a day to clean me and ward off evil spirits. Dad was horrified when he came home for lunch one day, to find me fast asleep and snoring heavily. Barely a month old, I had a shea butter glob on my forehead.

"Nana, what is that thing?"

"It's shea butter," she responded imperiously. Nana was very much aware that he knew nothing about babies and their needs.

"But Nana, Mary can't breathe," Dad said, a tad concerned.

"Who told you she couldn't breathe? Is that in one of your big books, huh?"

"Actually yes. That soft portion of her head will slowly harden but in the meantime, the thinness helps with the breathing process," Daddy explained.

"And what if she catches a cold huh? Because this school is on a hill, there is a breeze that could be damaging to a child and besides —the evil spirits are just waiting for a small opportunity to cause sickness and death so this shea butter will stop them cold!"

Dad just shook his head and smiled. You could never win an argument with Nana. When it had to do with me, she made sure everyone knew that she was the reigning authority. During the day she kept me indoors for fear of darkening my skin beyond an acceptable hue. When Dad asked what an acceptable hue was, she said:

"So that white people don't run away when they see her." There were few white people in Achimota at the time, and Dad says he could not recall seeing any of them running away from any black people. He couldn't resist asking her a question.

"Has anyone run away from you because you were too dark?"

"No…not yet anyway. But that's why you have to take precautions, Emmanuel. That's also why I am shaping her head with the cloth and hot water every day so that she will have a royally shaped head. You know, you can't have people looking at her thinking she is a nobody ohhhh? She is a somebody!"

Dad sighed again, remembering the ritual he saw Nana performing whenever she bathed me, which was four or five times a day. With her legs straddling the large basin, she would lay me tummy down across her outstretched legs and massage my whole body with a hot cloth while I yelled and screamed in pain and anger. Of course none of this fazed her. She would reprimand me in a firm but soothing voice. "Yes, now it hurts, but one day when your bones are strong and your skin is taut and unwrinkled, you will thank me, so shut up."

<<>>

When I was four months old, Daddy received a scholarship to study for his master's degree at the University of Sydney in Australia. While he was away we had to leave our beautiful bungalow at Number 14 and along with my older cousin Isaac who was staying with us, move to a two-bedroom compound house in Achimota Village—a huge step down from living on the Achimota School Campus. A compound house is one where several families live in close proximity, sharing a common courtyard space as well as toilets and bathrooms. Our compound house had twelve adults and nine children who shared one bathroom and one toilet. By eight months of age I was a professional crawler and began to explore my small world in that house, dirtying myself several times over each day and getting sick with malaria at least once a month.

My mother's maternity leave was over, and she had started teaching at the Anglican Primary School while Nana stayed home with Isaac and I. Several times a month, Mum was summoned to the Head Mistress' office and there we were: Nana with me strapped to her back with a traditional cloth, my neck lolling, eyes glassy, mouth drooling with fever. Her mission? To get money to take me to the hospital. Nana hardly ever had money of her own. Whatever she received in gifts she'd give away to someone who needed it more so every time she needed to take me to the hospital, she'd have to walk for half an hour to get to Mummy's school.

Of course, Mummy couldn't let her go off by herself so she'd always ask for permission to leave, which was given reluctantly, and

together they'd get into a taxi that would race us all to Achimota Hospital, hoping to get a doctor before I died of malaria. On the way, Nana would blow into my face chanting:

"The sky is claiming her ohhh…look at her eyes …staring up at the sky.

"*Yesu mogya nka wa nim,*
Yesu mogya nka wa nim",
May the blood of Jesus smite you evil spirits.

Needless to say, I survived all those attacks that Nana was convinced were sent by the devil, but I was a poor eater. Nana had a little trick to get me to eat. At around age two I'd started wondering where my Daddy was, and was told that he was on a plane (thus beginning a lifelong fascination with airplanes). Nana would remind me that the planes that flew overhead only stopped for those who ate their lunch and dinner. If I ate both very well, there was a good chance I would see my Daddy again. I was rewarded for all the lunches and dinners eaten under duress when Daddy returned in 1970, when I was about two and half years old. He immediately moved us to an apartment on the lower floor of a two-storey building belonging to a midwife. We didn't last too long there because of the screaming and crying at all hours of the day and night, as women went through the arduous process of pushing their babies out. As well, Maame Agyeiwaa, who lived across the hallway from us, had two maids that she beat for the smallest mistakes— like buying five plantains at the market stall instead of four or six, or looking at her the wrong way, or using the wrong pot to cook in, even though the food still got cooked. She would take a long belt to them and whip them across every part of their bodies. Even when they were writhing in pain on the floor, she continued

slicing their backs with her whip.

The only person she feared was Nana, so whenever there was extreme wailing, we'd stop and listen, trying to decipher if it was a woman in labour or a woman being whipped. One day, Nana left me in the living room, tied her cloth resolutely around her waist, put on what we called her 'no nonsense' face, and went to confront the monster. She pulled herself to her full height—under five feet and closer to four— reached out and grabbed the belt-like whip, and stared long and hard at Maame Agyeiwaa's plump, sweaty face. "Agyeiwaa, aren't these girls somebody's children? Do you want to kill them or what? What is one finger of plantain in the grand scheme of things? Huh? Stop this foolishness right now."

Maame Agyeiwaa apologized for disturbing her, not for beating the girls. Nana clearly needed more of an apology than that, and continued to stare her down. Agyeiwaa finally demurred.
"Ok, Nana. I know I beat them but I don't think it's too much. When I'm giving them instructions, they don't really listen and they keep doing the wrong thing. I'm tired of them, just tired of them."
"Maybe you talk too much," Nana offered.
Agyeiwaa sighed, clearly not agreeing with Nana. She wished she could be brave enough to tell Nana that *she* talked a lot too. Nana, sensing a resolution of sorts, could not resist the urge to throw in a proverb.
"You do not have to respond to a tiny annoying mosquito with a large hammer. You know what will happen? You will miss and hurt yourself. Let them get up, clean up and go and do their chores."

When Nana returned, Mummy teased her about her courage in confronting Maame Agyeiwaa, a woman whose husband was a Sales Manager for Coca-Cola and who owned three large stores in Makola and two vans that she used as rental vehicles, as well as large farms outside Accra.

"You're wondering why I'm able to tell the lioness that her breath stinks? It's because sometimes the stench gets so bad that if somebody doesn't say something, everybody will die. If the people around you are turning into animals and you do nothing about it, one day when they are fully animals, they will turn around and eat you up. Then what?"

Daddy moved us into a first-floor apartment just before I turned three. My brother Yaw was born a week after my third birthday. As the first-born son he was named Emmanuel Junior, and because he was born on Thursday he was called Yaw, one of the Ghanaian names designated for babies born on that day.

Dad was now working for the government and was assigned to act as a country representative for the American Peace Corps, for which he had to undertake an 18-month training program in New York. When he returned, I was sent to Lincoln International School, an American school for expatriate children and anyone else who could afford the expensive fees. Dad got a discount, so I was able to attend the school for about a year. I have fond memories of the place—cool colours on the walls, brightly coloured carpets, and piano music playing through discreetly placed loudspeakers. Most significant of all, it was the first time I tasted milk that didn't come condensed in a can. I came home one day to tell Mummy and

Nana about the white watery liquid that didn't taste like anything at all. Nana was wary.

"Emma, we have to find out about this thing the white people are giving to Mary oh? What if it dulls the brain? It will be hard to marry her off if she is soft in the head from drinking that thing."

"It's just milk, Nana. It comes from cows remember?"

"Don't talk to me like I'm foolish. Of course I know it comes from cows but since when did people start drinking the raw version, huh?"

She needn't have worried since Dad ran out of money, withdrew me from Lincoln, and enrolled me in St. John's Preparatory School, where no one had ever heard of watery milk. At least I still had my bike, which Dad had bought me while I was attending Lincoln. It had ribbons on the handles and was coloured yellow and green. I love green.

<<>>

By the time I was six, we lived in a lovely house in the town of Alogboshie. The property was beautifully landscaped and quite modern. There was a carport at the side of the house and a huge lawn. One humid September morning, Daddy's VW Beetle gave up the ghost and they had to figure out a way to get me to school. Mummy had to leave to her school, and Dad had to take the streetcar popularly known as a *trotro*, to work. The only way for me to get to school was in the company of Nana.

Once the realization hit me that I'd have to take her to school with me, I started hatching a plot against Nana. There was no way I was letting anyone see her, because she was old and they might think

she was my mother. What horror! Besides, she never did her hair at the hair salon and she never wore a dress like Mummy. I was by now well aware that crying was only the first step in putting something over on Nana. Crying couldn't last long because it would start to annoy her. The way to get to Nana was to let her think she was helping someone. This I knew from all the times my clothes and Yaw's would go missing because she'd taken them to the village to give to children who had no clothes. She said we had too much and it would go to our heads. So, I told her that I wanted to start a school with the neighbourhood children and teach them to read. Nana had had to leave school in the primary years, because her father thought it wasn't important to educate girls. She could read the Bible in the local language, *Twi*, and she knew the value of learning to read English just by virtue of seeing Mum and Dad succeed in their professions.

It took two days to repair the Beetle, and in that short time Nana and I had established our own school. Right in front of our house, about ten neighbourhood children sat in 'my' classroom, wearing my clothes, and being fed by my grandmother. I think Nana enjoyed it more than I did.

<<>>

Alogboshie was where my sister Esther was born. Surprisingly, Dad was in such shock from witnessing her birth that he walked around in a daze for several days after Mummy came home from the midwife's. Nana never let him near the kitchen; she made him hibernate and eat alone in his room, away from all the baby business. He was bossed around by Nana this way all the time,

not just when Mum had a baby. For instance, when he returned from the USA and asked for *kenkey* and fried fish, something he'd missed while in America, Nana refused and instead gave him sliced bread and butter.

"Now that your stomach is like the white man's stomach, you have to be careful. The grinders in your stomach will not recognize *kenkey* because of all the watery food you have eaten. If you're not careful, your intestines will knot up and pop out of your belly. Then you'll die. Did you hear that? You'll die and then the devil will be happy. So let your stomach get used to our foods by starting off with porridge, bread and butter—that's the heaviest food white people eat isn't it?"

I woke up one morning with my braids undone. This was unusual because Mummy had put them in just the day before, and I quite liked them. Come morning, my kinky Afro hair was standing on end and I looked positively unkempt. I ran into Mummy's room crying. One look at me told her who the culprit was. In we marched to Nana's room where she and ten-month-old Esther were lying down on a mat—Nana reading her *Twi* Bible, Esther tearing newspapers apart in delight.

"Nana, what is the meaning of this?" Mum asked.

"Her head was hurting," Nana replied, unconcerned.

"Did she say her head was hurting?"

"She didn't have to. Her sleep was restless and her brow was furrowed. A child her age should not have a furrowed brow; it shows she is worried about something."

"But Nana, it took me hours to put those braids in Mary's hair!"

"Really? I thought it took less than an hour since it wasn't very nice

anyway. Besides, she looks better with her hair combed out, don't you think?"

Mummy stomped out of the room fuming, dragging me along with her.

The afternoon was warm and hazy. After Nana finished feeding Esther, she went back to her Bible study. Esther kept on rolling on Nana's back as she lay on the raffia mat, so Nana came up with a perfect plan to get rid of her for a while.

"Esther, why don't you go and fetch me some water?"

She passed an empty mug to Esther who gurgled and cooed excitedly. She waddled out of the room with the mug while Nana congratulated herself on her plan to get some peace and quiet. She opened her Bible to Romans 15 and began to read about how Paul the Apostle admonished the church in Rome to be of service to one another. As she read she would let out murmur in delight at the miracles of the early apostles.

About five minutes after Esther left, she was back with the mug. She passed it to Nana who without looking took a drink.

"Good girl, go and fetch some more," she said to Esther. She was still reading Romans.

Esther got her some more water. Again, Nana thanked her and relished the few minutes of peace she was getting to have her Bible study. After the third drink from Esther's mug, Nana realized that she had no idea how a ten-month-old was fetching water. She gave the mug back to Esther and followed her closely as she waddled towards the source of the water.

The trip ended in the bathroom, where Nana watched in horror

as Esther dipped the mug into the toilet, fetched some water and excitedly headed towards Nana's room. She wanted to gag as Esther handed the mug to her. She murmured thanks but refused to drink. Esther started crying as she shoved the mug into Nana's face. Nana said 'thanks, you're a good girl, thanks, but no thanks'. Esther wouldn't let up. So Nana knelt in front of Esther, capitulated, and drank the toilet water. Nana told the story to the entire household in the evening.

"So that is why my mouth is all red. It's the palm oil I had to drink to get rid of the poison from the toilet. *Eiii,* maybe some of the witches in the village visited the house while I was meditating on the Word. Mmmhh… this world is a frightful place oh!"

Mummy laughed so hard she started crying. Esther had succeeded in doing what no one else could do: she'd literally brought Nana to her knees!

2

"If there is cause to hate someone, the cause to love has just begun"

1975 – 1977, England

In the mid-seventies, when I was just six years old, my father received a job offer in England with the Commonwealth Secretariat. The whole family, at the time Mummy, myself, brother Yaw, and sister Esther left Ghana and went to England with him. Nana, who'd lived with us ever since I was born, flatly refused to go with us to London and after much questioning, she confessed to a fear of flying. To try to convince her of the safety of a flying craft, we took her to the airport and let her watch planes take off and land at the modern Kotoka International Airport in Accra; all to no avail. Nana believed that if you chose to be carried up that high, your natural destination had to be heaven, and if you were lucky to be brought back alive, then God must not be ready for you.

My father's responsibilities were mainly to increase educational

opportunities for people in the developing world, and since the Commonwealth was made up mostly of poor countries, well—he was a busy man. From Trinidad & Tobago to Tanzania and Fiji, if there was a conference on education, my father had to be part of it. We had a steady stream of international visitors to our home in Chigwell, and now, on looking back, it developed a hankering for foreign lands in my siblings and I.

I can remember meeting all sorts of people who were escaping such dictators as Idi Amin in Uganda, for Dad had an unusual avocation: going to the airport after work and seeing if there were lost-looking Africans wandering the terminal. He would invite them home and they would stay with us up to a few weeks until they were connected with the African Students Union or their embassy, and then we wouldn't see them for a really long time. As a child, I can remember a constant stream of new people coming in and out of the house and Mummy always preparing an extra plate or two at the dinner table; she never knew who my father would bring home.

Our favourite family friends were the Khans. Azam and Shahana had three children: Bolaca, Shajeeb and Shalme who were exactly around me, Yaw, and Esther's ages. We'd spend Eid at their place and they'd spend Christmas at ours. Shahana made the most awesome basmati rice and curry and started us all on a love for foods from the Indian subcontinent. Her curried meats were delicious beyond words and as I write, I can almost taste my favourite curried chicken.

England was cold. In the seventies, that meant a lot of snow that

yielded many new options for playing. There was a field we had to cross to Limes Farm County School, and in the winter of 1975, that field was a deep and fluffy bed of knee-high snow that Esther sometimes disappeared in as Mummy helped us navigate our way to school.

My first day at the new school was not good. I got into class, got a smile from my teacher Ms. Collins, and was then 'displayed' before the class, who looked at me wide-eyed and curious. I didn't know why...I was only six.

'This is Mary, our new student from Africa,' said Ms. Collins.

Silence.

"Everyone say hello to Mary," urged a nervous Ms. Collins.

Murmurs of 'Hello, Mary' permeated the small classroom. Then she signed my death warrant with a question.

'Who would like to sit next to Mary?"

Silence. Shuffling of feet. Faces turned away guiltily.

It seemed like an eternity but suddenly, a blond haired boy about half way down the room said:

"I will!"

That was Guy. The second hottest Grade 2 boy this side of Essex; Stephen was the hottest but of course I didn't know that then. So I got to sit next to Guy, who forever became a good friend. He had a younger brother called Paddy—Patrick was the official name—but everyone called him Paddy.

Anyone who's been in a new school knows that after being introduced to your class, the next worst moment is recess time. The question of who to play with, loomed large before me as I walked out into the crisp September air. As I walked around aimlessly, I saw Yaw also looking lost, probably more than I was. He saw me and scurried over with tears in his eyes. As I wiped his almost

4-year-old face, we were surrounded by a bunch of children, all staring and pointing. One girl, the typical cheerleader type—she couldn't have been more than 8 years old—walked up to me and motioning with her hands, asked me to follow her. And so I did. What seemed like a sojourn led us to the girl's washroom where under the curious gaze of about five girls I was instructed by this alpha female to put my hands in the toilet. Now everytime I've told this story, I've had to stress it was the toilet, not the sink. People wonder why it was the sink and I have to say repeatedly that I honestly don't know. Maybe the children thought I'd make the sink dirty? I have no idea but they did explain it somewhat.

"We've got to flush the brown away…you're dirty."

So in went my arms, down came the plunger and whoosh came the sound of about ten gallons of water from some treatment plant in Essex, designed to wash away the brown dirt on my body. As I fought back huge tears, the girls flushed a couple more times, and when they realized I wasn't getting any cleaner, they gave up. I wasn't interesting anymore so they left me alone in the washroom. My first emotion was one of shame. Then it turned to anger.

Shortly after, fear took over as I realized that I was a target of some sort. I was clearly very different but I had no way of changing the difference that was setting me apart. The scene is so vivid for me now…I wonder, is it vivid for them too after over thirty years? The recess ending bell went and we had to go back to class. Mummy was waiting by the school fence for us at the end of that day and one look at our faces told her we didn't want to go back.

Dad was mad as hell. How dare they do that to his daughter? What did they think she was? A toy? I'd never seen him so upset before, but my mother was oddly resigned. She seemed powerless and yet as she tucked us into bed that night, her bedtime prayer ended

with "Lord, remind us that if there is cause to hate someone, the cause to love has just begun." I opened my eyes and looked inquiringly at her.

"One of your grandmother's proverbs. Does it make sense?"

I smiled. Not really, I thought. Perhaps it would make sense when all my enemies were crushed.

My father was in no mood to forgive anyone just yet. He marched to school with me the following day and asked to see poor Ms. Collins.

"They are just very curious Mr. Apea. You see, they haven't seen a black person before. They were just experimenting," was her reply to Dad's question about why it happened.

"Well they shouldn't experiment with my daughter!"

<<>>

I settled in nicely, once the horrors of the first few days were over. I was quite a show off sometimes. I always wanted to be first to do something and when it was announced at assembly that there was an audition for the Christmas play, I prepared myself. I had to be Mary because she was the main character in the Nativity story and I didn't do back up. So, hoping that this was a prelude to an eventual Oscar, I prepared like no one else. I memorized not just Mary's lines but the shepherds, the wise men and the angels too. I harbored a secret hope that something devastating would happen to all the cast members and then I would have to do the play all by myself; how delicious! So I strutted my stuff on the day of the audition and eagerly awaited the announcement after lunch.

"The wise men are Guy, Richard and Mark. The shepherds are Katy,

Melissa and James. Jason is King Herod, Joseph will be played by Stephen…"

At this point, I could contain the excitement no longer. I knew the next major part was Mary and I'd get to play her next to our resident hunk, Stephen.

I was so excited that I didn't even hear the next announcement. The one where Mrs. Collins told us who was to play Mary. Suffice it to say that on seeing everyone else's reaction, I knew it wasn't me and I was livid!

Why not? I shouted in my head. Who on God's earth was going to be a better Mary? I can't remember her name now but I do remember that she was a very quiet girl. No wonder I had forgotten she existed. What went wrong? I knew all my lines, I knew everyone's line even before the play had begun! She knew nothing, I knew everything…or so I thought. I boldly went up to Ms. Collins and asked why I didn't get a part. I must have sounded quite annoying.

"Well not everyone can get a part, Mary. There are twenty of you and only nine major parts," she explained.

"Besides," she continued. "There were no black people in Bible times."

"But …but…I really wanted to be Mary," I said weakly.

"I know, I know," she soothed. And then she got a conspiratorial gleam in her eye.

"You know, I think you could be the narrator since you know the whole play."

She was right with that last comment, and discarded as I felt that I didn't even get a walk on part like a Hebrew woman in the market place or in the temple in Jerusalem, I knew the offer of narrator was better than nothing. I ended up behind a screen, narrating the

whole story since many couldn't remember their lines on the day of the play. And all because there were no black people in Bible times?

From that day onwards, my best friend Cathy and I came up with a name that we thought was clever for the girl who played Mary. Fake Mary or FM for short. I cannot for the life of me remember her real name now. What a pity.

<<>>

I made some amazing friends at Limes Farm County School. Lisa, who was quite popular got to pick two friends to take for birthday treats at the movies. The new *King Kong* movie had just opened all over London and everyone who mattered was going to see it. Imagine my surprise when I got asked to come along with Cathy to see it with Lisa; several girls wondered why.

"How come she gets picked? She's black."

Lisa lived on the east side of the hill so we walked over to her house after school, met her parents and then set off to the movies. What an experience that was! I'd never been to the movies before and the movie itself, filled with Hollywood glitz and make-believe was amazing. Afterwards, we had cake and I got asked many questions from the adults there—I don't think they had seen a real, live African without a grass skirt or a spear in one hand. They also asked how I got to England and seemed shocked at my answer; at which they murmured:

"Fancy that…Africans in planes."

<<>>

Cathy was the sweetest freckle faced girl and her family, Dad, Mum and Billy were warm and loving to me. I never felt black when I was with them, just Mary. One day, I overheard her mother telling mine about how some of their neighbours moved out because we'd started walking their streets.

"If niggers come here, what's going to become of our neighbourhood," they'd said.

Needless to say, Cathy's parents stayed put and until we left England, we remained close friends. My favourite memory of her parents and how kind they were was on July 7, 1977. My school had qualified for the District Sports and I was the representative for the 400-meter race. I was pumped and ready to run and then my mother had a baby just a few days before the day of the race! My father was away on another of his trips, this time to Arusha in Tanzania so I had no one to come and watch me decimate the competition. Unbeknownst to me, Cathy had told her parents that neither one of my parents could be there so they planned to come and surprise me. We boarded a bus to take us to the site of the games, somewhere in Essex, and of course everyone sat by their best friend. Cathy and I were sitting at the middle of the bus. That was quite cool and it wasn't too far from Stephen and his gang. I just thought I'd die from 8-year-old desire. The bus chugged along and everyone was engrossed in his or her third grade fantasies when Liam, an annoying freckle-faced boy yelled loudly enough for everyone to hear.

"Who's got sardine sandwiches?"

Dead silence.

Cathy nudged me. She knew I loved sardine sandwiches.

"Oy," she whispered. "Did you bring sardine sandwiches?"

I froze in my seat.

"Yes," I mumbled.

"O my God, what are we going to do?"

We both sat paralyzed as Liam, Jack and Robin made their detective way from the front of the bus towards the back, inspecting everyone's lunch boxes looking for the offensive sardine sandwiches. Cathy's eyes popped out in fear of what would happen if we were discovered.

"Quick, where are they? Give them to me!"

I thrust them at her like they were hot potatoes and she immediately dropped them like hot potatoes and kicked them fast behind me. My very sharp ears heard my beloved sardine sandwiches careening towards the back of the bus and my mouth watered for what could have been. The sardine detectives got to us, paused a while as their noses detected a faint smell of fish and just as quickly dismissed it. Cathy couldn't like sardines. The black girl? Maybe, but would Cathy sit by her if she'd eaten sardines?

I breathed a sigh of utter relief as they continued their detective quest. Cathy and I knelt on our seats and cheered the boys on like we had no idea where the sandwiches were. Before they got to the back of the bus, there was a big whoop from Jack whose pseudo canine senses had detected the fish. The bus erupted in hoorays as he held it to his nose and acted like he was about to puke and stared accusingly at FM. She shook her head vehemently and held her lovely ham and cheese sandwiches up for everyone to see. No one cared. We all knew who had the sardine sandwiches and it was FM! Revenge was so sweet, if mean. Cathy and I gave high-fives and congratulated ourselves on her perfect kick that landed the evidence right at FM's door. A wicked thought occurred to me. Did Mary in the Bible like sardine sandwiches?

We arrived at the games in high spirits and it didn't take long for my race to be called. Imagine this: I am making my way towards my lane to start my stretches and pumps when I hear a voice in the crowd yell.

'What's that nigger doin' 'ere?"

'Go back to Africa!"

"Mary, go get them!" a third familiar voice said.

I swung my head round to the source of that third voice, and saw Cathy's parents waving frantically. I've never loved Cathy's family more. My eyes smarted from the tears and anger that seemed to course through my body like waves of torrential rain. How dare they call me nigger? I had never been more determined to do my best and as the referee yelled for us to get on our marks, my legs seemed to take on a new life form as I sped around the tracks like a pack of cheetahs was after me. I sobbed as I ran, burning up the track with all the frustrations possible for an eight-year-old to feel. I felt like I was running for all black people in the world—and Cathy's family too. Surely, the hopes of a whole race rested on my performance, did they not?

I won gold.

<<>>

Our three years in London were filled with such memories of people, places, silly games and unpredictable weather. We played *knock down ginger* on our neighbours—a game where the children in the neighbourhood would press the doorbell and run away. After a couple of times, we'd move to another street and try it again. Stupid stuff but it was totally fun and we hardly got into trouble. Guy and Paddy would come over and play on the weekends and we went over to their home too. We made friends

with another lovely family from Iceland—the Wests. Their children Melanie, and Eydis, along with Yaw, Esther and I, used to go to the 'forbidden forest'. Actually they were woods and not that forbidden but for our imaginative minds, it helped to make it forbidden. We would play hide and seek and make all sorts of noises to mimic wild animals. They were white and we were black. Oddly enough, I don't think it mattered to us or that we ever talked about it.

We had a lovely church that became home for us. The Ilford Elim Pentecostal Church was mostly white with a sprinkle of Caribbean nationals and we loved it, especially getting to it. We'd leave our home at 37 Northdene, walk down the winding path to the nearest train station called Hainault, then the train would take us through to Fairlop, then Barkingside, then Newbury Park and then Gants Hill. At Gants Hill, we'd hop out and take Bus 150 to Ilford since Ilford was on the British Rail line and not on the underground. For Yaw and I, each of those stops was something to look forward to. Fairlop sounded like we would see a county fair every time our train passed through. Barkingside sounded like there would be lots of dogs there on any given day. We liked dogs; our parents just didn't think we could be responsible pet owners. Newbury Park sounded very uppity, like Lord Newbury lived there and only his servants were allowed to stop there on Sundays. Gants Hill sounded like it belonged to the Gants Family who had to lug water up and down the hill. They would probably welcome strangers to help them with their farm chores. Such were our fantasies.

On a typical Sunday morning, we were usually the only people on the platform and being Sunday, train service was every half hour. We'd stand on the platform waiting and just about five minutes before the train would arrive, Esther would start clutching her

groin area and start crying.

"What's wrong?" Mum would ask, praying it wasn't what she feared it was.

"I – wanna- pee-pee."

"Now?"

"Y-e-s – now."

So we'd miss the train because Mum would be off finding a toilet for Esther. And being Sunday, there was sometimes no guard to open the one toilet at the station. So, the solution was one of: either let Esther wear a diaper or we leave home early enough to miss at least one train. Since Esther was likely to take the diaper off at church, Dad and Mom tried the latter. It wasn't long before the biting cold, while standing on the platform after missing one train too many, won out over the diaper. Esther wore diapers on Sundays till she turned three. Amazing that it took her that long to stop pulling that prank.

Being black and therefore looking different from everyone else everyday began taking its toll on all of us. Mum was very unhappy, Daddy was stressed because Mummy was unhappy, and for us children, we could never predict what would happen on the way to or from school. My father decided to make a drastic change and announced it one evening over dinner.

"You'll be going back to Ghana at the end of the school year," he said, as Mummy smiled like the Cheshire cat. "I'll stay here on my own and visit at holiday time."

What? Without Dad? Back to Ghana? But wasn't that where everyone was poor? That's what all my friends said at school.

I had mixed feelings. On the one hand, I was going to miss Lisa and

Cathy and my newly acquired boy friends (hoping they would one day become boyfriends). On the other hand, Ghana held certain warmth…and I remembered that it was a place where everyone — especially Mummy—was happy. None of us children said a thing but that may have been because only I understood much of what our father had said. I couldn't wait to tell my teacher, Mr. Redfarn. Mr. Redfarn was the best teacher in the whole wide world. He was my grade three teacher and he seemed to wear the same suit each and every day. He looked out for me, appreciated me and I never felt 'black' in his class. When I told him that my family was leaving, he was visibly shaken. He invited our whole family over for dinner and asked us a very interesting question.

"Will Mary find a good tree to study under?"

This was not a trick question. From all the documentaries and films made about Africa, it was no wonder that all Mr. Redfarn knew about Africa was that anyone fortunate enough to get out of Africa shouldn't want to go back there. After all, you'd be lucky to get an education and even luckier to get a tree to do it under.

"She will study under the tree that I studied under," replied my Dad without a beat.

Mr. Redfarn did not suspect any sarcasm in the response. What a sweet guy. He was satisfied that if Dad had been deemed worthy to have a job at the Commonwealth Secretariat, situated in Marlborough House on Pall Mall, a short walk to Buckingham Palace, well then, that tree he studied under had to be good enough, even if it wasn't Oxford or Cambridge.

If not for the fact that we were going to be on a plane, I do think I would have really been sad to leave. Besides, I was beginning to think I was less black every day, so what was the point of leaving?

3

"We're back!"

August 1977 – September 1977

Mummy, Yaw, Esther, John and I left England on a blustery day in the summer of 1977 when our new brother John was just about four weeks old. We hardly remembered Ghana and couldn't speak any of the languages we'd left knowing just three years before. We had exchanged letters a couple of times with our maternal grandmother, Nana. She had gone to the local teacher and asked for a translation into English, of a letter she recited in *Twi*, the local language. Most of her letters were sad. Crops had failed and her hair cream business had put her in debt. As well, Sisi Ama, her second cousin had died of shock when her husband presented her with a second wife who was a year older than Sisi Ama's youngest daughter! The list of woes was endless. We remembered Nana quite well but sadly, these stories of woe diminished her in our eyes. The Nana we had left behind was always in charge and knew everything and everybody. This new Nana sounded weak and

desperate, in need of us to look after her. Just as well we were going back, I thought. I wondered what she'd look like now.

For the trip, I wore a cream coloured dress that had long flowing sleeves and a huge collar, a Shirley Temple classic. My hair was done up in two pony tails and I had new shoes since it wouldn't be good to arrive in the place you had left looking poorer than when you'd left it. That's what I heard Mummy saying to my father as she explained why she had to go shopping all the time. Dad had decided to send us back because he felt that we'd never get the best of anything if we remained in someone else's country. We could be bright and yet never get to go to a grammar school. We could have talent in acting but would never get to be any of the main characters. It was time to go where he thought it'd be an even playing field.

Yaw and I bounced up and down in the airplane; we could hardly contain our excitement. Esther was doodling on a scrapbook Mummy had brought along, while John was fast asleep for almost the entire trip. We flew out of Gatwick airport on what used to be *British Caledonian* in the mid morning. The stewardesses were so nice; they gave us colouring pencils and toys and made us not want to ever leave the plane. By 7pm, we started descending into Accra and I peered out the window. Ghana seemed so dark—there were hardly any lights on, it seemed.

Touchdown. We were 'home'. Mummy looked so happy that it made us feel happy, even though we felt so tired. Yaw and I helped to carry some of the baby stuff as the air stewardesses helped Mummy navigate the pram from the locker they'd put it in. We

45

were helped down the stairs into air that was musty with heat and water and a slight breeze that smelled like cooked yam. As we descended the stairs, we heard people shouting and calling out Mummy's Ghanaian name, Ama Adobea; they were standing at a lookout point in the terminal and could see us exiting the plane onto the tarmac.

"Ama Adobea gyi maam ah?'

'Yeye oh. Eche Mary!'

I heard my name! Mummy had stopped at the bottom of the stairs and was waving frantically at people on the balcony at Kotoka International Airport. She yelled back to them.

"Ene ebeh ohhhhh"! We're back ohhhhh!

Back to Ghana. Where it seemed like we were celebrities because everyone wanted to hug us, talk to us, take pictures with us. I hadn't felt so wanted since I was born! I heard a language I vaguely remembered. It was being spoken in excited tones all around me, some assuming I remembered the language and therefore understood all the questions they were asking. When my blank stare conveyed my inability to understand, well-rehearsed English replaced Anum as the language with which to communicate to us.

"How *a* you?"

"London fine?"

"How is Queen? You see *ha*?"

I looked around for Nana but no one looked like the woman I remembered. Had she forgotten us? What did she look like now? Would she be happy to see us?

As I looked around, hoping to have these questions answered, the throng that had come to the airport to welcome us to Ghana burst into song and one older woman, short of stature, piercing dark

eyes and high cheekbones, just over four and half feet but clearly a leader, made her way through the crowd. She hugged a crying Mummy, then turned to me. She bent her knee slightly—I was quite tall for my age, took my hand and looked straight into my eyes and said:

"*Akwaaba. Wer Kam.*"

Welcome. Only one person could say that with so much meaning. That…was Nana.

<<>>

Oddly enough, I don't remember the drive to where we were to live for the next couple of weeks. I just remember that because we were deemed special, we sat in the best car. This was my grand uncle's Peugeot 504. Most of the relatives hailed *trotros*. I vaguely remember being smothered by hugs and kisses and lots of loud noises. It seemed like everyone in Ghana was loud—laughter was loud, sneezes were loud, talk was loud. No one seemed bored or depressed, just boisterous and full of life. To top it off, there were no lights it seemed, anywhere. Yaw and I clung to Mummy for fear of being swallowed up in all the people who were clamoring to touch us and hear us talk. When I got a chance to get a word in edgewise, I asked Mummy why it was so dark, why no one was turning on the lights.

"The government turns it off. There isn't enough electricity so they turn it off some nights and turn it on other nights so there's enough to go around."

I wondered what we were missing on British TV.

We drove on a bumpy road that seemed to be neverending, on and on through dark streets with no streetlights but with people

still walking around and finding their way by the light of street sellers. Yams and fried turkey tails, fried plantains and peanuts, coconuts and mangoes…all still for sale in the city at nine in the late evening. We were to stay at Mummy's uncle's house in an area of Accra called Kaneshie. Papa Lawyer as he was called was a *big man*, where big in this instance didn't refer to his frame but to his position within the family and the community. As such, he'd stayed at home and waited for us to be brought to him instead of joining the rest of the clan in making the journey to the airport. The driver of our car honked very loudly as we approached a metal gate painted bright green—so bright you could still see it in the nighttime. At the sound of the honk, a chorus of voices was heard coming from the house in words that now mean something to me but at the time sounded like noise.

"*Ehmo Ebe ohhhhh*". They're here ohhhhh.

Every exciting statement in Ghana seemed to end with ohhhhh. There was a mad rush as we were again engulfed by a sea of laughing, screaming, hugging people who seemed to know who we were and expected us to understand them. I felt horribly inadequate. Yaw continued to cling. Esther whimpered sadly as she clung to Mummy's bosom. A very tall man made his way towards us and tried to take Esther from Mummy.

"Kweku, hold her for me," Mummy said to the tall man, who was forever referred to by us all as Mr. Long Man.

He smiled at us, showed us his palm and asked us to high five him. A lovely looking woman wearing a *kaba* and *slit*—the traditional cloth of the Ghanaian woman led us to the living room, plumped up some sofa pillows and pointed for us to sit. That was Papa Lawyer's wife who everyone called Mama Yaa Afanso. Papa Lawyer himself had big bulging eyes and looked very stern

although every so often, a sliver of a smile would pass his face and then he didn't look so scary; I just knew he liked me. Everyone sat looking at us and speaking to us in Anum but suddenly, a hush fell in the room—Nana was coming in. As she walked in, a path was automatically created for her. She sat in a comfortable seat and told everyone of the great deeds of God. One of these deeds was apparently the bringing of Ama —that was my Mummy's Ghanaian day name—and the children from the land of the white man, back to the country of our birth.

"In the days of old, our elders taught us wisdom through proverbs, so I will remind you of the one that says that 'no matter how long the night, the day is sure to come'. Ama and the children were away from us for so long that it seemed like night. But today, does it not feel like the day has come? If this is not God, then who is it who does such great deeds?' She said all of this in Anum while mummy translated for me.

No one answered verbally but there were umms and aahhs and very knowing nods. Everyone seemed to know that this God was so powerful. This was Nana's cue to continue.

'They went up in the sky, disappeared in the clouds and then have reappeared. It is like when Jesus will come again is it not?"

Again, umms and aahh's and knowing nods. Nana was on a roll now.

"We will praise and thank the Lord for this mighty deed which we have witnessed. Everyone pray!'

At that terrifying command everyone raised his or her voice in prayer—some yelling, some meditating, some singing. It was a prayerfest the likes of which the world—at least my world till then— had never seen. I seriously wanted to sleep and so did Yaw. Esther was already gone out like a light. I was so jealous of her

ability to sleep in the midst of all this noise. Mummy was in her element. She was praying, crying, singing, arms raised in gratitude. Mummy was really glad to be back home.

That night, I slept in the same room as Nana. I don't know how that sleeping arrangement was thought of but after prayer and food, Mummy took us to go and take a shower. Brrrrr…the water was cold! Yaw and I endured it and quickly afterwards, slipped on our pajamas. Then Mummy asked me to go to the adjoining room and sleep on the mat that had been prepared for me. I did what I was told and found that Nana was already there.

"Ei Abena. Wo ji mwa?" I knew my Ghanaian day name was Abena and it was wonderful to hear Nana refer to me as such.

Huh? I thought. What on God's earth was she saying?

"Eche ohhhh. Abeka edeni mi eyi amo ohhhhh"

The ohhhhhh gave this sentence away. She must be excited or something so I decided to give it a shot.

"Hi Nana," I said in the Queen's English.

"Her ro," she replied.

"Hello," I said.

And then she smiled even more broadly.

"Mwanso wo ka edeni me eyi amwa?"

Huh?

"Bale. Kakabi le eh, ene ebeh Ghana su ene beka Anum kaaaa?'

Huh?

"Beh de me yo."

She then pulled my mat closer to hers and patted it. That was easy then, I figured. She must have meant for me to come and lie down beside her. So I did. And she placed her right hand on my back in a protective manner that I've never forgotten.

So I went to bed having learned one new Ghanaian phrase: *Beh de me yo* probably meant 'come lie beside me'. Now where was I going to get to use this phrase? I had no idea that by the end of the week, we would be heading to Asamankese, at that time a town of about two thousand people with intermittent running water and nice people who didn't speak my kind of English. My one phrase would have to be re-jigged since telling strangers to 'come lie beside me' was not a decent phrase for an eight-year-old to be uttering!

<<>>

Mummy's family was large and like most Ghanaian and African families, the family unit and its subsequent bonding was ultra important. In the first few weeks of arriving in Ghana, I was starting to get a handle on who everybody was and how the naming system worked. I knew my name Abena meant I was born on a Tuesday and Yaw was born on a Thursday but I learnt something new about 'house names' as they were referred to. Firstly, everyone had one. You couldn't be born on anything but a day and secondly, boys and girls had different names even if they were born on the same day. This meant it could be one of about fourteen names that every Ghanaian child had. Of course each tribe put their own slant on it so if I was from the Fante tribe, I would be called Araba instead of Abena which is the *Twi* tribe version. So, boys born on:

Monday were called Kojo,

Tuesday Kwabena,

Wednesday Kweku,

Thursday Yaw,

Friday Kofi,

Saturday Kwame and

Sunday Kwesi.

Girls born on:
Monday were called Adwoa,
Tuesday Abena,
Wednesday Akua,
Thursday Yaa,
 Friday Afua,
 Saturday Ama and
Sunday Akosua.

Mummy had an older sister called Sisi Yaa Anto. She had four children: Adwoa, Stella, Kofi and Kwame, all older than me. Nana was married to Sisi Yaa Anto's Dad who passed away of something or other while she was pregnant. To remember her sorrow at the birth of the baby, Nana decided to name her 'Anto', which meant 'didn't meet'. Basically, she was calling her 'the Yaa, who didn't meet her father'. Names in Ghana are so very important and when you hear someone's name, you can usually surmise something about the person's life. Most people also had a spirit name and this was the name that they believed would follow you spiritually. For me, I was given the name Asabea, a version of Asarebea, which means 'a place of healing'. It was my paternal grandmother's name and all who knew her said as I grew, I reminded them of her. Ghana being a patriarchal society in so many ways, imbued men with the responsibility of 'naming' their children and so all my siblings at this time, were named after illustrious and beloved people on my father's side of the family.

Nana was the eldest in her family of three brothers and one sister and this respect was accorded to her in very visible ways. The

eldest brother was Papa Kwabena, also known as Appiah John and legend has it that he was the first person in Asamankese to buy a car. Infact, the Peugeot 504 by which we were driven home from the airport belong to him. It had been brought all the way from the large bustling town of Asamankese where the family had 'emigrated' to after a war with another tribe near Anum, the original homestead. He was a cocoa farmer with one legitimate wife and several concubines to his name. He was so rich he had two houses. There was the family house fondly referred to as 'old house' and then what everyone called 'new house'—a two storey building made of bricks in the newest part of Asamankese. So, a house of brick, and a car made him a most popular man and there was no one in Asamankese who did not know Appiah John —his official name. He was so rich that when his younger brother showed promise beyond the 'standard seven' level and passed his Cambridge Exams, Appiah John paid his tuition to go to London, to Grays Inn to read Law. He came back as Papa Lawyer. This name was so that no one would forget our illustrious son—the one who had gone to London to study the Queens Law, to come back and show us all how to live in a civilized society. Teacher Kwaku was — you guessed it, a teacher. He was the third brother and the youngest sibling and always struck me as still looking for his own mother. Nana treated him like a baby and he seemed to love it. According to Mummy, their mother had died while Teacher Kwaku was still a baby and this was supposed to explain his dependence on Nana, I guess. Then there was Nana's sister who was called Maa Yaa. She seemed shy all the time. She had four children with whom we became very close: Auntie Hieneh, Auntie Adjo, Auntie Chaama and Uncle Boadu. She was always looking happy, seemed to lose her composure when Nana was around but then again, so did

many other people in the large compound house we called the Old House.

So that's the direct line, but if you know anything about African families, you do know that there's no such thing as a family made up of father, mother and children. There are always cousins who are several times removed. Nana's first cousin was Maa Akua. She was so dark skinned that her teeth shone like she had perpetual teeth whitener. She never seemed to wear a blouse or shirt, she always just had the traditional cloth high up over her bosom. I guess it was very hot. Maa Akua had five children: Auntie Kumia, Sisi Yaa Yaabi, Serwa, Yaw and Mr. Long Man. Auntie Kumia's daughter was Julie and we got along so well that she spent long summers with us in our house in Accra. Sisi Yaa Yaabi was fair of skin and had a twinkle in her eye. I could just imagine her as a wayward teen, catching the eye of every lothario in Asamankese. She had two children. The other cousins were in and out of old house so we didn't get to know them too well. Another first cousin of Nana's, Papa Titi, who was Maa Akua's brother also lived in Old House and was quite a character. I don't quite remember him talking, just grunting. He had the biggest nose I'd ever seen and when he sneezed or passed gas or did both at the same time, you had to run for cover; it seemed the whole town shook with a 6.8 on the Richter scale. He was a big man and even on the concrete floors of Old House, you knew when Papa Titi was prowling the earthth—there was no mercy from his pounding feet.

So it was to this mélange of characters that Mummy and Nana took us, on one very humid Saturday morning in September 1977. We made our way to the government transport station to board

one of the long buses that plied their trade all across Ghana. General Acheampong was in power with his Supreme Military Council and there was much tension in the country. Even at six in the morning, it seemed like there was so much life already—had anyone even gone to bed?

"Beh li doh," said Nana to Yaw, Esther and myself. By this time, only the first week, I was beginning to get it. She meant 'walk this way'. I whispered the translation to my siblings and with Mummy taking up the rear, we wove our way through the early morning bustle of the transport station. *Bofrot*, a doughnut-like pastry was on sale, as was *kohkoh meko*—a kind of porridge made of millet and hot tiger pepper. The *obroniwherewu* merchants were busy hanging up their second hand clothes and as they shouted in their shrill voices *"obroni"*, 'Wherewu', I thought it very funny; I'd learned that *Obroni Wherewu* meant a 'dead white person'. As drivers revved up their engines, their assistants who were called mates, hollered out to passersby to join their bus by clapping their hands, clicking their tongues and sucking their teeth—anything to get the attention of would be passengers. If their bus filled up first, they got to leave. Mummy asked one of the mates for the queue to join for Asamankese. He pointed to the east side of the station, way on the other side of where we were. We began the arduous journey and while Mummy carried John securely on her back, Nana did the same for Esther. Yaw and I had to face the torture of the trek so he and I vowed we'd pay John and Esther back for all the pain and suffering we had to endure because they got carried and we had to walk!

It was no comfort to finally sit in the bus, have it start up and weave

through the maze of station chaos, only to have someone stand up at the front and announce that he was a preacher. Could we give him some of our time? Well we couldn't very well say no could we? For one thing, Ghanaians are painfully polite. Secondly, most Ghanaians of any religious persuasion believe that nothing of God is to be trifled with and if you do not give respect especially to a man (or woman) of God, well, hell or whatever your bad place is called has your name written all over it. Thirdly and most importantly, Nana wanted to listen and she gave him an enthusiastic 'Amen' followed by a proverb.

"It is easy to defeat people who do not kindle fire for themselves. Preacher Man, please help us kindle our fires!"

That's all he needed and the preaching began. Of course I didn't understand a word he was saying. I was only beginning to understand (or possibly remember) simple phrases like thank you, which had to be preceded by please. In Ghana, every sentence seemed to be preceded by please and I was not quite sure why. If you needed to ask someone for directions, you'd preceed the request with the word 'please'.

The preacher looked hungry but I bet he was saying that he was hungry for the 'Word'. He wore a tattered pair of shoes that were chafed at the front. His laces didn't even match and they seemed too short because I noticed some eyelets that weren't lucky enough to get laces. The shirt he was wearing was definitely *oburoni wherewu* and it was worn under a leather jacket. In thirty-degree temperatures, he must have been baking in that offensive piece of red leather. But then everyone was looking at him and admiring it—I could see their looks of amazement at his ability to afford a leather jacket. I wish I'd understood what he was saying because the bus crowd was giving him such encouragement.

"I know *brada*…say it again"

"*Ei*, isn't the Lord guud?"

"Mmmhhh…if not the Lord, then WHO?"

This fired up the preacher and he paused mid sentence and started a hymnal. Everyone, as if on cue, picked it up and suddenly, the bus was filled with the African version of American Negro spirituals—this mournful rising of voice, crescendo-ing precariously to a peak of joyful desire, only to be arrested by one lone voice from the front, carrying the descant higher and higher and then being rescued by the throng in a captivating acappella that would rival the Harlem Gospel Choir. O how glorious!!

Of course after this outpouring of belief in the one true God, it had to be followed by prayer. And like many of the prayers I was to hear in Ghana, it had an introduction, a thesis statement, a body and then a conclusion and this time, in English that was not half bad!

"Oh God, maker of heaven and *'eart*, the *'eart* is your footstool, heaven is your *trone*, from everlasting to everlasting, thou art God."

A pause; with plentiful amens coming from every sector of the bus at strategic points in the prayer.

"You are the God who save Isaac from the *onwilling* hand of his *fadder* Abraham.

AMEN

You are the God who parted the Red Sea.

AMEN

The mighty Red sea was parted, and it was you.

AMEN

You are the Lord who opened Moses *mout*, even when he did not know he even had a *mout*. But you gave him the *mout* to *spik* to

Pharaoh.

AMEN

And Pharaoh listened.

AMEN

He listened to Moses because you oh God, gave him *mout* to *spik*.

AMEN

You are the God who made Noah to build *de* ark.

AMEN

A big and mighty *ting* that he build. But you O God help him build it.

AMEN

And the rain fall on the *'eart* and only Noah *savive.* Everybody die. Noah *savive.*

AMEN

As for Joshua, if you O God did not help him blow *de* trompet, Jericho will still be there.

AMEN

But he was your servant and he listened to you.

AMEN

Samuel hear your voice at night. It was you O God who do not let him be sad when he left his *moda* so early in life.

AMEN

Because O God you were his *fadda* and his *moda.*

AMEN

And you did mighty *tings tru* him.

AMEN

Ei, who is like onto *dee?* If I was to go on…

"Halleluyah *brada,* go on," yelled a voice from the middle of the bus.

No please don't go on, I thought. At this rate, we're still in the Old

Testament and barely past the books of Moses and haven't gotten to the prophets yet. There was *no way* we were going to get to Revelation and this was only the beginning of the prayer. Needless to say, the Lord heard *my* prayer and granted us some sort of a reprieve. The pastor finished his introduction and then with his thesis statement, he delved into the mother of all prayers. "This is why we *sev* you. This is why we worship you. This is why we praise you. You are a great and mighty God."

God must be quite the patient individual because I could have sworn that from the center of Accra, past the popular roundabout known as Circle and on towards Achimota, this man not only preached but he ended with a prayer that not only exhausted him (his face was beady with sweat) but it exhausted those of us who listened and maybe did not quite understand!

By the time the bus got to the bustling town of Nsawam, Yaw and I were both very fast asleep. Nana was swatting flies away from me when her cloth hit my face by mistake so I woke up startled.

'Are we there yet?' I asked.

"Ene befo," Nana responded.

I looked at Mummy imploringly and she translated.

"Nana just said that we're not there yet."

Another useful phrase to store in my vocabulary. The bus slowed and then we were deluged by masses of people selling everything under the sun—underwear, dog chains, deep-fried turkey tails (which I learned that very minute was called *chofi)*, and 'designer' bread. Apparently, Nsawam was famous for its breads and people would travel from far off just to buy their bread. Once the bus came to a stop, all of those wares were shoved in our faces, everyone begging us to buy their goods and no one letting up. This was a tough decision I thought. Who would we buy from? I waited to see

what Nana would do.

"Hey," she haughtily motioned in their collective direction.

"Mama, buy mine," implored an older woman in a bright green outfit with *chofi* arranged precariously on a tray that sat even more precariously on her head. About five more *chofi* sellers tried to pummel their way through.

"How much?" Nana asked in her imperious tone.

"Please Mama, just for you, a special rate today. One for fifty *pesewas*, two for eighty *pesewas* and if you buy three or more, I will give you each one for 30 *pesewas* please."

"*Ei,* your stuff is expensive. Why would I buy one *chofi* for fifty?"

"Mama, please that's why I've given you a deal. If you buy more, please, I will reduce it. The oil for cooking, it is now very expensive—it comes from Ivory Coast."

"I don't care if it's from America, that *chofi* is too expensive. I would have to work a whole month to feed my family on your Ivory Coast *chofi!*"

I was so hungry I didn't care how much the *chofi* cost but Nana was taking this way too far! Yaw and I looked at Nana, hoping she would stop this 11th century haggling and get on with the business of buying. At the sign of a little bit of strife, a few more *chofi* sellers launched into their own marketing campaigns.

"Mama please, mine is forty *pesewas* each," a crafty looking teenage girl plunged in.

"And yours too, does it come from Ivory Coast?" Nana scathingly questioned.

"Erm…yes Madam," she replied, unsure of the correct response.

"So then why is yours cheaper?" Nana went in for the kill. " Is it because your oil is very old and dirty and smelly?"

"Oh please Mama no," the poor child said, broken and contrite.

Nana continued looking around for another victim willing to be tortured. She was surprised to find that most of the sellers had found passengers on the bus who were not going to give them the fifth degree about the oil they used to fry their *chofi* so they were busy bargaining with them instead. Nana had no choice but to go back to her initial victim.

"Hey, give me five *chofi's*…you said twenty *pesewas* each didn't you?"

"Oh please mama, I said thirty."

"Make it twenty five and lets hurry up, the bus is about to leave."

The *chofi* seller quickly wrapped five *chofi's* in a plastic bag and tossed them back to Nana while Mummy quietly bought some Nsawam bread that was smothered in butter and we all breathed a sigh of relief. We were going to have lunch!

"Ayen," I heard the *chofi* seller mutter.

"Hey, did you call me a witch? Look at her face that she is using to call me a witch. Same to you!" Nana shouted after her.

We passed villages that seemed to blend one into another. Some with corrugated roofs and mud walls interspersed with brick buildings that also had corrugated roofs. Everywhere I looked, little children were running around with hardly any shoes on, happy faces reflecting a joy that seemed tied to the blazing sunshine that seemed to be part and parcel of a Ghanaian day. Over there was a mother with a baby on her back, a cutlass in one hand, a walking infant being held by the other hand and a load on her head. How did she do that? There were some stretches of road where we'd see nobody, not even farmers coming back from the farm. With nothing to look at on the road, I looked farther away, past large tall trees that seemed to go on forever and wondered if

there were tiny men who lived in the land beyond. As I wondered these things, Yaw woke up, drooling on his own shirt and rubbing his eyes furiously.

"Are we there yet?" he asked me.

"Ene befo," I responded triumphantly.

Asamankese seemed sunny and dusty. It seemed everyone was shouting for something or other and unlike Accra, no one seemed like they were in a hurry. Our Government Transport Bus made its winding way to the station, honking noisily and kicking up dust at every turn. It finally screeched to a stop and let out a belch that sounded very rude; it made Yaw burst out laughing. We shuffled out into the blazing sun and tried to stay together. Mum and Nana held our hands and we shuffled through the crowd at the lorry station and when we finally felt like we could breathe again, we saw some smaller buses, filling up really fast and looking horribly crowded. I didn't fancy sitting next to some sweaty stinky person. I spoke too soon! We found ourselves in one of those buses with Nana on the aisle part of a shabby, well-worn seat. I could even feel the metal that used to be covered by foam! A man with a sleeveless undershirt known as a singlet, was near the window and I was in the middle. Talk about a sandwich! I wondered how long I could hold my breath and still live another day; the man smelled like he worked in a pig farm or something close to that. Then I thought of a brilliant plan. I would bury my face on Nana's shoulder. That would ensure a clean source of oxygen for however long this journey was going to take. I had barely thought of this mind-blowing plan when I saw Esther moving from Mummy's lap and onto Nana's lap, lying down in such a way that prevented me from 'borrowing' Nana's shoulder! I resisted an enormous urge to

slap the brat but she quickly shut her eyes and pretended she was fast asleep. I couldn't believe her cunning. I then set about trying to control my breathing and to this day, anytime I am under water and having to hold in my breath, I lose it because I can smell that man!

Mercifully, the trip to Old House, Mummy's family's homestead, took barely 15 minutes. Or maybe it was 3 minutes. I have no idea since I was somewhere very low on Maslow's hierarchy of needs; the part where I am just existing to exist. Breathing was my self-actualization. The little bus wound to a stop right beside a gutter and the mate yelled out *'Awele Awi'*. I was later to find out that this meant 'the chief's house'. Mummy got out first with John and Yaw, then Nana, still holding Esther followed and I literally sprung out from the bondage of the man's armpits and bounded out of the small bus. We had to wait outside while our bags were retrieved from what seemed like the bowels of hell and then the bus sputtered off and we were left standing beside the gutter with more bags than we could all carry and two sleeping children under 4!

In what I was to learn was typical, Nana called out to some young children who were playing nearby—not by name—just 'hey' and they came over and picked some of our bags up. We managed to get the rest of our bags and then we crossed the badly tarred street through an alcove and through a doorway that was very cave like. This took us into a large expanse of living space that had a concrete floor and many rooms coming off of it. Old House was a 'compound' house and many houses in Ghana are still built this way. There is a communal central courtyard around which there are rooms. At one corner, there are the washrooms and on the

opposite end of the washrooms are the cooking areas. Each subset of the extended family usually has an area within this cooking area to use for their own purposes. Old house had two openings with which to get in or out of the compound. I say opening because there was no actual door or gate. People just walked in and out and sometimes, they really didn't come on an errand at all. They just walked in, said a greeting, and inquired after everyone, one by one and they exited through the other opening. There were no such things as cell phones and I didn't know of any village homes that had land lines to make sure you knew who was planning to visit; they just came. Barely had we stepped foot into this concrete space than the shouting began.

"*Emwe ebe ohhhhhh!*"

"*Ama ebe oh!*"

"Mary! Yaw! John! Esther!"

These were all shouts of excitement as our extended family competed with one another to shout the loudest greeting and to hug the life out of us. I was carried by a big guy and led to a stack of chairs near the middle of the concrete compound and after what seemed like an eternity, the process of a formal welcome began. Since Nana had been living with us and we had been surrounded by some family in Accra, I had picked up quite a number of Anum words and I could sort of tell what was transpiring. One of the men asked if we could hush for a word of prayer and this of course was preceded by song. After the song, a prayer thanking God for bringing us safely was given and then a loud Amen and then everyone was laughing again, slapping one another on the back and then Nana stood up.

"We are not bringing bad news."

"Amen!" said everyone.

"We are bringing greetings from Accra, from the entire family and are here to show our little white people where they really come from. We need them to realize that a family is like a forest; when you are outside, it is dense, when you are inside, you see that each tree has its place. They will get to know everyone in this dense forest of ours!"

"Amen," said everyone.

By this time, some little children had brought us water that was so amazingly cold that it stung! I didn't see a refrigerator anywhere around so how could they keep it this cold in this sweltering heat? I heard Nana's voice droning on, talking about the white people. Then it hit me. We were the white people! Somehow, they said it with a hint of endearment.

"We are glad that you are not bringing bad news," chimed an older woman who I later found out to be Maa Akua. "We have heard how the Lord carried Ama and her children on his wings from the land of the white man and has brought them back home, safe and sound. Glory be to God for his almighty provision."

"Amen." responded the throng.

I looked around the room, which was sparsely decorated except for a few black and white photographs. The men in the pictures all had their hair parted in the middle or the side. The women all seemed to have a hand on a Bible or purse, on their laps. They all wore traditional cloth but since it was black and white pictures, there was no way to tell how colourful the outfits were. I noticed something else too. Some of the pictures had 'x' on them in red. I wondered why. The day passed rather uneventfully since by this point, we were so travel weary that Yaw and I couldn't even think of any fun tricks to play on anyone. By six o'clock, the sun had set and because there were no televisions in Old House, everyone was

expected to take a bath and then go to bed. Mummy took us to the bathroom and brought in buckets of cold water for us to swish and swash over ourselves. It was cold but so refreshing. Esther didn't enjoy hers much. I could hear her moaning and groaning the entire time she was being scrubbed. Maybe it wasn't the water but Nana scrubbing her like she'd been in a mud bath all day!

What a relief to finally lie down after such a day. The events of the day came crashing back to mind and the vividness of the landscape we'd observed through the bus window was rich in its diversity. I still hadn't seen snow here and part of me missed that. Part of me too was glad that I hadn't seen any boots, winter jackets or mittens. Was this what Nana seemed to be thinking or saying whenever her words sounded like she felt sorry for us? About the only thing I felt sorry for—at least at this time—was the fact that I still struggled to understand everything they were saying. But I knew it was only a matter of time before I was one of them; I was going to make sure of it. Mummy was so happy here that I knew we were all going to be happy.

4

"Things are to be tried; an old lady cooked stones and they turned into soup"

1977 – 1988, Ghana

Accra was our home base and during the school year, we were enrolled in Association International School, a private school that was very close to the airport. Yaw was in class one and I was in class four, in a school so big that our first day felt like we'd landed in a new country. There were multiple classes for every grade and they were named after rivers, lakes or countries. I was in Class Four Densu, named after the river Densu.

My teacher was Mrs. Abankwa, and on the first day, she smiled coldly at me as she peered through glasses that were perched on her broad nose. She stood at the front of the class with a cane in her hand, pointing to words and sums on the board and screaming down the length of the large classroom. It was really odd being in a class full of people who looked like me but didn't sound like me.

Mrs. Abankwa was no Mr. Redfarn that was for sure. She banged her cane all day, made us stay inside for break time if one person did not finish the work on time, and she hardly ever called on me to answer any question, even if I had my hand up the entire time. I did not like her.

One day, as we waited in the classroom for her to return after lunchtime, I looked around the room. I was shocked to find that everyone was absolutely quiet, even though there was no teacher in the room. My best friend Michael was sitting behind me and he smiled wanly at me. Mrs. Dapaah the Head Mistress, made her way noisily to our classroom and announced that Mrs. Abankwa had been taken ill and would not be returning for a few days. No one said anything. We were going to have another teacher for those few days until Mrs. Abankwa could return. She then left the classroom. We rejoiced by clapping our hands silently under the table, smiling broadly, pumping our fists in the air...all with not a sound. Our new teacher was the daughter of the Head Mistress. She had just arrived from America and was studying to be a teacher. We loved her totally. She was young, fun and she smiled at us. All her lessons were fun and she turned everything into a game.
Ms. Dapaah was in her early twenties, full of spunk and energy and she was fine...very fine. We would see some of the male teachers pass glances at her whenever we went for assembly and we'd giggle.

On the day Mrs. Abankwa was to come back, I had an incident on the way to school. I was so sick to my stomach at the thought of that curmudgeon coming back that as soon as I spied the school at the end of the long tarred residential street, my stomach just gave

way and I threw up. All the hot chocolate and bread I'd had for breakfast came out onto my seat in the car, and onto my freshly starched, burgundy and white school uniform. As the driver screeched to a halt and Mummy jumped out to clean me up, Yaw committed a copy cat crime and heaved all over Mummy's back as she hunched over to reach me.

"What is wrong with the two of you? Or is it the hot chocolate? Maybe it has expired," was her explanation for this sudden turn of events. It wasn't uncommon to buy powdered chocolate that had expired since America and England shipped us containers full of expired food that was called 'AID'.

For the next two weeks, all my lunches went uneaten as I struggled to keep things down amidst the fear that was Mrs. Abankwa.

Finally, I could take it no longer and told Mummy.

"Mummy I don't like that school."

"Why? It's a good school."

"Mrs. Abankwa is cruel. The other day, she threw chalk at me just because I answered her question before she had a chance to call on someone."

"And why didn't you just wait eh? I know you—you're always in a hurry to show off!"

"Well, she never calls me!" I said in exasperation. "She says I think I'm white and that I should stop speaking like a British person because we are now in Ghana."

There. I'd said it. I really was trying desperately to lose the British accent since I felt so out of place. And from the tone of Mrs. Abankwa's voice, if I didn't lose it, it would make me come across like I felt I was better than her. What a confusing thing — here in Ghana, we looked like everyone else but just because we didn't sound like everyone else, some people took offense. I guess

it wasn't too different from being in England where despite the fact that we spoke like everyone else, we didn't look like everyone else. I wondered if I'd ever belong.

Mummy was teaching at another school called Achimota Preparatory School and we were immediately withdrawn from Association International School in the middle of the school year. I went into Class four at Achimota Preparatory and quickly made some new friends—Rimmel, Yvonne, Leticia and Celestine. This school was smaller so it didn't take us long to get to know everyone else. Having Mummy in the school was amazing too and for lunch, we'd huddle around her desk eating *kenkey*, a kind of white corn meal, along with some fried fish and *shitto*.

No one in this school seemed to care that I still had remnants of an English accent that revealed itself in all the weirdest of places. Instead, we were embraced and encouraged to work hard and participate in all sorts of sports and extracurricular activities. I joined the girl guides and went camping in the Achimota forest, winning every conceivable badge that was available to be won. I knew how to light a fire with no matches, could climb a tall tree to run away from wild animals, and had memorized the entire girl guide code and rule book even though no one told us to do so! I wanted to give the Guide Leader a reason to invent an award for the most ardent Girl Guide on the Planet and I knew I would win!

We had a long playing field just adjacent to the Kindergarten building of the school and each afternoon, we'd practice our running in preparation for sports day. The whole school was divided into three teams, named after flowers: Alamanda, Hibiscus

and Rose. Everyone wanted to be in Rose and definitely not in Alamanda. When the list came out, I was in Alamanda. What sacrilege! We met in our groups and that was when I noticed why no one ever wanted to be in Alamanda; somehow, all the uncool kids managed to get put in Alamanda. How on earth did I get put in there? I was convinced it was rigged but there was to be no switching for any reason. I set about trying to put Alamanda on the map, feeling once again that a whole generation's pride (and not just that of an ethnic group!) rested on my shoulders. Although I won all my races, it wasn't enough to pull us out from third place and I promised God I'd make an offering—a human one—if he put me in Rose next year.

The offering was Yaw, who mysteriously got placed in Alamanda the year I got into Rose.

There IS a God.

<<>>

My Class Four teacher, Mrs. Djabatey, had a baby towards the end of the third term. Although she was an okay teacher before the baby, her hormones must have gone out of whack after the birth because I could have sworn she'd grown horns and a beard when she got back.

"Everybody line up to show me your marks since I've been gone," she yelled one very hot May morning.

Yvonne and I were in the second row so we twiddled our fingers, watching what was going to happen to those in the first row. First up was Kenneth, whose nickname was Kaunda after Kenneth Kaunda the weepy president of Zambia. He always got six out of ten for almost every assignment no matter how hard he tried.

"Stretch out your hand," Mrs. Djabatey said.

Kenneth did and got a sound rap on each palm. That looked like it hurt. He passed by a pram that had Baby Djabatey in it and acidentally shifted it. The sleeping baby woke and let out a yelp and Mrs. Djabatey's nostrils flared, emitting fire and toxic sulphurous smoke.

"Come back you foolish boy! Don't you know babies need their sleep?"

Then why did you bring your baby to school, I thought.

Poor Kenneth respectfully pushed the pram closer to Mrs. Djabatey's desk, went back for a second rap on his knuckles and quickly shuffled to his seat while trying to hold back the tears. Slowly, each member of the class that sat in the first row got the stick and then the entire second row got up. Henry was usually the ringleader in anything rebellious, and he'd passed round a piece of paper with something written in his characteristic chicken scrawl suggesting a plan of attack. We all lined up after Henry and after each whack of the stick, the baby would let out a yelp. Mrs. Djabatey would pause the torture and gently rock the pram. The baby would be settled and then Mrs. Djabatey would continue with her whacks. As more of us got our whacks, the baby cried louder. She looked baffled and we pretended to look baffled too. She had no idea we were pinching the poor thing after our whacks. Hey, it was Henry's idea.

Let the child pay for the sins of its mother.

<<>>

Mr. Awude was my class six teacher and he was the best. It seemed he had just two sets of clothes—his casual wear which was

comprised of brown pleated trousers and a cream coloured shirt, and his 'serious' wear which was a dark brown suit, a white shirt and a blue tie. We could always tell how hard a test was going to be by the kind of 'wear' Mr. Awude had on that day. If he walked in wearing his suit, we all relaxed; it was going to be an easy test. If he came in his casuals, the Lord help us; it was going to be brutal! To this day, I have no idea why it was so; perhaps the effort required to dress in a suit sapped him of the vital energy with which to write a difficult test?

After every test, the classroom seating arrangement was changed to reflect the intellectual hierarchy evident in the rankings. This is something I cannot imagine ever happening in any of the North American schools in which I've taught. Facing the class, you could tell who the smart ones were and who the not-so-smart were because the highest ranked would always sit at the back row at the left corner. The second in class would sit in front of them and so it would snake along, coming up to the front of the class and down again towards the back until the last in class, the one with the lowest grade would be sitting at the door, right in the front row on the far right of the room. I spent most of my sixth grade year at the first place, occasionally switching spots with Emefa or Worlanyo for first, second and third spots. And being me, I cried every time I was not first in a test.

One Friday, after a particularly grueling test where Mr. Awude had accompanied his 'casual' wear with an unusually stern face, I trudged to the water fountain in a bid to hide my tears at coming in second and also to get a drink of water. I bent over the fountain, drank my fill, and turned around to find Kwame-with-the-weird-head staring up my skirt! I slapped his head hard and stormed

off. How impertinent and lecherous! Leticia met me outside the classroom and wondered why I was fuming.

"Was it because you didn't come first in that test? It was hard!"

"No," I lied. Well, that too but there was a more current reason.

"That boy, Kwame-with-the-weird-head was actually looking up my skirt."

"Maybe he likes you."

"I guess things are to be tried since an old lady cooked stones and they turned into soup." I replied knowingly.

"What?" Leticia asked.

"My grandma says that proverb every time I don't want to try something new—it's a way of reminding you that if you try things, the impossible might happen."

"So Kwame-with-the-weird-head could actually become your boyfriend, if he just tried?"

Gosh Leticia could be thick, I thought.

We both laughed so hard. The thought that Kwame, the boy who always sat next to the door because he was always last, thought he could score with the girl who always sat the furthest from him was such a joke.

I don't hang with loser boys. I have bigger plans.

5

"The Child of a Lion is a Lion"

At eleven I entered my first year of boarding school, where I wore no underwear for a week, a miracle that I never told anyone about. It came about because the school prospectus for Form One students told us to bring six pairs of underpants and six bras. Dad took one look at the list and then at me and said:

"You're only eleven, why would you need a bra, let alone 6 bras?"

I had no idea either and frankly, at that time, the thought of wearing a bra was disgusting. If I wore a bra, that meant I had breasts. If I had breasts, that meant I could get pregnant. Ergo, no bra, no pregnancy and I wanted to keep it that way for a really long time. So instead of six bras, I was allowed to double up and buy six extra panties to bring the total to twelve, which by midterm was down to ten. I suspected eagles were swooping down to the courtyard, and making off with just mine; probably to use in lining the nests for their young. England's Marks & Spencer still makes the best cotton underwear.

Senior Sandra, the Form Five student in charge of our supervision

was shocked when while conducting a routine Saturday morning inspection, she found that I had a five-pack set of frilly underpants in my school trunk. They were brand spanking new.

"Hey Mary Apea, is that all yours?"

"Yes please."

"So, you're wearing one now, there are three here and is there one hanging in the courtyard to dry?"

"Yes please."

"So you have *ten* pairs of underpants?"

"Yes please."

"With your small buttocks, why do you need ten?"

No answer seemed the right one. I just shut my mouth. It looked like the conversation could go any way at this point.

I shuffled from foot to foot nervously.

"Put the underwear you've never worn on my bed. It's your punishment for having ten pairs while your seniors don't have as many."

What?

I didn't say a word but quietly took the five-pack and walked to the other side of the dorm, popularly known as 'the inner chamber' where all the Form Fives slept. I threw it on Sandra's bed and uttered a pretend curse on her—that she wouldn't pass her final exams and her buttocks would itch each time she wore my underwear. She continued her inspection, punishing a few more people who had to fetch her morning bucket of water for the next three lifetimes. Others were punished to walk behind her until she graduated. It seemed the lucky ones were those who had to fan her and scare mosquitoes away while she studied. I began to think I got off easy until my remaining underwear started disappearing. No one else seemed to be complaining about their lost underwear

and no one admitted to seeing mine. I was down to one pair, the blue one with white trimming. I was so afraid to take it off that I wore it for two days, turning it inside out in a bid to pretend it was a different pair each time. Ghanaian girls don't do that. I gingerly removed it on the third day, washed it lovingly and hung it out to dry. This was Monday morning.

What was I thinking? Today was gym with Miss Amponsah, another curmudgeon of a creature who enjoyed torturing all form one girls. I walked sullenly from the Form One building to the gym, wondering how I was going to enjoy today's class given the shape and length of the gym uniform. I was in Clark house and the girls in that house had a gym uniform that was a white sleeveless top attached to a blue flared bottom that ended mid thigh. Yes, you get the picture. With the bending down exercises we had to do in order to stretch, and God knows what else, my bum was definitely going to be seen one way or the other. I sat in the changing room, waiting for most of the girls to finish chit chatting and leave the room so I could quickly change. When I thought it was all clear, I quickly pulled my school uniform over my head and reached for the gym uniform. Before I could pass it over my shoulders, I heard a curious voice.

"You have no underwear?"

I spun round, using the moment to quickly pull the gym uniform over my nakedness to see Mercy staring at me. She was quietly changing in one of the stalls and so my infrared senses had missed her entirely. "What?" I said, sounding like she'd asked the most stupid question on earth. Considering that Mercy was one of the smartest students in Form One, I should have been slapping myself.

"Well, it's obvious. You're not wearing underwear and there isn't

one on the bench, so chances are, you don't have underwear."

She's way too smart for her own good. She's making me hate her, I thought.

"I usually keep a spare one in my gym bag. Would you like it?" she offered.

Gosh, I really do hate her now. I knew she was being kind but really?
"No thank you. Tempting as the offer is, we both know it's not hygienic but I really appreciate the offer. Just don't tell anyone ok?"

She told everyone.

By the end of gym, even the boys—who had a separate gym class from the girls—were drawing pictures of underwear on pieces of paper, cutting it out and dropping it off at my desk.

Thelma was the most mature of all my Form one friends; she had already turned thirteen by the time we turned twelve. She comforted me and said maybe it wasn't so bad not having underwear because sometimes, your 'parts' have to breathe. I was actually lucky, she said, because I was giving my 'parts' more freedom than others did. She just cautioned me to sit very ladylike and even offered to let me practice while she 'marked' me on a good sit or a bad sit. I told her that I needed the lessons for only one day because I had washed the last pair and they should be dry by the time I got back to the dorm. After lunch, I raced back to the dorm. I hadn't loved underwear so much as I did right then and I couldn't wait to get into them. I bounded through the doors that led to the courtyard and raced to the last but one clothesline, located my cream towel with the green lines and —

The underwear was gone!

I shrieked till my lungs felt like they were going to explode! What was I going to do? This airing of my 'parts' was now an indefinite

process? I passed by Senior Jane's room to ask if there were any letters for me. Surprisingly, there was and this really cheered me up. Apart from Dad who sent me postcards from every country he visited, and my grand uncle, Papa Kwabena who wrote twice a term and always reminded me to 'write as soon as practicable', I hardly received a letter from anyone. I hungrily grabbed the letter from her and noticed a British Stamp and on the back flap, surprise, surprise—

Cathy ! My best friend from London, the one who'd had my back all those years ago when I was teased for being black! I missed her. I could hardly breathe. It had been so long and although we had kept in touch intermittently, I had only heard from her about once a year. I tore the flap open and pulled out a lined piece of paper with Cathy's familiar scrawl. This is how I remember it:

Dear Mary,

I miss you lots and wish you were here lots. Billy has a girlfriend he is planning to run off with and Dad has got cancer. Is Africa still hot? When are you coming back? My new school has got lots of boys and they are all dishy. There's this one called Antonio. I think he's from a place in America called South America because he is very hairy. We've been talking about loads of things that are funny but exciting. Maybe I will tell you some of them next time. Robin had to move because his family got evicted and FM is now in a West End play. She is actually quite nice when you get to know her and she still talks about the sardine sandwiches. I tell her I believe her that they couldn't be hers hahaha. Did I tell you FM was in a play? She is what they call an understudy so when the real actress doesn't come,

she gets to play that part. I think she will be famous one day and then we can say we played a prank on her.

London is very cold and it still snows. The Bay City Rollers don't make good songs anymore and I'm not sure I like the Beatles anymore either. My favourite bands are now Police and Siouxsie and the Banshees. Siouxsie is a punk. She is a girl who doesn't care what other people think so I like her a lot. Last time you asked me what I wanted to be when I grow up. I'm not sure but I like Siouxsie a lot and I think I'd like to be a lot like her. Mum says there are lots of jobs in the shops so when I'm done my GCE's, I can go work there. They give you discounts at C&A and British Home Stores. Hey, I can get you a discount when you come back! When are you coming back? It's no fun without you and because you were black, everyone looked at us when we went anywhere! Please tell me about your boarding school. I hope no one is your best friend because you're still mine.

All my love,
Cathy

I walked dejectedly to 'A' Dormitory, a place that felt like prison, took off my uniform in full view of everyone, put on my nightdress, plunked myself on the thin mattress and sobbed softly. I loved Cathy but she was far away and I had to have another best friend in Ghana; there were incredible challenges—like the underwear crisis—that Cathy would just not get. In England, I never ran out of underwear. Afua, my other best friend from Obuasi, reached over and patted me on the back.

"I can sell some of my canned milk and corned beef and we can bribe some of the peanut sellers to go buy you some underwear,"

she offered. I couldn't be consoled.

"I know you won't wear mine but what if I cut up some of the fabric from one of my dresses and we make underwear for you?" she offered again.

Afua was nothing if not rich, and creative. Oh, and count very unselfish. You see, apart from our uniforms, we were only allowed a traditional costume for church on Sundays and five non-school dresses. They had to be decent but there was no restriction on the colour or style. Afua was prepared to cut one of hers up for me?

"No, that's okay," I murmured through the sobs.

"But what will you do?"

"What I did today."

"But…everyone knows." Afua was very concerned.

"Well, I'll just have to act like I found them wouldn't I? Besides Mummy will come to visit on Saturday and I will get her to bring me a few on Sunday. I'm more afraid of explaining the loss to Mummy than walking around in this godforsaken place with no underwear on!"

<<>>

One Monday following an exeat—we had one every six weeks where we were allowed to go home for the weekend— I sat in the humongous dining hall of Achimota Boarding School. With four hundred or so other students, I waited for my turn to ladle the thick, yucky, *Tom Brown* porridge into my bowl. The first bell rang for announcements. Being a form one student, most announcements hardly concerned me but I had to listen anyway. It felt like a never ending cycle of persecution made all the more poignant by Scripture Union prayer meetings where we (i.e. persecuted Form One students) were told to 'turn the other cheek' and wait for our

redemption on 'that day'. *What day?* Every day seemed accursed, with my friends and I subjected to interminable labour and no food in the dining hall. I tried to focus on the announcements. As usual, they had nothing to do with me: all Form Four students had to meet in front of the bookstore after fourth period; Janice Manu was to report to the Prefect in charge of chapel; All Kingsley House Girls were to collect their new gym uniforms after lunch. Just as I was beginning to heave a sigh of utter boredom, I heard my name.

"Mary Apea of Clark House should see her visitors outside right now."

Me? Visitors? Why? What was wrong? Was someone dead? It was barely seven in the morning and I had a visitor? This was very odd so I even forgot that I had not had any sustenance (in the form of yucky *Tom Brown* porridge) and I bounded outside. There stood Nana, in traditional cloth with her walking stick.

"Nana, what are you doing here?" I asked in Anum.

"I'm here to visit you and to speak with that girl, Cynthia, who is always eating your food in the dining hall—it's no wonder you're all skin and bones—look at you!'

Oh dear God no! There was no way Nana should be let loose near Cynthia. She was a fourth former, large and mean who made it a habit of joining my table almost every day and eating my food. Afterwards she'd send me to her table to go and pick up her food, I'd bring it back to her and she'd eat that too! Nothing was beyond limits for this girl and there were many days on which I'd go back to the dormitory hungry, angry and drained. She was evil incarnate but she'd be worse if at all possible, if Nana was let loose on her.

"I don't think she's in school Nana," I quivered.

How had this old woman been let loose from our home in

Abelenkpe? Where was Mummy? Did she know Nana was going to war on behalf of an unwilling victim?

"Well, I'll wait for her," said a resolutely defiant Nana. And she proceeded to sit comfortably on the ledge in front of the dining hall to wait for Cynthia. I felt numb. My face must have been contorting in fear because anytime soon, breakfast would be over and everyone would come streaming out of the dining hall towards the classrooms. I felt sure that someone was bound to say Cynthia's name in passing, and Nana would get up, guns blazing and give a whopping slap to that girl.

"That's for eating little children's food," she'd say, as a resounding whack would pass Cynthia's face. "Next time, I'll sound you even harder and push your face into next week, you evil witch'!

I offered a prayer up to God, asking him to deliver Cynthia from Nana because that meant delivering *me* from Cynthia. I even offered to fast to show how earnest I was; of course, fasting wasn't that much of a sacrifice in my boarding school. I did it all the time without wanting to!

Students streamed out after the bell went and as Nana searched through the faces for someone who ate little children's food, I tried to look like I didn't know who she was. Slowly, the stream of students thinned out and Nana, looking frustrated turned to me.

'I know you didn't want to show her to me huh? When did you become such a mouse? Don't you know that the child of a lion is a lion? Do I look like a mouse? If you don't stand up to bullies, they'll keep on mistreating you. The next thing you know, she'll be asking you to wash her underthings."

Oops, too late. Done that, but no way was I ever going to tell Nana!

"You're lucky that now, the schools are very good and so you can attend a school the Queen would send her child to. I'll be back," she

83

said menacingly and proceeded to gather her top cloth around her waist. I walked with her to the school gate. After the ten-minute walk, she prayed for me and asked God to help me so I'd stop being a wimp. Gotta love Nana's prayers—empowering and at the same time demeaning, especially as she didn't know the half of what I had to do just to survive in the jungle of boarding school. She did however leave me with a smile on my face.

The days passed in a very slow blur. I'd read that one usually experienced this in extreme hunger. *Captive Bride* by Johanna Lindsey was very informative even if it was a trashy romance novel. One day, I announced to no one in particular that I was going to do something before I died of hunger. Auntie Lucy was Dad's cousin and she lived about half an hour from our school gates. She was awesome and she sold bread. I figured I'd run away from school—in between the time we woke from siesta and dinner time. I'd hurriedly complete my chores and holding my broom, walk away from Clark House pretending I was going to sweep someone else's allotment – as if!

On the day of the great escape, I prepared very carefully. Looking nonchalant with nary a backward glance, I darted in and out of classroom blocks, one moment looking busy by using the broom to sweep the floor, the next moment, running like I needed a toilet very badly. Before long, I was at the Achimota golf course, a bare dirty green landscape that was definitely not a good place to hide. By this time, I'd ditched the broom in my hiding place ready to be used as a prop on the return journey. I now looked like a

respectable secondary school student, perhaps sent by a senior to deliver a message to another senior in another boarding house. I didn't look any student in the eye for fear of giving away the fact that I was a runaway. I passed behind Mr. Asensu's house, past Mr. & Mrs. Asante's and then lo and behold, there was Auntie Lucy's! I ran like the wind, inhaling the smell of fresh baked bread even before seeing the sun baked earthen oven that occupied a large space right behind the house. With her eagle-like eyes, she saw me from afar and shouted.

"Mary!"

And then almost immediately thrust the bread into my hands. I dug into it like there was a famine approaching. She encouraged this gouging by reminding me of how thin I looked.

"*Ei*, look at you, all skin and bones. What do they feed you at that school they call a first class institution?"

"Nothing," I said with bread stuffed in my mouth.

"Eh?"

"I said nothing. They feed us nothing."

"That's impossible. Why do you think Colonel Utuka and Afrifa all have children there? Those government people will not send their children to a school that will not feed them. You don't know how lucky you are."

So lucky I have to escape from school to get some food to eat?

When I was done stuffing my face, Auntie Lucy helped me hide bits of bread in my pockets and where my breasts should be. I ended up having disproportionate breasts but she assured me that by evening, I would have eaten all my breasts away and I would be flat again—my normal self. Such a comforting thought. She saw my slight displeasure at having bread for breasts and breadcrumbs all over my uniform.

"At least I'm letting you see what you will look like one day when everything has appeared in the right place," she says.

I prayed earnestly that God would be a better placer of body parts than Auntie Lucy because otherwise, I would be a freak for life.

One scorching Thursday, the crusty taps in the school stopped running. Nothing new there. Whether it was the Volta Lake drying up, Satan drinking up all the clouds or whatever, the water situation was really getting bad. The toilets were all so full and buzzing with flies that you couldn't even go near the bathrooms. We had to walk over a mile to fetch water from a well and then when we brought it back, the lazy seniors —Cynthia included— sitting on the stairs leading to Clark House demanded we hand over our buckets of water. With this state of affairs, I could literally go for days without bathing and sometimes, Akos, Barbara and I would wonder if perhaps we could find some other place closer to the well to bath before walking back to the dorm with no water in our buckets. The thing was, there were boys also fetching water there, so it'd be tough to do that.

Akos and I dragged ourselves to the *chopbox* room where all our provisions were kept. It was even tortuous trying to eat because there was no water to drink afterwards. All of us knew that if you ate *gari* and didn't wash it down with water immediately, you would look six-months pregnant in way less than six months. We sat wearily on our *chopboxes*, wondering what to do next.

"Scripture Union prayer meeting will be starting soon," Akos reminded me.

"Yah, so?" I asked petulantly

"You *paa*—don't you want to go and pray or something? At least it gets us out of the dorm and we won't get sent everywhere by seniors."

And there are a few hot guys in there too, she carefully neglected to add. She didn't want God knowing that we had ulterior motives for wanting to 'fellowship with believers'.

"Have you ever had a miracle happen to you?" I asked her.

"What kind?"

"I don't know, but the real kind. Like something that was so impossible but it still happened".

She didn't answer but sat deep in thought.

"Have you?" she threw the question back at me.

"Yes."

"Well…what was it?"

"Lots actually. One time we were driving through Kaneshie and my mother mistakenly drove the car into the gutter. She screamed 'Jesus' as we felt one side of our Datsun 120Y dip into the gutter and we all yelled too. Suddenly, the car seemed to jump out of the gutter back onto the road."

"Are you serious?"

"You asked for a miracle story."

"But I didn't say make one up!" she hit me playfully.

"I'm serious " I continued. "I do remember it happening but I don't know how it happened. My grandma says if you have faith, you can move mountains."

"Mmmmhhh, if I had faith right now, I would be making water flow through these pipes so we'd get some water to drink," Akos said sadly.

"Maybe you do, you just don't know it." I said it as a dare.

Getting out from the 6 by 8 feet *chopbox* room, we made our way

about two meters to our left where the two outdoor taps were. We giggled nervously; we knew that this was something profound. We were actually going to pray for a miracle. What if it happened? What if it didn't? Who cared?

We placed our hands—both—on the first tap and prayed.

"Lord, we are thirsty and we haven't had water in a while. We believe that you are more powerful than anything and we ask that your Holy Spirit will release power into this tap and cause it to flow with water. In Jesus name! Amen!"

We opened our eyes and looked at each other. This was the moment of truth. Akos's piercing white eyes looked fervent and eager. I wondered what mine looked like. All I knew was that now, I wasn't sure of any miracles. My faith now wavered so badly it felt like it was hanging by a gossamer thread. Without speaking, we turned the tap slowly.

Shockingly, the water began to flow.

And we stood staring.

Someone in one of the dorms heard the beautiful sound of running water and screamed.

"The water is running!"

An army of students rushed out from every part of Clark House with buckets, pails, name it, any container was good enough. We were shoved out of the way, still in a trance, while the water flowed and then before the first bucket was filled, it stopped.

Akos and I looked at our wet feet.

We'd just witnessed a miracle.

And we were still thirsty.

6

A Sounding in Asamankese

Living in Accra made visiting Asamankese feel like a holiday of sorts, especially after a hectic term in boarding school. In Asamankese, our mornings would start when we'd hear vendors touting their various wares, calling out for people to come and buy breakfast on the go. We were soon to learn that many people ate breakfast sold by these sellers. Porridge, both white and grey—the grey was made with the usual corn as well as tiger pepper. It was so hot you cried just at the thought. There was also rice and beans with pepper, *kenkey* and fish with pepper and fried plantains and beans, with pepper. Every thing was hot—pepper hot and spicy hot—but Nana had prepared us so well that it wasn't bad at all — we survived it—anything to prove we were really Ghanaians.

There were some rocks outside Old House that were perfect for viewing the rest of the town from. They were outside one of the

cave-like entrances to Old House. An added advantage was that it was close to the chief's house, a concept that took some getting used to. If a chief was like a king—and a king lived in a palace like Buckingham Palace—then this chief's house was quite odd. It was definitely not a palace although the reverence accorded it by the townspeople belied it's sparse grandeur. There were all sorts of rituals one had to go through just to go through the front door, and I found it hard to see what all the fuss was about. The scariest thing about the Chief's house was a stone at the entrance that was supposed to be possessed and if you touched it, you'd die. I had so much to live for that the thought of testing this never crossed my mind.

Papa Kwabena lived in New House and had a decent toilet with a real toilet seat so we never needed much goading to go and visit him. On our very first visit to Asamankese, we'd hardly had a chance to meet him since he had been busy on his cocoa farms on the outskirts of the town. During this December trip though, we made the 10-minute walk to his house and the house help excitedly announced that we had arrived.

"Ebele emo hebe" – bring them in, he said.

We entered an ornately decorated living room where Papa Kwabena and his friends, all wearing traditional costume were huddled around a checkers table, drinking beers, smoking, laughing, generally living some sort of a good life. He called to us. "Come here."

That was cool, I thought. He spoke English. We were finally meeting an older person in the village whose English was not only passable, it could be understood!

"Hello Grandpa," we politely said, as his friends looked on

admiringly.

"*Ei*, you children have grown ohhh. Speak English so my friends will know where you come from."

I wanted to say we came from Ghana and looked quizzically at him. Or were we really from some other place? What to say? I looked at Yaw, he looked at me and we both wondered if we should sing, dance or just plain chant a rhyme. We sang the Persil automatic advertisement we loved on British TV. How stupid was that? Obviously not too stupid for those listening to us because they burst out in applause and yelled for an encore.

We felt like stars. We sang Persil Automatic (*makes your washing clean, you do what's clean and you do what's bright*), Mars (*A mars a day makes you work, rest and play*), and then we sang The Bay City Rollers' *I only want to be with you* and all this while a small crowd was gathering outside the living room to listen to us. Mum thankfully came to our rescue after the fourth rendition of Persil Automatic and we couldn't have been more grateful. We were running out of songs and yet the audience was screaming for more. We bowed, they clapped, we bowed, they shouted for more, we bowed and then Papa Kwabena held up his hands to stop the audience. He had a profound announcement to make.

"Mary wants to be a doctor."

One of his friends responded with a word that I just can't seem to spell—it sounds something like 'Enhh?' and has dips and turns and is a bit nasal. When Ghanaians use that word they are actually asking 'really?'

"Yes please," I murmured demurely. I was learning fast that the word 'please' had to be added to every sentence, even when you were not asking for a thing.

"And Mary, tell them what kind of a doctor you are going to be."

"Please I want to be a doctor who helps women have babies."

Claps were heard all around the living room as my grandpa and his beer-swigging friends endorsed my life's ambition.

"So, as you all know, it will be an honour for our family when Mary becomes a doctor. I will bequeath a plot of land to her, to be used to build a hospital to be named after her Grandpa—The Appiah John Memorial Hospital for Maternal Health."

Deafening applause filled the entire 2-storey building as Papa Kwabena declared his pleasure at his granddaughter's dream. There were also jealous glances at this announcement; I was not his only relative after all.

Papa Kwabena kept his word—I got the land.

I didn't keep mine. Well, not quite.

We learned to carry water in buckets. This may not seem like a feat, I know, but when you consider that this water had to be in an aluminum bucket, on your head, well, you get the picture. I must have had about a thousand tries before I could take one step without the water spilling all over my clothes. It was so much fun. In the evenings, we would gather on the steps leading up to Nana's rooms. She would tell *Ananse the Spider* stories, scaring us while laughing at the looks on our faces. Mosquitoes were rampant and we, waging war on those nasties, punctuated her stories with slaps and ouches. She didn't seem affected by them. Mummy would come in after a long day of visiting Auntie this and Uncle that— boy did we have a lot of relatives—seemed like every older person was related to us. One evening, Mummy had to go and help at a delivery even though she's not a midwife; like that mattered; in

those days, almost any older woman was expected to help at a delivery and it was an art that seemed to be handed down from mother to daughter. She came back exhausted. By this time, I was getting quite good at Anum and so as she recounted the experience to one of her cousins, I eavesdropped, understanding every word.

"I tell you, she was lucky ohh," Mum said.

"*E-n-h?*"

"Yes—she could have easily died. And then who would have taken care of her other eight children?"

"'Then it is the will of the gods that this one died oh?"

'The will of God, not gods! How many times will I tell you that there is only one true God?"

"As for you Emma, you've gone and filled your head with all this one-God business. I know there is a supreme being but don't you know there are many others? Smaller ones?"

"I'm not going to argue with you—I am exhausted—let me sleep," Mum begged.

I ran away before I could be spotted but kept wondering how someone could have eight children and still try to have more. There had to be a way to stop having children if you'd had enough.

There was no electricity those days in the Old House and we saw our way around with lanterns and candles and for us, it was spooky and fun. This felt like going camping and there were all sorts of silly games we could play in the dark. One evening, we heard that there was a show on the television at New House so we all made the trek there to watch a sitcom called *Osofo Dadzie*. There were about thirty people watching this small 13 –inch black and white TV —most of them outside the living room area, standing outside and peering through windows. Since we were Papa Kwabena's

relatives, we were allowed in the room where the television was perched on a table. All the children sat cross-legged on the floor. The drama was entirely in *Twi* so it was a bit difficult to understand but basically, a man had two wives and each of them tried to outdo the other one in trying to gain the husband's affection. It got so competitive that they tried to sabotage one another and a child of the first wife died in the process. The second wife thinking she had 'won', triumphantly went to church to praise God for her victory. Everyone branded her a witch so her husband subsequently left her, and the first wife and the husband lived happily ever after. Everyone was so engrossed in the drama that they sounded like a support crew – giving 'ei's and 'oh's' at the appropriate junctures, clapping when good overcame evil and hooting at the second wife when she was led away in disgrace. Such was the substance of most, if not all local dramas, comedic or otherwise; it had to have marital strife, accusations of witchcraft, extra-marital affairs, local boy branded stupid goes 'abroad' and comes back with a car, tortured stepchild grows up to become a doctor while spoilt brat child gets hit by a car and maimed in the accident. Another staple was one where a beautiful woman couldn't have babies (it's always her fault) so her husband married a second wife who treated the first wife with disdain because she (second wife) was so fecund that she had a baby barely nine months after her engagement. The first wife, full of sorrow went to church, got delivered of the demons who had captured her womb and taken it to a shrine in *Obosomase*. She then conceived and named the child Samuel (as in the Bible). Suddenly, her husband's love returned and they lived happily ever after. On the way home after watching such dramas, people would be talking about all of this, putting themselves in the shoes of one or more of the characters and

wondering what they would do in that character's stead.

"Me, I would have beaten her *paa*," one would say.

"As for me, if she took my womb, I would have taken hers too and her childrens' wombs too…*kwasia*!" It hadn't taken me long to learn that *kwasia* meant something or someone that was utterly stupid (It is indeed true that the first words you learn in any language are the rude words ones).

"But isn't it the right thing to do? To ask God for forgiveness eh? All of these things are because people have forgotten the God of Jacob," some pious person would add.

"What are you talking about? Listen, even when the God of Jacob is with you, sometimes the other gods get you ohhh? That God of Jacob sometimes doesn't listen to black people like us. If he did, would some of us be so poor?"

I had another encounter with African superstition one particularly hot, dusty day. Over the years, many Ghanaian friends I've told the story to have had similar stories to tell. Mr. Koduah was the next richest man in Asamankese after Papa Kwabena. He owned three bakeries and two tipper trucks that plied their trade from Asamankese to Kade and Akwatia, sometimes going all the way to Accra. Everyone who sold bread in Asamankese bought it wholesale from Mr. Koduah's Bakeries, aptly named 'The Only One Bakery'. They then sold it by the roadside or the marketplace. Everyone revered him, some jealously, and it wasn't long before the rumours about his wealth reached small ears like mine. Mr. Koduah was a practicing wizard apparently, using black magic to conjure money from things like pots and pans, car parts, suitcases and generally anything that could hold anything.

Kwabena Atta, a scrawny boy who lived behind Old House told

me that Mr. Koduah had a sore on his left leg, somewhere around his ankle. As long as this sore festered, Mr. Koduah's money kept multiplying so we started plotting to find a way to see this powerful sore. We recruited a few more children from the neighbourhood and planned a soccer game, just at the time we knew Mr. Koduah would be getting out of his Peugeot and making his slow way to his bungalow off the Asamankese High Street.

The day arrived when our plan was to be put into action. Yaw and I, to get away from Old House without Esther following, pretended we were going on an errand. We scampered to the left entrance and escaped through the cave like opening, ran over the rocks in between the chief's house and Old House and down the hill to the small park behind Mr. Koduah's house. We were last to arrive—Kwabena was there along with Mary Agyeiwaa—a plump girl around my age, as well as Ata Addo and his twin sister Ataa. Together, we waited. Around five in the evening, we were rewarded when Mr. Koduah's Peugeot pulled up to the front and we saw the house helps rushing out of the house to go and carry whatever produce had been purchased on the way home. We immediately started kicking the ball to one another and by the time we were close to Mr. Koduah, we heard voices shouting and telling us to be careful; we ignored them. Ata kicked it close to Mr. Koduah's left leg and that was our cue to rush and pick up the ball, pull his trouser leg up and come face to face with the money producing sore. We all rushed to the man's leg and literally knocked him over amidst cries of *buei!, ei!, buei!, ei!* We looked with anguish at one another, knowing that we hadn't seen a sore and yet we were going to get the biggest beatings of our lives! By the time I was able to get my wits about me, everyone was gone, even Yaw! I stood face

to face with this big man, surrounded by nosy people who'd heard the commotion, and wanted to stick their noses where they didn't belong. Actually, anyone who wanted to see me get my come-uppance was there. I had to act quickly.

"I'm sorry," I whimpered to Mr. Koduah, who was being helped up by some two men who had mysteriously appeared by his side. Mr. Koduah glared at me.

"Why are you and your friends so bad? And where are they?"

"I don't know," I said softly, looking around me for my so-called friends and Judas Iscariot brother!

"Mmmmhhhh, they are like Jesus' disciples eh? Betraying you and leaving you to your accusers."

The man read my mind—what a genius! I decided to continue the penitent act since it was beginning to look like this was the only way out of this predicament.

"Why did you all decide that it was best to play football around me, so close to me?" he asked.

"I don't know," I lied.

"Ahhh, I think you know. Mary Abena Asabea Apea"—the saying of my full name sent shivers down my spine—"my children tell me you are a clever child. You read a lot and you talk a lot too. Now don't lie to me and tell me that you don't know why you and your friends decided to kick a ball at me. Did you think I felt like playing a game of football with you?"

That game was clearly over and I figured that since we had just one week left to spend in Asamankese on this holiday break, I couldn't lose by telling the truth. So I put my most innocent face on and said very slowly.

"I wanted to see your sore."

"My sore? What sore?"

"The one on your left ankle."

"My left ankle? I had no idea I had a sore on my left ankle." He turned to look at his family and while some laughed, I noticed that some of the older women were not amused. Instead they were looking me up and down like I had put a bad taste in their mouths. "Hey! Somebody give this foolish girl some bread and let her go back home," he shouted in the direction of the onlookers. Almost immediately, a plastic bag with two loaves of bread was thrust into my hand and I was led away towards the street. I dared not look back and ran as fast as my legs would carry me. Panting like a dog, I almost bumped into Nana in the courtyard of the Old House as she made her way towards the kitchen area. I held up the loaves of bread for her to see.

"And where did you get this?" she asked.

I couldn't respond; I was still running and although I'd come to a stop, my voice would just not come out of my mouth.Only loud panting.

"I said where did you get this? I don't like little girls picking things up from some place and bringing it home—that's called stealing and our people don't steal."

I took a deep breath and explained.

"Mr. Koduah gave it to me."

"Mr. Koduah gave it to you? Why?"

Time for another lie? I had to stammer through my next statement.

"I'm not sure—I met him on his way into his house—when I was playing football and he said I was clever and asked someone to bring me bread."

That wasn't a lie was it? He did say all those things!

"Oh, that's nice although quite unusual. It is a good thing. The

Lord will surely bless him." She patted my head and I basked in the glow of her admiration, wondering how long it would last when—

"Hey, Mary...I've heard!"

I spun round so fast that my head hit Nana's jaw! There behind me was Sisi Yaa Yaabi, my fair skinned aunt who seemed to know everything that went on in the town of Asámankese. I nursed the bruise on my head, forgetting Nana must be hurting also.

"What are you talking about?" Nana demanded.

"Ask her!" Sisi Yaa Yaabi challenged.

O God, save me I thought. I opened my eyes wide to feign innocence, swallowed a gallon of spit and held my legs together to stop myself from urinating in fear.

"Mary, what did you do?" said Nana in that voice that signified the calm before the storm.

No lies this time. Straight truth.

"Kwabena told me Mr. Koduah has *sika-aduro*—you know—the witchcraft that makes people get plenty of money."

"*Tschew*, look at her explaining *sika-aduro* to me—*kwasia*," Nana interjected.

" - and it was in a sore on his left leg so we made a plan to see it. We decided to play football near him so that when the ball got close to him and we went to fetch it, we would pull up his trouser leg to see if the sore was really there."

"And?"

"We didn't see anything," I said sadly.

"And then he gave you bread?" Nana said incredulously.

I nodded vigorously.

Nana looked at Sisi Yaa Yaabi. Sisi Yaa Yaabi looked at Nana. I swung my head from one to the other, trying desperately to read their body language. Did they believe me? Was I off the hook?

More importantly, did Mr. Koduah have *sika-aduro*?

Nana pulled me close to her and delivered a knock on my head that rang through my skull. I actually heard the knock inside my head and felt it move into each of my two ears. No wonder they called it a *sounding*! As my ears rang, I heard Nana yelling at me.

"Next time, don't go and poke your nose into other people's business, especially when it has to do with money. Listening to stories like that is not a good way to become wise. When you have your finger pointing at someone, don't forget that you have three pointing at yourself. Next time, you'll get an even bigger *sounding*!"

I nodded, agreeing to every word she was saying although my head felt like it was on fire.

"And the fact that I'm *sounding* you doesn't mean Mr. Koduah doesn't do *sika-aduro;* throw that bread away!"

I did what I was told and then Nana did a very odd thing. She gave me one cedi to go and buy bread from the lady across the road who buys all her bread wholesale from 'The Only One Bakery'. And as we all knew, Mr. Koduah owned the 'The Only One Bakery'.

Why were old people so odd? Or was it just Ghanaian old people?

We traipsed around Asamankese during the day, jumping on lizards and poking goats with sticks. There was a river we were warned about repeatedly. It was called *Ebuchen* and it was apparently a god that swallowed naughty children. Every time we were heading out, Nana would yell out in Anum.

"Don't go near *Ebuchen* you hear? Especially as you've been naughty already today!"

We'd ignore her of course and make our way down the main street, through various vending stalls, through some thick brush to

within twenty feet of *Ebuchen*. The river wound round and round the bushes and seemed to have no end. I sometimes wondered how dangerous it was because there were some kids swimming in it. They were definitely bad kids.

Christmas in Asamankese was different from what we'd experienced in England. We didn't have a Christmas tree and there were no presents. Santa Claus was called Father Christmas but no one dressed up like him to ride the streets in a sleigh. It was all very odd. Instead, along with other children in the town we wore chains of small crackers round our necks, caroling through the streets—or paths—of the Anum section. We sold paper hats and eggs, sang English carols to adoring crowds and performed at church.

Christmas lunch was *fufu* and chicken and this was quite the treat since all year, we ate just fish and no chicken. It was simple but so refreshingly different and after our first Christmas, we'd almost forgotten how it felt like to have an English Christmas! One Christmas day, we came home from church to New House to find a goat tethered to the main gate. Now bear in mind that a goat in the main compound of a house is nothing unusual in Ghana—goats tend to wander freely in the outer compound of many rural houses. However, this was unusual in that no one knew where this goat was from. No one knew how it got there, and so a period of unease ensued. In many parts of Africa, it seems everything for which there doesn't seem to be a logical explanation is the work of Satan. So this goat, young, healthy and tethered to the gate was an object of wonder and fear, simultaneously.

By evening, a meeting had to be called to ask what to do about it. One said to throw it out. But, another argued, that's some serious meat! That goat could feed the entire household several times

over. But, another argued, what if the goat has an evil spirit and after eating it, everyone dies? Maybe this is a way for the devil to wipe out entire sections of families that are destined for greatness. And, another one continued, this happened to a friend of a friend of a friend and all the men in that house became impotent and the women became barren. Just as the voices were raised in consternation, a shuffle was heard. Everyone turned round to see an entourage made up of a decently dressed elderly man and three women. Everyone got up to greet them as was the custom, and then discreetly left the elders to sit with these visitors. Turned out the goat was a gift from these people who had traveled from Kumasi but on their arrival in Asamankese, everyone had gone out to church—even Papa Kwabena—who went to church only on Easter and Christmas day. Meeting no one, they tethered the goat to the gate with the intention of coming back in the late afternoon to personally pay their respects to Papa Kwabena, the intended recipient of the gift.

I'd learned another lesson that day. For my people, the unknown, the unexplainable, the unusual and the non-conforming were always a cause for concern; Satan always did it.

The day before we left Asamankese after one of our many visits, there was a comedy of errors, Nana-style. Old House seemed pretty quiet since all the adults were out at market, and the children were all playing outside. Yaw and Esther were digging for ants outside in the sand. I was skipping rope with Agyeiwaa who was so much fun that I didn't mind that she could barely jump rope. The sun was

about to set and so there was a little bit of movement in and around the cave-like entrance to Old House. As Agyeiwaa and I wiped the sweat off our brows, we saw Papa Kwabena hurriedly rush out of the compound house. He didn't even say hi or acknowledge my presence. That was quite odd; I was his favourite, or so I thought. About half an hour passed. We'd gone to play with Esther and Yaw to help them catch more ants but we got fed up. We came back to our 'base' to jump rope with two other girls Adwoa and Ama, when I saw Papa Kwabena's wife walk hurriedly into Old House. She didn't say hi either to acknowledge my presence. That was *very* odd. I pretended that I wasn't very curious and asked the girls if they wanted to go home so I could walk them back. They agreed and we started hopping over little gutters filled with spirogyras, narrowly missing buckets of dirty water being thrown by women who'd just finished their dishes or laundry. It was a treacherous journey to say the least! I said my byes to each of my friends and ran like wild fire back to Old House.

Even before I got there, I could hear voices raised in anger.
"And so why would you call Amoakoa?" Papa Kwabena was saying. Amoakoa was his wife.
Nana raised her voice, as if she wanted the whole world to hear her.
"Because you are an unfaithful husband, that's what you are!"
"So can't a husband have some alone time away from his wife?"
"If you want to be alone, you don't bring your girlfriend to my room, assuming I won't be there!"
"But I built this room!"
"*E-n-h*? Is that the thanks I get for raising you and making sure you are able to stand on your own two feet?"
Silence. Dead Silence.

"*Maanum,* I am sorry for saying that. What I mean is, I am a grown man, with grown up needs. If one woman cannot satisfy those needs, what am I to do?"

"You are to pray!"

There was laughter from Papa Kwabena; a very hearty laughter that rang through the whole compound. Although the rest of Old House seemed quiet, I knew everyone was home listening to this exchange with bated breath. How dare Papa Kwabena stand up to Nana?

"Nana, all I am saying is that if I want some time away from my wife, and you find out, please don't send someone to go and fetch my wife on the pretense that I need her right here, in the same room in which my girlfriend is waiting," pleaded Papa Kwabena.

"Over my dead body," the wrinkled old woman said. "I will not let such abominations go unchecked. Take that harlot away from this place and send some of your house helps to come and disinfect my room with an antiseptic liquid…something strong like Dettol. I cannot stand the smell of sexual impurity!"

Nana marched out of the room with Amoakoa, both holding their heads up high. They headed towards the exit of the compound house where Nana assured her that she would be well taken care of ;wasn't that what the family promised when they sent emissaries to engage her in marriage over twenty six years ago? Amoakoa thanked Nana, clasping her hand in gratitude while tears flowed freely down her face. Nana walked back resolutely and stood outside her door as Papa Kwabena and the harlot also came out of the room. The harlot hung her head in shame while Nana rained insults on her retreating back.

"Shame on you! No wonder you can't find a proper man! Hey, if

you think this man will stick with you, let me tell you, you're not the first ok? He will drop you like hot yam. Do you know you aren't the first?"

She spat after them while murmuring under her breath and then she slowly made her way to her room. As if on cue, the entire compound came back to life. Suddenly, water needed to be fetched —even at this late hour—and church arrangements needed to be made; anything to allow inhabitants of the Old House to mingle and gossip about tonight's show.

The verdict was unanimous once again: Nana 1, Papa Kwabena 0. Nothing ever changes, I hear.

7

"Stay home, there is a big, big coup"

Form Two in boarding school was like a glorious awakening. Being thirteen and having twelve-year-olds doing what I was required to do for a whole year made me feel so good about myself, in an oddly stupid way. I could wake up a full two minutes after the morning bell went, lounging lazily in my bed and watching the Form One minions running as if their lives were in danger, which I guess they were. After I'd counted to 120 seconds I'd slowly get out of my bed, grab a towel, underwear, and a sponge bag and then take a lazy stroll to the showers, making sure to practice shaking my bottom the way I'd seen the seniors do. I'd get to the showers and perhaps a Form One girl would have just got in and I'd say this sentence with attitude every single time.

"Excuse me! Who told you to get into the shower before me?"

At which query the minion would scamper out and then I'd feel bad and ask her to get back in the shower and finish quickly. On

several occasions, I confessed (to myself) that I wouldn't be a very good senior; I wasn't mean enough.

I had a new chore in Form Two—wiping the A-court. This was the expanse of cream tiles on the right side of the middle stairs. Clark House, which was the name of our boarding house was a large imposing building, whitewashed with blue window trimmings and gables. It was reminiscent of all the colonial buildings erected along the coast in the early part of the twentieth century. From the front, there was a large blue wooden door and when you entered, there were two floors comprised of four large dormitories, or dorms for short. The dorms upstairs were called A Dorm and B Dorm and the ones downstairs were C and D dorms. All form one and two students were usually in A and B and from Form three upwards, you could be placed anywhere. You'd enter Clark House through the large blue doors, then a tiled forecourt and that would take you to a staircase so grand that the first time I watched *Gone with the Wind*, I thought it'd have made a good substitute when Tara burnt down. On either side of this staircase were the courts that led to courtyards where we'd hang out, hang our laundry, do our washing and also visit the boxrooms that housed our *chopboxes* filled with *gari, shitto* and canned fish of all types. After the afternoon siesta, many students would go to their *chopboxes* and have a little snack before starting the evening chores. I used to wish my daily chore was to clean B-Court since everyone hung their stuff out to dry in A-courtyard so there was a lot of traffic in A-court; it was always dirty. Still, it was better than being a toilet girl, the nastiest Third former job ever. You had to scrub the toilets and empty waste paper baskets and such, and as you can imagine, when there was no water, it was deadly.

For our classes we got to be in the Form Two block which was closer to the boys houses so that was cool; we got to see more boys! In the second term, we had a tutor for English who was a University of Ghana final year student. I think he was replacing one of our English teachers who had gone on maternity leave. He was less than 5 feet tall with a wide head and very heavyset eyes. He looked mean and he was mean. During one English class, he called my friend Afua to his desk to collect her work. She walked fearfully to his desk and as she waited to be handed her notebook, she placed her hands on his desk; no intent to be rude, just a casual placing of the arms on a structure that promised rest. He slowly looked up from his marking and gave her the dirtiest look.

"Take those paws off my desk."

Afua and I asked God several times why people like him don't die from boils to the head.

I had my period in Form Two. I was sort of expecting it and was upset it had taken so long. Everyone else was having it or had had it—Kezia when she was a mere eight years old! Nana of course had told me to watch out for it and when it did come, to make sure I never talked to boys again. According to Nana, talking to boys after your period 'had shown up' was a guarantee of pregnancy. Mummy was less dramatic, if that was at all possible. Since Form One, I had been cautioned about cleanliness, the need to always have an ample supply of sanitary towels, the need to change underwear often and discreetly...blah, blah, and blah. When I actually saw the stain for the first time, I couldn't remember one thing Nana or Mummy had told me—it was like they'd never told me this would happen. I had this uncanny feeling something was

wrong and the first thought was that I was bleeding internally from eating too much *gari*. Or was it the spinach sauce from two days ago that had something chunky in it that looked like meat? Or did a senior feed me glass in my sleep? I went to one of my fountains of wisdom—Afua.

"Wait, tell me step by step," she said as we lay on our four-inch thick foam mattresses in the afternoon heat of A Dorm.

"Well, I went to the bathroom and you know, pulled down my pants to urinate and there was this red stain."

"Well, have you seen this kind of stain before," she asked like a doctor.

"No, silly! Of course not! Are you going to tell me what it is or not?"

We heard Senior Gloria get up from her twelve-inch thick foam mattress (one of her own 4 inch mattresses and two confiscated from some hapless Form One girls who now had to sleep on pieces of plywood) in the inner chamber of A Dorm and make her way to our beds. We immediately shut up, closed our eyes and pretended to be breathing softly, feigning sleep.

"I know some of you were talking," she said. "If I hear one more word out of you before afternoon siesta is over, you are dead meat, you hear me? You will scrub the whole house from top to bottom till I can lick the floor and not get sick."

We stifled giggles since we were thinking that it might not be a bad way to kill her off. After we were sure she was safely ensconced on her bed, Afua dared to open her mouth.

"I'll have to check after the siesta bell goes. Are you still wearing the underwear?"

"Yes."

"*Kai*, you're really dirty *paa*! What Ghanaian girl does that? You

should have taken it off and washed it!"

"Well, now you tell me!"

We didn't realize how much our voices carried...all the way to the inner chamber of A Dorm to Senior Gloria's ears.

"Mary and Afua with your big mouths, you've been punished to scrub the whole house tomorrow. See me when the siesta-ending bell goes," shouted Senior Gloria from the A-Dorm inner chamber. After the bell rang to indicate that the siesta was over, we totally ignored Senior Gloria who was now snoring and we ran to the bathroom and I showed Afua what I meant. By then, it was more than just a stain and Afua declared that I had begun my trip into womanhood. She cautioned me to stay put—like I was going to run around while leaking—while she fetched her box of implements a.k.a tampons. She explained how they worked and said they were way neater and more comfortable than walking with pads in between your legs. I had never seen tampons before and was quite apprehensive. They looked liked bullets. What if they exploded inside me? All the Form One, Two and Three girls loved us the next day. There was an announcement in the common room in the evening that, for talking excessively when they should have been sleeping, Mary and Afua had been punished to scrub the whole house so no one else had to do their chores that day. That meant any cleaning to do with all the dorms from A through to D including their inner chambers, both courts, the landing upstairs, the magnificent stairs, the two hallways running to each House Mistress' home as well as the bathrooms and the toilets. As we filed out from the common room, we had various looks from our classmates. Some pretended to be sad for us but most were happy and whispering.

"Ei, you *paa*, how dare you talk when seniors say you shouldn't

talk?"

I cared and didn't care, all at once. I knew I would be horribly tired by the end of the marathon scrub session but I was oddly bereft of feeling. Maybe it was because I suddenly felt like a woman, not a girl. Women were strong and took every challenge in stride. Children didn't do that; they broke down and cried. And with the tampon safely lodged within me, I had ample evidence that the journey had begun. Punishment didn't scare me. I was a woman.

No woman no cry. Thanks Bob Marley.

<<>>

If Form Two felt like heaven, then Form Three was indescribable. At this rate, I thought I'd probably be in the proverbial seventh heaven by the time I got to Form Five. Now my lie-in after the morning bell was heard at 5:30 am was five minutes long! I was filling out in all the right places and I'd even acquired a Kohl pencil that I would use to outline my eyes when no one was looking. Barbara and I were on the same dining table that first term—table B 20—and since we were third formers, we did get quite a bit to eat. We had a fourth former on our table who was about six feet tall and very soldier like; his name was Archibald and all he did was grunt. A Ghanaian called Archibald. Imagine.

One morning, after we'd dragged our sorry behinds to the dining hall after a particularly tiresome morning of singing *O Jesus I have promised* in chapel, we saw Archibald get up, climb the prefects' table and take over the microphone.

"This afternoon will be the first tryout for all students interested in joining the army cadet corps. Meet at the Cadet Square in front

of Livingstone House at 3pm sharp…oh, and girls are welcome." Barbara and I looked at each other in mock shock. Turns out I was shocked that Archibald could speak words that could be understood, and Barbara was shocked that girls were welcome to tryout. Needless to say, we were both at the Cadet Square at 3pm that afternoon, ready to begin our careers as army cadets. I had no idea why I was there —I lie —I did have an idea why I was there. Barbara needed a friend to be with her and I thought it'd be a cool way to meet boys—tough boys. We got there and saw Archibald looking like a soldier in military type fatigues. He was yelling at everyone to get in line, stand at ease, jump up and down, stand at ease, get in line…I was tired just at the sound of his voice. This was not worth it I thought, but Barbara was lapping it all up; all this in searing thirty degree Celsius temperatures. We were released to our dorms just before 4:30 in the afternoon and I felt a cramping in my calves, a sure sign that my body had actually done some work. "That was amazing!" Barbara said, beaming and glistening with salty sweat.

"Are you crazy?" I said, barely able to walk from the strain on all the muscles in my body.

"Why? Didn't you enjoy it?"

"Yes I did, like a bullet to the head!"

We laughed so hard I thought I'd pee on myself.

"Listen Barbara. It was fun while it lasted but I've never thought I wanted to be a soldier. Air force maybe—its sexy—but army? I hate people yelling at me and I can't stand standing in 30 degree temperatures unable to scratch myself or twitch or lick my lips. I just can't handle it."

"That was just today Mary, stop being lazy and lets go back tomorrow. You'll see it'll be easy the next time around."

Why do I listen to my friends? I was carried off the cadet square the next afternoon having fainted in the 35 degree Celsius temperature after a particularly grueling jog around the school campus, a perimeter of at least a couple of miles while hauling what felt like a sack of yams strapped to my back. I guess the upside was that I was carried off to the sick bay by strong boys and hauling the sack on my back made me straighten my back...which made my bust firm. Since the whole point of joining the cadets was to meet boys, getting a firmer bust was a bonus so I think I came out the winner.

Even though I lasted just two days. Whatever.

Before long, Form Four arrived and suddenly, we were picking our courses to allow us to be in Arts or Science. Actually, you didn't get to pick. You took a math and science exam at the end of form three and if you did well, you were in the Science class, meaning most of your classes were science based. If you were in Arts then that meant you took Humanities and Arts courses. Of course you could decline this 'prestigious honour' as my friend Akosua B did. She was incredibly bright but had decided even at that very early age that science was not for her. I ended up in one of the science classes—4S1— with Afua. One morning in the first term, we saw a student being led towards our room by Miss Trudy, our Literature teacher. He was introduced to us as Robert and had just arrived from the United States. Everyone was enamoured by Robert who spoke American English and was very shy. Before long, we'd coerced him into joining our posse and that made us incredibly cool. One afternoon as we sat at the Snack Square having some bananas and peanuts, we got talking about family.

"So where do your parents come from?" I asked.

"From a town called Asamankese," Robert replied. His American accent made Asamankese sound like Arsemankiss!

"Really? So do I."

"No kidding," he replied in that very American way that was so relaxed and lazy sounding.

We became kin from that moment on, hardly knowing that there was an amazing story behind the kinship. Mummy was the one who revealed it to me one Sunday evening when she came for a visit.

"Mummy, there's an American boy in my class and his name is Robert. He says his mother is from Asamankese."

"Last Name?"

"Kumi. Do you know any Kumi's from Asamankese?"

"There are many," she said unfazed.

"His father was in the Foreign Service," I continued.

She dropped the bowl of *jollof rice* she had brought for my Sunday evening meal. It was a good thing it was still in the trunk.

"Is his mother called Bedu?"

"Yes," I said excitely. "Do you know her?"

"Of course I know her." Then she proceeded to clean up the mess she'd created in the trunk of the car.

I waited for more information. She didn't give it.

"So how do you know her," I prodded.

"Sit in the car, its too hot and this could be a long story."

We both sat in the car just in front of Clark House as Mummy told me how Robert's Mum, Bedu was so beautiful and had been the belle of the whole town of Asamankese. She even won a beauty contest. Everyone wanted to marry her, even Daddy. *My father?* She nodded. So he asked for her hand in marriage and she

gave him the twice over and said he wasn't suitable—she had seen better. Alas, Daddy went back to university, determined never to ask a girl to marry him again!

"So how could I marry him when his family asked for my hand in marriage? Bedu had so many offers so it made your father look so unsuitable!"

I looked sadly at Mummy. She looked like she'd been transported to a sad place in time.

"Papa Kwabena sat me down and told me that although your father did not seem—what do you people call it—cool? Yes, he was definitely not cool, but he was studying science and that meant he knew the positions of the stars and could tell you deep and mysterious things about the universe."

We chuckled at that. Being a budding scientist, Papa Kwabena's description of Daddy's abilities sounded to me like Daddy read horoscopes!

"You know, there was a guy I wanted to marry? He was cool. He had an afro," Mummy said wistfully.

"Do you know where he is now?" I asked.

"Yes. I hear he works at the gas station in Asikuma!"

We laughed quite uncontrollably, tears running down our faces. Asikuma was a step down—way down—from Asamankese and to think that at one time, Mummy had actually thought of picking petrol boy over Daddy? She gave me a hug and we held each other close.

"I'm a lucky woman…I made the right choice."

"So you see Robert, you and I were meant to be brother and sister. Maybe you can teach me to speak American?" I said to him the following Monday.

Absolute power corrupts absolutely, and this was never more evident than when my friends and I became Fifth Formers. We could braid our hair, wear make-up, not wake up when the bell went at 5:30 and generally not lift a finger to do anything.

Everyone acquired a 'small girl' to do the running around, fetching of water, cutting of toenails and any other inconsequential thing that created a huge power gap between you and another person. I acquired two form one girls who became my 'small girls'— Akosua D and Elizabeth, the latter so mouthy that if she couldn't carry two buckets all at once, I would have fired her from the coveted position of Mary's small girl! One day, to cheer them up as they complained about how awful their Form One lives were, I sat on the front steps with them, telling them my Form One story of the missing underwear. At least it made them laugh. I neglected to add that after Afua offered to cut up her dress to make me underwear, we giggled softly into our pillows and then lay quietly in the November heat. Each of us, unbeknownst to the other, remembering a time when life seemed unfair. Mine was when we went to London without Nana. Afua's was when she found out she would probably stay an only child. For each of us, the sense of loss would haunt us for several years.

It's hard to believe that all of these sometimes mundane things happened before, during and after living under a military regime. In 1979, while I was just ten years old, Jerry John Rawlings and a

bunch of other military people took over the country—guns and all—in a coup d'etat. All the adults were terrified, but the kids were thrilled that we were seeing more than one airplane in a day! The air force planes would whiz by with a whirring sound that felt like it would burst your eardrums, and then another would follow close behind. It was so exciting we'd sit outside watching them. We even sang songs about the coup d'etat. My favourite was sung to the tune of 'Bridge on the River Kwai' and the words went like this:

Stay home, there is a big big coup
Stay home; there is a big big coup
Stay home, I tell you stay home
There is a very big coup, in town

Rawlings has overthrown, Akuffo and his men
The SMC is no more
Akuffo and his men, have been shot
By firing squad at Teshie Nungua!

Such childhood bliss while all around us, there was chaos. Food prices had gone up, everyone was afraid of going beyond their house gates and no one knew what was going to happen from day to day. At boarding school, we hardly knew what was going on but we did know that when you had visitors and they brought you food, you had to guard it with your life. We usually ate with our fingers unless we were in the dining hall and then we'd use cutlery. So, together with our friends, we'd hold pieces of paper under our chins to catch whatever errant grains of rice dared to escape our mouths. Oddly enough, since Rawlings spoke so eloquently and was young and charismatic, many started calling him Junior

Jesus, sort of matching the actual initials in his name—Jerry John. After his second coup (this guy had nine lives), he came to Achimota School and we raced to go and hear him speak at the Assembly Hall. We all—actually just the girls—thought he was cute so we were very much in favour of a revolution. He was dashing and handsome; this made it so much easier to embrace the revolution. Planes were everywhere but it seemed you couldn't get a flight out of Ghana to England or the USA. We heard rumours of judges being murdered, only to find out they weren't rumours. The murders had actually happened. The price of food was ridiculous—one day, *kenkey* would sell for 50 *pesewas* and the next day, if you found it, you'd be glad to be paying four times the price! A new word entered the lingo—*kalabule*. Not sure now what English word is synonymous with it, but it's a word that sort of means corruption and hoarding. Everyone was hoarding because you didn't know when you'd get another one of whatever. At school, we ate *kenkey* made from yellow corn; a clear demotion since yellow corn had been always known as livestock feed. I guess it was now good enough for humans.

If it was at all possible to get thinner, I did and now my collarbones poked out from my shoulders like hangers. I wasn't the only one who looked like this. Everyone now had *Rawlings chain*, a poking out of the collar bone that could only happen in extreme hunger and years later when I heard some stupid fashion model whine about how lucky hungry people in Africa were—because they didn't have to try too hard to lose weight—I'd feel like throwing up. Being hungry was not funny and it definitely was not cute or pretty. Why would anyone want to be in a state where you stopped talking, laughing, or dancing because it took too much energy and you didn't have enough to last through the day?

At home, we ate twice a day, the earlier meal a kind of brunch that happened around eleven in the morning. It was supposed to last us till around five p.m. when we'd have the second meal that was supposed to take us through the night to the following morning. It was a blessing that we hardly had electricity too. That way, you went to sleep early since there wasn't much to do but talk about food, and that was not terribly helpful. Then one day, we heard that the government was changing the currency because of inflation. I had no idea which government it was—it seemed we changed them as often as I undid my braids. As usual, there was no system for handling this change and utter chaos ensued. People were fighting in the streets for food and for the first time in a long time, Mummy cried. I overheard she and Nana talking.

Nana: Why haven't you told your husband eh?

Mummy: I have and he wants us to come back to London.

Nana: So why are you still here then?

Mummy: How can I leave you *Maanum*?

Nana: And why can't you? Look at me, I don't have much time left and if I become thinner from hunger, I will not look that much different. Besides, God always had a plan for us when the Word encouraged us to fast. Now we know how to do it!

Mummy: But who will look after you?

Nana: What kind of question is that from someone who was virtually born in the church? *E-n-h*? You shame me by asking such a question. Look at your white children—they are hungry. *Ei*, how long will you stay here? Until you are carrying a dead child? You have these precious ones—some are not so lucky with their children so don't be foolish and lose them. Boys are scarce in this

family.

Mummy: Tomorrow I will go to P & T and make a phone call to him to send us a package of essentials because I do not want to go back to that cold place ma. I can't live there.

Nana: Even for your children?

Silence.

<<>>

P & T was the abbreviation for Posts & Telecommunication—a raggedy place that was clearly built pre-independence. This was where you went to make an international call. It was falling apart. The booths that housed the telephones still creaked—its floors and doors—and it stank. Many a phone call was placed from this edifice and they all seemed to happen the same way. We would have to leave very early in the morning to brave the crowds and traffic heading to Accra. Mummy would bundle us all into our van with BraTeye our trusted driver, and we'd have been briefed on our mission: let Daddy know you are hungry. We'd sleep on the way because it was so early in the morning so by the time we got there, we'd all be very groggy. Yaw and I had to walk inside by ourselves while Mummy and BraTeye carried Esther and John in. We'd huddle together in one corner, Mummy with her arms around us like refugees complete with our blankets waiting for our docket (a number) to be called. Just as we were drifting off into Neverland, we'd hear:

"Emma Apea, call to Emmanuel Apea, London, Booth 4!"

Mum would slap us awake, we'd lick our lips and run into Booth 4 only to find the line dead. No one would apologize for the call being mysteriously dropped. No one cared. It was a surprise there were even any workers there at all at that time of the morning. So

off we'd go back to our huddle, this time slightly more awake and then we'd hear:

"Emma Apea, call to Emmanuel Apea, London, Booth 13!"

And that was way on the other side of the hallway so we'd run, bags, blankets and what not, trailing us as Mummy ran fast enough to catch this call. It was a joyous occasion when we'd hear her say:

"Praise the Lord darl."

Ewww disgusting. They still called each other darling. We continued to listen to only Mummy's side of the conversation.

"Yes, we are all well."

"No, the package has not arrived, who did you send it through?"

"I haven't seen her."

"Yes, the van is running well but the Nissan is broken down and there is no money to repair it."

"No, the children are back home for the holidays— in fact they are here, eager to speak with you."

Then she'd pass the phone over to me first.

"Hi Daddy," I'd say in my chirpiest voice. At that, Mummy would give me a stern look and point to my Rawlings chain. Ah, yes, I'd forgotten to act very very hungry. Voice falls an octave lower…

"Hi Dad." (No energy to say the whole word 'Daddy').

"Yes Dad."

"Yes sometimes…but I am always hungry." Mummy gives me thumbs up and points to my Rawlings chain again.

"We all have Rawlings Chain, Dad."

"It means our bones are showing through our skin."

"Thank you Daddy." (The promise of food gave me enough energy to say Daddy instead of Dad)

I pass the phone victoriously to Yaw who doesn't even bother with the pleasantries.

"We are hungry," he announces to Daddy. Mummy is beaming now and gives him thumbs up.

"Yes Daddy. We are hungry," he says to a question from Daddy. Daddy could have asked if William Shakespeare was his best friend and the answer would have been the same.

Then Daddy asks something that throws Yaw off. He looks imploringly at Mummy since this part was not on his Hunger Games script. Mummy whispers something in his ear.

"Yes Daddy. Thank you, Daddy. We are hungry," he says like an automaton.

Then he passes the phone to Esther like it's a viral disease. Esther just looks at the phone and smiles. Mummy whispers to her.

"I love you Daddy," in her cutest most I-want-to-plunge-her-in-a-toilet voice. Why didn't Mummy give me those lines? I hate being the whiner.

Mummy grabs the phone from Esther and continues.

"Yes, darl, we all miss you." And then she chuckles a bit and I see a little girl in her eyes and hear that same girl in her voice.

"I will go and look for Auntie Martha to collect the package and the money. You know, now the exchange rate is one pound sterling to five thousand cedis."

"Mmmhhh, who knows how long this will take?"

"But God is good and we will continue to pray."

"Thank you and God bless you too."

We'd walk out triumphantly from the booth. We had succeeded in making Daddy feel guilty that he was in London with the Queen while we were holed up in Ghana with Junior Jesus and his gang!

<<>>

Meanwhile, the economic situation worsened. We continued to receive essentials from Daddy—powdered milk, money, flour and sugar—it was ridiculous that these items had to be sent from London before we got a nutritious meal. The other alternative was the free powdered milk that the Americans were sending down in boxes. Eating it gave everyone gas and this was not good gas! The changing of the currency was in full swing but Mummy had still not been able to change any money. As such, we bought all our food from the market on credit. One day, Mummy came back from the market empty handed, looking devastated.

"Where is the cassava for the *fufu*, Ama?" Nana asked.

Mummy replied so softly that we had to strain to hear her.

"They wouldn't extend credit to me anymore. I've borrowed so much, they won't give me anymore."

"Ei Jesus!!!!" Nana the drama queen dropped on her knees and started crying and praying. Mummy walked dejectedly to her room and flopped on the bed. Nana followed, having done her prayers and supplication and ready to annoy someone.

"What else have you done to get some new money?"

"Maanum, I told you. I've asked around to see if anyone has connections because that's the only way to get the new money. No one in their right minds queues up at the banks anymore."

Nana would not let it go. "But Nii Amu next door got some money. Why don't you ask him where he got his?"

Mummy sighed. Why didn't Nana understand that she was trying? Just then, there was a knock at the door.

"Come in," she said tiredly.

No doubt Kwasi the househelp was at the door wondering if he had to cook anything. Everyone was hungry and she had just one bag of cornmeal left. There was no way it would last the whole

week if we started eating it today.

"Please Madam, there is a gentleman here to see you."

"Who is it?"

"Please I don't know but he knows Mary and Yaw—he asked for them by name."

Tschew! Mum sucked her teeth. Who was this worrisome person? She really did not feel like talking to anyone and there was a good possibility that he was here to ask for money or food—two things in very short supply in this house.

She gathered her cloth around her waist, adjusted her scarf and walked out wearily from the bedroom. There in the sparse living room, decked with striped plastic chairs and awkward side tables with elephants under them, stood an equally sparse man with large glasses, an extremely strong jaw and an awful smell.

"*Ei* Mr. Latse!"

"Hello Madam."

"Please sit down. Kwasi, bring Mr. Latse some water." Kwasi ran to do Mummy's bidding. Nana slinked away looking wary. She also wondered what he was there for and guessed it might be for money. Well, he was out of luck because we had none.

"So is Mr. Apea doing well in London?" The young man was trying hard to ignite conversation.

"Yes he is," Mummy replied. "And how are your brothers?"

"Joseph is teaching at Presbyterian Boys School in Legon and Jacob is in our hometown. He has opened a mechanic shop and is employing many people."

"That is good to hear. Jacob was a very good mechanic and infact, Mr. Apea's Volkswagen continues to run smoothly because of him. So what have you been doing since you stopped tutoring the children?"

The young man shifted uncomfortably in his seat, making a scrunching sound against the plastic cover.

"I completed my undergraduate degree in Mathematics from Kumasi and have been teaching part time in Achimota and Accra Girls Secondary School…as well as working in the bank."

Mummy perked up. "That is good. You have done well."

An uncomfortable silence ensued. Mummy allowed it to continue as Kwasi brought the water in and the young man guzzled it noisily. As soon as he was done, mummy plunged in.

"So how can one get some of the new currency?"

"Madam, unless you know someone in there, there is no way." *Like she didn't know.*

Then he moved forward in his seat.

"Maybe I can go with you. That might help."

"Mmmhhh…I will think about it." Mummy didn't look convinced.

Mr. Latse continued to sit there but no offer of food came. After about fifteen minutes, he must have figured this was not his lucky day and asked for his leave. Mummy readily gave it to him, murmuring her thanks for his dropping by to say hi. She left him at the door and he bade us all farewell as he slinked away, trousers falling off at the waist. I surmised that Rawlings chain was probably happening to his hips.

Kenkey today.

Banku yesterday.

Definitely one of the two tomorrow. Kenkey and Banku were made from corn which continued to be the cheapest thing in town these days.

<<>>

A week later, we were all still eating cornmeal.

"Kwasi!" yelled Mummy from the back of the house where she was trying to coax some of our tomato plants into giving us fruit.

Kwasi appeared before her like a genie.

"Do you remember where Mr. Latse lives in Anumle?"

"Yes Madam."

"Go and give him this letter and tell him it is urgent." She turned away and continued to tend to her tomatoes. Kwasi vaporized into thin air…poof and he was gone.

One week had cleaned Mr. Latse up. He no longer had the pungent odor of a skunk and he didn't look that hungry. He came to the house early on the morning after Kwasi had delivered the letter, with a briefcase that looked like it belonged to the Governor of the Gold Coast *circa* 1935. I got the impression he needed to look important, like someone who worked in the bank.

"Where are you going?" Nana implored Mummy in her bedroom.

"Our last cornmeal is today's portion. I think it's time I tried to battle it to the front of the crowds at the bank. I need to get this new money and Mr. Latse will help me."

"Why do you think he will help?"

"I don't know that he will help but I've got to try something. Besides, the money as it is now is useless anyway. I need to do something."

"What did Auntie Martha say regarding the package Emmanuel sent us from London?"

"She claims they seized it at the airport."

"She's such a liar," Nana retorted.

"Yes, I know but what can I do? You can't squeeze milk, money, sugar and flour from someone who says she doesn't have them."

"And 'Auntie Jesus' had to go and get herself arrested by carrying illegal drugs from London to Ghana instead of smuggling food!"

Mummy and I
(1968)
(and my massaged head)

Three month old me
(1969)
(and a better angle of
my head)

Daddy and Mummy on their wedding day at the Aggrey Chapel. (1967)

Daddy the Inspector of Schools.
(Note the retro beard and glasses)

Sisi Adjo and I standing beside Daddy's venerable VW
Beetle.
(1972)

A view of a busy street in Accra.

New House: Papa Kwabena's Homestead

Our House In Accra

Nana
(1965)

Papa Kwabena

Papa Lawyer

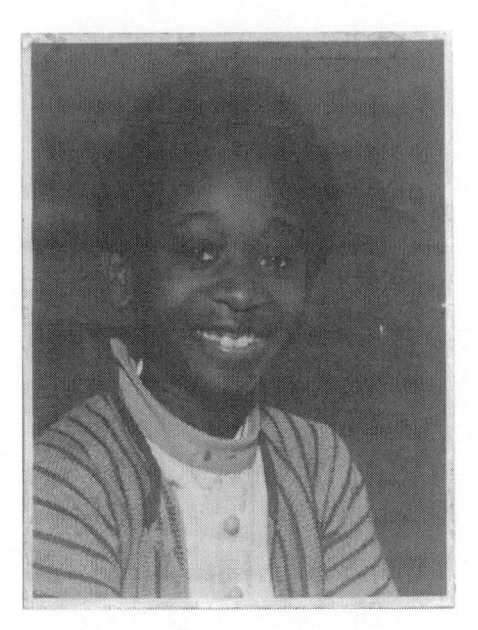

My School Photo
(London 1976)

Esther, Me and Yaw
(London 1976)

Achimota School, Accra, Ghana

6th Formers chilling in the dormitory.
Top: Barbara and Thelma
Bottom: Me & Reinette

"Nana please!" Mummy motioned with her fingers to her lips. "I don't want the children to hear that."

"Why? They've got to know that some people are foolish. I will confront Auntie Martha when I see her at church and as for 'Auntie Jesus', I will die before they let her out of Ussher Fort Jail. *Tschew* – foolish woman," Nana concluded and walked out.

Mummy and Mr. Latse set out before the cock crowed. We all huddled around Nana wondering how long it took to die if you didn't have food. We missed Daddy but had heard that no flights were being allowed into or out of the country. The last time we'd done our P & T phone call to Daddy, he had purchased tickets for us to leave. When Mummy went to the British Airways office, they told us there were no flights allowed out of the country. Daddy couldn't come in either, so in this most crucial time, Daddy wasn't near. Nana held us close and started praying:

"Lord, there is nothing impossible for you. You fed the children of Israel when they didn't know where to turn. We trust that you will do that again this time because you have never failed your people. Let this be a witness to these children; that you are a God who never fails. Let them never forget this day when your people prayed and you answered."

And then followed about fifteen minutes of unintelligible tongues. We dozed off. Hunger coupled with unintelligible tongues can do that to you. The day passed uneventfully. We all just walked around listlessly. Corn meal for brunch and dinner was not exciting and with no electricity, even our favourite children's show *Children's Own* was not on. We didn't even tell each other scary stories and most telling was the fact that we didn't play our favorite game *Making people laugh*. Around 8pm, the front gate creaked open

and we all listened quietly. A dirty disheveled woman with tears streaming down her face walked towards us. It was Mummy.

"Emma, what happened?" Nana was first to raise the question we were all dying to ask.

No response from Mummy.

"Emma, talk to me. What happened?"

Kwasi rushed to the kitchen and fetched some water for her. As we all crouched around her, shocked at her appearance and sad that she looked so violated, the whole world felt like it was caving in. She started to tell us softly what had happened.

"Mr. Latse and I got to the bank quite early, around six but there was a huge crowd already. We pushed our way as far as we could but still could not get close to the door to even go in. Everyone was screaming and yelling at the top of their voices and it felt very scary. I was tired of pushing and fighting so I sat on a short stone wall behind the crowd. When he saw me resting, Mr. Latse asked me to give him my bag of money so he would continue to push through while I rested. I thought it was a good idea since I was very tired. I watched him push through and for a while I could see his head pushing through the crowd and then no more. I prayed that he would be able to get through and waited. And waited. And waited. At 2pm, there was a voice on the loudspeaker announcing that the bank was closed and everyone started to disperse.

I waited, praying that he at least got inside before the bank door closed, only to find that by the time the crowd had dispersed, I was the only one there. I was the only one still waiting for my money, and Mr. Latse was nowhere to be seen."

Nana put her hands on her head and let out a wail that cut through the thin night air.

"*Buei!!!!!!!!!!!*"

We all started crying—Me, Yaw, Esther and John. Maybe they had no idea why they were crying but I did. There was no more corn meal and what money we'd had, although useless, was no more. Mr. Latse had done us in.

Skunk!

We huddled together again that night. All except Nana who knelt by the bed praying endlessly; she prayed for everyone. I dozed off last, wondering what hungry people do in this state. Would we start eating each other? Who would we eat first? Esther looked the juiciest because she had managed to retain some baby fat. John was a rascal—in body and attitude. No one would eat Nana. She wouldn't taste good.

The dreaded morning came. Mummy called us all and told us to be patient as she looked for ways to feed us. We drank water for breakfast, lots of it. BraTeye came to find out if Mummy needed some errands to be run. She looked like a warrior this morning; gone was the sadness in her eyes and the soft jaw from the day before. I could have sworn she was getting ready to fight the British with Yaa Asantewaa and the Ashanti army, what with the fire in her eyes and the square shoulders. She spoke fast.

"Is there petrol in the van?"

"Yes Madam."

"How much?"

"About fifty cedis worth."

Mum looked like she was thinking. Then she had a brainwave. "Siphon the few liters left in the van and take the petrol to the Lorry Station. See if anyone will buy it to top up their taxis."

BraTeye run off to get the Jeri-can to siphon the petrol. Less than two hours later, he was back home with some of the new currency. We all jumped for joy but calmed down when Mummy told us it was only enough for the day's meal. She sent Kwasi off to the market to buy some cassava and fish and with that, we had a good meal in the mid afternoon. As Kwasi pounded and Nana kneaded the *fufu*, she sang *God is good, all the time.* I wondered what tomorrow's miracle would be, since there was only so much petrol—and it was virtually gone after today's siphoning. That evening, we had a Bible study and Nana reminded us of God's providence. We sang songs, prayed and asked God to 'do great and mighty things again'. We went to bed hopeful.

<<>>

Ratatat! Ratatat!

The rapping on the door would not stop. Who was it so early in the morning? Mummy quickly put on her morning gown and stepped out into the walkway that led to the front door.

"Amos!" she shouted. We all jumped out of our beds, not caring that Uncle Amos would see us at our nastiest so early in the morning. The best uncle in the world—and the richest—carried us all one by one and gave us the biggest hugs. At each turn, he would say how big we'd grown and how well we looked. What a liar!

"Emma, how are you all?"

He was handsome, tall and so funny. Uncle Amos was Dad's best friend and they had known each other since their days in high school when Dad was the wimpy kid and Uncle Amos was cool. He protected Dad all through their high school days and they both ended up at the University of Ghana at Legon. Since then, they'd

worked at the Ministry of Education prior to Dad taking up this new post in England. He was such a busy man that the last we'd seen of him must have been at least a year ago.

"What brings you here?" Mum said, trying to look like she had our lives under control with not a care in the world.

"Well, Emmanuel called to tell me to check up on you. He's been very worried and says he hasn't heard from you in a while."

Mummy teared up. We all teared up. Uncle Amos hugged us all. It was too much for Mummy to bear and she just broke down crying. "We have no money Amos. Someone duped me of my last few old currency notes."

"What? How?"

"It's a long story but suffice it to say that we had nothing left so I took a chance and it backfired. I owe the market women so much that they refuse to give me any foodstuffs on credit. I don't know what to do for Mary as she goes back to boarding school next week; she needs some provisions to take back with her, you know…milk, sardines…."

Uncle Amos stood up.

"Is Nana here"?

Of course she was here. She was probably hiding in the bedroom, listening to every word that was being spoken.

"Nana!!!!" Mummy called for Nana who took her sweet old time to appear, like she was far away when the summons came.

"Ei Amos!" said Nana, like she didn't know he was there.

He gave her a bear hug, his six-foot frame bending very low to her under five-foot frame.

"Nana, I am taking Emma to the market to pay off her debts so can you let the Kwasi follow us so he can bring some foodstuffs back?" Nana didn't need to be told twice!

As she waltzed around the house singing *This is the day that the Lord has made*, we mimicked her voice and her moves as her bony frame danced a dance we'd never seen before. Mummy too came home a different person, smiling and carrying many bags filled with food. Uncle Amos had also given her money to tide her over, promising to return in the next few weeks to see if she needed anymore.

"Hey, go and help Kwasi with the bags," she said to my cousins Adwoa, Stella and I. We had goat meat and *fufu* that day and oranges for dessert. We were rich!

8

"The Good Old Days of Fate"

Almost Every Sunday Till 1988

A mosquito buzzes by my ear, urging me to wake up and warning me that it's still hungry. I hate mosquitoes. I roll over and use my arm to ward one off, with as much energy as is possible in this body of mine. As the humidity envelops my body, I am painfully aware of the fact that I still haven't had much sleep and it's almost five am. The cocks are going to start crowing, the swish-swash of the neighbourhood brooms are going to be heard and then I'm going to really have to wake up. Today is Sunday and in this house, you have to be dead not to go to church on Sunday.

'"Mary," and then a pregnant pause.

"A-B-E-NA!!!!!!!!!"

That was Nana for sure. Only she would put that special inflexion on my day name indicating that she'd called you once before, and

if this time you didn't respond, there was going to be hell to pay. I scurried out of bed, rubbed my eyes and passed my tongue over my teeth and lips to make it look like I'd been awake for a while and quickly made my way to the backyard. Adwoa and Stella, my older cousins, were already there, faces scrunched up in anger at being woken up at five am to sweep. I joined the sorry pair and without as much as a hello, added my broom to the swish swash that was beginning to become the anthem of our Abelenkpe neighbourhood. As dawn broke, the pitter-patter of feet joined the swish swashing of brooms and very soon afterwards, voices were raised in greeting.

'*Maa chio!*' Good morning!

Mo ho te sen?" How are you?

I responded that I was fine to everyone who asked. After all, it would be awfully rude not to. You would elicit some concern from the person who'd asked after your health, the wrath of your parents and in my case, the wrath of Nana. I wouldn't risk that on any day. As we gathered the leaves to go and throw away at the garbage dump, the songs from a nearby church wafted through the air. Some churches had taken to starting really early—by about seven in the morning. Early bird catches the worm they'd say. And in this case, the worm was the tithes and offering that could come pouring into the coffers, no matter how poor the parishioner. If you waited till ten in the morning to start church, well, you'd get hardly anyone. Many church services tend to take an average of three or four hours. So mathematically speaking, a service that starts at 7 a.m. will likely be done by 11 a.m. And afterwards, there's visitation, where all the sick people get a visit from at least ten members of the church. The parishioners deliver food, and clean—all the while singing loud songs. Tambourines will shake

142

right in your face, as if daring the demons invading your body to dare stand in the face of all that noise. And then there's the prayer. Before the visitation ends, a prayer has to be said for the sick person and this again can take the form of songs, meditation, more songs, and even more meditation. So you see, 'church' doesn't really end till about mid afternoon, by which time you are exhausted. If there was any reason for us to dislike church, that was certainly it!

But Nana liked it. She liked it a lot. She especially liked testimony time. This was the part of the service where anyone could go to the front and say something the Lord had done for them. It's supposed to inspire, encourage and give glory to the awesome power of God. And most of the time, I think it did exactly that. Nana's testimonies were always long winded; she was walking by the roadside, a car almost hit her, she thought she saw the driver, last week she almost got lost, the cocoa trees on her farm were being vandalized and on and on. In fact, she would sometimes sit on the stage at church throughout her testimony because she had so much to say—and she needed a comfortable place from which to say it.

Nana said she was born when the rains fell very heavily, with emphasis on the heavily. Of course that could be 10 June 1901, 24 July 1910 or even in some years, it could have been Dec 5th. Needless to say, it was tough coming up with family trees for class assignments where I had to list my grandma's age. What do you put for D.O.B? When the rains fell heavily? And when you throw in the fact that one person's heavy is another person's light, well… the whole equation falls apart.

Nana was short. Even as children we thought she was short,

probably no more than five feet tall but since she never had a full-scale physical exam, her vital statistics—birth date, height, weight and such are all left to speculation. She was born in Anum, a tiny village on the banks of the Lake Volta that had, what Daddy referred to as 'a magnificent past'. *Past, all right.* The last time we visited the village it was hard to imagine the 'magnificent' in Daddy's statement. It probably had no more than a hundred families, there were few cement buildings and none of the roads were paved. We had trudged up to the one secondary school— founded by Presbyterian missionaries—on top of the hill and from that vantage point, I saw what daddy had been talking about all along. For down below, from the aforementioned vantage point at the front of the secondary school building lay the Volta Lake. Pristine clear with a few islands dotted on its calm surface, it was a sight to behold, even for my pre-teen mind that lived for just song and dance. I was overcome with emotion so great that my legs could not hold me up and gave way. My buttocks felt the impact of a jagged rock as I fell as if to my knees in abject worship. Why were the villagers walking around like this was no big deal? I looked at Dad; he was in a trance. I drank it all in and when I thought I could not take anymore in, I turned to Daddy who said:

"Isn't it magnificent?"

"Yes Dad. Yes it is."

"Long ago when our ancestors traveled downwards from the central part of Ghana and—by the way, did you know that the Anum tribe, part of the Guan Clan was the first group of people to arrive in what is now modern day Ghana? The Ashanti and Fanti are considered Guans too."

I shook my head. I had no idea since all I was learning in school was British History; the Battle of Trafalgar and how and why King

Henry the eighth felt the need to dispose of some of his wives by beheading them. Apart from the fact that it was interesting, how was that ever going to help me? Why weren't we being taught stuff like this? I was so glad that my father was on holiday from his work in England; at last, here was someone who would answer all my questions and not tell me to shut up.

"Well, the Guan are believed to have begun to migrate from the Mossi region of modern Burkina around A.D. 1000. You know what A.D. means right?" I nodded. "So moving gradually through the Volta valley in a southerly direction, they created settlements along the Black Volta, throughout the Afram Plains, in the Volta Gorge, and in the Akwapim Hills before moving farther south onto the coastal plains. Along the way, they fought wars and some were captured. The few who remained had to decide whether to move on or to stay until very soon, remnants of the Guan could be found almost everywhere in Ghana. Did you know that the Gonja are also Guan?"

"Really? But they are way up north."

"Yes, but archaeologists have found plenty of evidence that there was significant activity all around the Akwapim region during the iron and bronze ages."

"Why are there so few of us though?" I quizzed.

"That's a really long story but apparently, the Anum people camped around the Volta Lake for a really long while and built settlements there. One day, legend has it that the god of the Lake got very angry with the lack of sacrifices and it overflowed its banks causing the people to run as far away as possible. This led them to the top of one of the many hills surrounding the lake and as you've noticed, we're on one of them! By the time the danger seemed to have subsided, there were only five of them left!"

"And five in our language is Anum!"

"Yes. Our people decided to name themselves after the number of people who were left to tell the tale. They then moved around till a group arrived in Asamankese, which is where your mom was born."

"Just five? Dad, is that a true story?"

Dad smiled, his black beard giving way to pearly white front teeth that had a slight forward incline. He scratched the beard thoughtfully as if wondering how to broach this tough question without lying.

"Well just like most stories, as it gets handed down from generation to generation, a little piece of it is lost. It's never going to be the same you know? I think it's true that the lake overflowed its banks but you know I don't believe in gods of lakes, rivers and trees and such. I believe there is only one true God and he is the God of all those things. I think it's possible there were five people left but you know, our families are so patriarchal that it could have been just five men that were left and many women— they just wouldn't have counted the women."

I thought about this one last comment. The Bible too, had that habit of counting men only. I wondered why, when women did so much work and were so strong. Take Nana for example. I can't imagine her not being counted especially as she was born to a family that claimed some royal connection. Actually, I heard she'd been asked to be the Queen Mother, a common term with a meaning quite unfamiliar to Western Civilization. It's not exactly the mother of the Queen (or King) who gets called the Queen mother in traditional African societies; the Queen Mother is a hereditary title that runs through a particular family

line. It turns out that when Nana was in her fifties, it was her turn. The job of queen mother was in complete opposition to what Nana believed since it combined ancestral worship with some pagan rituals. Nana had been 'saved' through the work of some Scottish missionaries and was not about to abandon her new God. Early in the 20th century, missionaries were quite a common sight in the Gold Coast as Ghana was then called. Nana, along with a couple of other ladies met a missionary called James McKeown. He was a Pentecostal and a believer in healing through faith. Their church was called "Faith' but its constant use and Ghanaian mis-pronunciation caused it to become adulterated to sound like 'Fate'. So I remember hearing Nana talking about the good old days of 'Fate' and how there were so many healings when they used to attend 'Fate'. There were days when they were going to go hungry and they would go to church, pray and by the time they got home, there was food waiting for them. Nana soon became one of the leaders of 'Fate' and in her typical no nonsense take-charge way, she soon became a force to be reckoned with in the church. Sadly, the missionary had a falling out with some other members, the church split and one faction became the Church of Pentecost. She stuck with this latter incarnation without ever forgetting 'the healings that happened in 'Fate'.

Mummy and her older sister Sisi Yanto were brought up in the faith, sometimes spending days fasting for this or that. The church was to Nana what a bar is to a drunk— it was her source of sustenance (albeit spiritual), camaraderie, a sense of shared purpose and a place where she felt like she could be herself. We were constantly hearing of miracles and healings, some sounding so preposterous that you truly did need faith to believe them. She knew of mad people who'd been healed, babies born with more

than five fingers—the extra ones had shriveled in fear after the members of the church laid hands on the afflicted child. One such healing I kept hearing about was something called Nantwi Pompor – which translated literally means 'cow's boil'. It was an awful growth that would protrude out of the side of one's neck and there seemed to be no cure for this except by using herbs and praying till it disappeared. Every day, it seemed we were introduced to people who'd experienced life-changing events that would buoy anyone's faith. I don't recall ever wondering if these stories of healings were true or not. Those people who recounted these stories seemed sincere so it was difficult to believe that a miracle had not occurred.

So on this Sunday morning, we all got ready for church at the Abelenkpe Assembly of the Church of Pentecost. Abelenkpe is a suburb of Accra and is notable for the Achimota Business College, which is supposed to turn out the best secretarial staff this side of England. Mum and Dad were lucky to purchase a piece of land just opposite the school and had built a five bedroom home that was inhabited by not just our immediate family but anyone else who needed a place in Accra to start off what they hoped, would be an illustrious career. Our house was always full of people, relatives as well as people who called us their relatives. On this particular Sunday morning, Adwoa and Stella wasted time in the bathroom as usual, my brothers Yaw and John tried not to bathe, my little sister Esther prettied herself as best as she could for the grueling marathon of church. Of course Nana had the house help up around five in the morning starting the afternoon meal so we'd eat as soon as we got back. Dad and Mum were also very active in the church so they usually left very early—around eight or so—to help set up. I pulled on a long skirt, making sure my knees were covered for

this conservative throng and tied my hair up in a pompadour (this was the hairstyle made famous by the Marquise de Pompadour, lover of Louis XV of France. The hair is swept up from the face and held high in a turned up bun). Dab of lip-gloss, puckering of the lips, and I was ready to join the rest of the family in the long walk up the hill to the little wooden church with the one door; as soon as you tried to leave, everyone would see you and you'd feel bad… so you just had to stay.

As we passed street sellers with freshly fried yams and *shito*—a hot peppery sauce that sometimes had shrimp in it—I wondered if we'd be able to sneak off and buy some in the middle of the service. Mummy was good that way. She'd give us fifty *pesewas* for the offering plate and give us an extra twenty *pesewas* for whatever. That whatever was usually boiled corn, bananas and peanuts or yam and the peppery *shito*. I salivated at the thought as I quickened my footsteps to keep up with the rest of them. Our modest kiosk in front of the house was closed today since it was the Sabbath. Adwoa had Esther on her back. Yaw and John were running and Nana was briskly taking up the rear, ensuring that there was no one left behind.

"Maa chio."

"Maa chio"

The greetings continued unabated. Every so often, someone we knew would actually stop us and in stilted English, say: "How are you today" and smile broadly while waiting for a response.

"Very well thank you," one of us would respond quickly.

"Good. Very good. It is good that you are speaking English so well. English is the language of the queen. The more you speak English, the more you become like the Queen of England."

Yah. Right.

<<>>

The church was a one-room building made of wood. It couldn't have been more than 80ft by 80 ft and it had a watered sand floor. What this meant was that each morning, one of the church members would sweep the floor and sprinkle water onto it to settle the sand and dust. There was a makeshift stage on which a crude drum set was placed, along with some bongo drums, dozens of tambourines, a large cello-like instrument that was played using another instrument that is hard to describe. There was always a large offertory bowl to collect the offering. Parishioners would sit on the wooden benches that were arranged in neat rows from about a quarter of the way down the front of the church with an aisle in between. When facing the pulpit and stage, the women would sit on the right and the men on the left. I always wondered why but never got an answer that seemed rational.

"That's the way it is."

"Because men have to sit here and women have to sit there."

"So that the men will not be tempted by the scent of a woman."

"Just shut up. You ask too many questions!"

That last one was Nana. I vowed to ask Daddy. He was more likely to give me an answer that made sense.

The sound of music emanating from the church made us quicken our steps as we made our way past Black Cat, the seedy motel responsible for the downward spiral of Abelenkpe's previously moral upright citizenry. Nana was already speaking in tongues and made me wonder. Didn't the 'spirit' only take a hold of you in the church? She motioned for us to hurry up because praise and worship had begun and so we did. One of the ushers, Brother

Cephas ran towards Nana, took both of her hands in his and bowed slightly. He was a small man and had a beady nose that made him look a bit hawk like and quite needy.

"Praise the Lord, Nana."

"Halleluyah. Cephas how is your wife?"

"Please Nana, she is fine, by God's grace."

"And when is the fifth child coming?"

"In a couple of months Nana. We pray daily that the Lord will give her a safe delivery and that he will continue to give me strength in my masonry job."

"We will pray with you," encouraged Nana.

And then Cephas would lead her in to her special spot right in front of the church on the very first row of the women's side. As children, we had to sit at the back or on the sides, where some benches had been placed for 'latecomers'. Also at the back were people who had been *bor asen*—a term meaning 'nailed to the cross' or crucified when translated into English. Basically, they were those who had committed big sins—usually sexual and had been found guilty of said sin and were undergoing a restorative phase until such a time that they would be found worthy to join the rest of the congregation. I often wondered why anyone would endure that and not just leave the church. There were at least fifty more churches in Abelenkpe alone, a small suburb of Accra! I wondered how they could bear to sit there, all lonely and forlorn, knowing that everyone was wondering if it was fornication, adultery, incest, major slander, theft of farm produce or fighting in the market that had gotten them that sentence.

We shuffled quickly to take our seats beside the crucified, just as the fever pitch singing and dancing subsided and the next phase began.

"Praise the Lord."

"Halleluyah."

"PRAISE THE LORD!"

"HALLELUYAH!"

"Sons of God."

"March Forward."

"Victory."

"Through the blood of Jesus."

"If you don't go to heaven?"

"Don't blame Jesus."

"Blame who?"

"Blame yourself!"

This was the litany that was scattered inconsequentially throughout the service in a bid to wake people up, ignite passion, and get a frenzy going. We loved that part of church.

We sang many of my favourite songs of praise and as was the custom, when the spirit fell upon you, you'd go to the front to dance. We all felt this was so important because that's what David did in the Bible. When his heart was filled with gladness, he praised God and danced and he didn't care who saw him do it. And I guess for us, it helped that the typical African has music running in his bones; it's quite impossible to hear music and not move a part of your body. By the time praises were over, the humidity in the wooden building would be so high it would be difficult to measure the actual temperature. Needless to say, the sweat pouring off people's faces, arms and necks could have been harvested for the salt content! White handkerchiefs would be whipped out to mop it all up and papers previously placed in Bibles to mark a particular place—like bookmarks—would be made into make-shift fans to cool our bodies down…but not our spirits.

The pastor would stand up like he was going to war and start the "Sons of God" litany. Then some old lady at the back (I always feared it would be Nana teleporting from the front of the church to the back), would raise a funereal sounding dirge and then everyone would have to stand again and sing with her, in support. Then we'd all sit again while the leaders on stage conferred as to the best course of event for the next four hours. And then would come testimonies.

One after the other, historical accounts (some as recent as in the past hour) of God's derring-do's, were recounted. This one saved from drowning in a river while he went fishing, that one's wayward prostitute daughter finally giving up the evil life and giving her life to the Lord—at which point, said wayward daughter would shyly come to the front to have pastoral hands laid on her to prevent her from going back to her previously sordid life. My favourite today was the testimony of the lady who could not carry a baby to term. She'd tried everything—faith healers, traditional medicines, white man's medicine, secretive sexual positions (this said in a way that didn't sound abnormal). Nothing worked till she went through fourteen days of prayer and fasting. She came off the fast, she and her husband 'met' and like magic, she was now here to tell us that she was expecting her baby in five months. Why did she wait this long to tell us? She didn't have to explain that, you see. Everyone here understood why she waited that long to tell anyone about finally being pregnant. She was convinced one of her relatives was secretly eating up the babies in her womb each time she got pregnant. So now at four months, the baby was presumably too big for the evil mouths to consume it.

"Praise the Lord," murmured a chorus of fat ladies in the third row from the front.

"Mmmhhh, the Lord has visited his people again."

"So rejoice with me," the lady with the testimony said. "For God has not let me be ashamed. I will now also have a child for my husband."

Why isn't she having the child for herself, I wondered.

"AMEN!" chorused the entire church. I was one of them.

Then we were commanded to pray for things that happen without warning, things that the devil sends to impede our progress, sudden death, and sudden accidents, sudden everything. I prayed about the death of Bob Marley since it fit all of these categories. For me, it happened without warning, his death had impeded my progress in learning the words to his every song, it was a sudden death and it was some sort of a sudden accident. I didn't even know before his death that he wasn't Ghanaian; what with the show of grief in the streets of Accra, it was hard to believe that Bob Marley wasn't Ghanaian. I still harboured a hope that one day, someone would discover that his ancestors had come from Ghana. I yelled and prayed against all of these sudden things and when I was done, my 'Marleyed' mind drifted off to a place where it started humming to *Buffalo Soldier*. It probably came out loud but who was to tell? The church was so loud no one would have heard me.

I opened my eyes to see if anyone else was tired of praying and screaming and noticed one of the crucified, writing in a small notepad. No wonder he was damned. In the middle of a prayer, he was writing? My eyes scanned the rest of the room. In the

second row on the men's side was one of my favourite uncles. Actually, just an older man but you know in Ghana, anyone older than you is an uncle or aunt. This man played the cello that didn't have a bow and his nickname was 'Ayefro Kunu' which translated literally means 'The bridegroom'. No idea why he was called that name since he was old and had been married for a really long time. He was always smiling and wearing the baggiest pants I had ever seen. I'd heard through the grapevine that he'd been deported from Germany after hitch hiking through the deserts of Libya, being thrown in jail in Egypt and stowing away on an oil tanker off the coast of Spain. He managed to wiggle his way into East Germany where he scrounged the streets looking for second hand goods, got a job in a factory and was even collecting *arbeitslosengeld* in West Germany. How he collected welfare while being a non-resident of West Germany and also being an illegal immigrant in East Germany was a mystery and for some people, a miracle worthy of praise to God. Maame Konaba was directly on the opposite side, on the women's side. She was tall and imposing with burgundy lipstick and a big *gele* hat on her head. When she'd first joined the church, Mummy was the only one who'd speak to her since many of the women said she dressed like a jezebel. She owned a couple of stores in Makola, the biggest market in Accra and was constantly traveling outside the country to buy gold brocade, jewelry and anything basically too expensive for the average Ghanaian to afford. Now she was quite accepted, after purchasing and donating musical instruments to the church. She gave a testimony a year ago about how the police ransacked one of her stores thinking she was smuggling drugs. By God's grace, they found nothing. I wondered—was that because there was nothing to be found or was that because the police were incompetent? Of course when I asked

that, I was told to shut up.

So I did.

Right behind Ayefro Kunu was Brother Noah. He had such an unusual face—the kind that looks both sad and happy. I think it's his eyes. They look sad but his mouth is always in a smile. He has a photography business so every day after church, you'll find most parishioners waiting their turn to have their pictures taken. Ghanaians love taking pictures and many will immediately pose when they see a flash in their faces. He has one of those cameras that need the photographer to cover his head with a black cloth and when they see him lift one hand, they know that's when you put the biggest smile on. He had the most awesome customer service too; he'd bring the proofs over to your house and then your favourites would get printed. I've heard Mummy and Nana gossiping about how eligible he is, and I think they are plotting to find a wife for him. Adwoa was not amused when they hinted that he was a good catch. I stifled a laugh as I remembered the way she acted like she'd rather puke all over herself. Time to get out of the Church for some fresh air!

As I try to look pious while leaving so no one will ask me where I'm going, I see 'Auntie Jesus' outside. This is mom's friend who currently bears this most holy of names just because she acted as Jesus in one of Mom's plays. The women's fellowship, led by mummy tends to put these plays on because many of the women can't read; reading the Bible is therefore not an option for them. Being mommy, she had to devise a plan and what better way to get the message across than to act it out. And Mummy is a good actress—you just have to wake her up as she dozes, to see her own version of a horror flick. 'Auntie Jesus' is bubbly, gregarious and

quite rich. Since she wasn't in Ussher Fort Jail as Nana had hoped, I thought it a good idea to be nice to her—she passes you a few cedi notes when you smile and are extra polite to her so I didn't fail her at all.

"Hello Auntie," I murmured in my most humble voice.

"*Ei* Mary, how are you?' She spoke English fairly well, having finished some portion of High School.

"I'm very fine thank you auntie."

"And are you studying hard in school"?

"Yes please Auntie. I came first in my class," I didn't add that this was only in Home Economics a.k.a cooking class, and that only the girls take that. Also, that Nana thought it was ridiculous that I came first in a subject for which I seemed to have no practical aptitude at home. *Whatever*.

"Very good, very good." She paused, seemingly lost for words. I looked away, as if I was shy.

"*Ei*, you are growing *paa*, even your breasts are coming."

Coming? Where from, or maybe more importantly where to?

I chuckled softly, acting very shy but inwardly quite horrified. She may be Mum's friend and her nickname might be Jesus but that did not give her the right to talk about my breasts.

"That means we will have to look for a husband for you quickly, otherwise…" her voice trailed off.

Otherwise what? The breasts would 'come' so much they would fall off? Looking down at my early teen bosom, I lamented the fact that this was not even a mere possibility.

Auntie Jesus laughed like she had said something profoundly funny while slapping me on the back. I was not amused but laughed heartily.

"*Ei*, you young people eh. Look at your hair, when are they going

to let you braid it?"

"When I am in Form Five Auntie."

'Ei, that is in a long time *ohhhhh.* That means you will have to look like that for a long time."

Like I didn't know. It was a source of annoyance to my friends and I that we had to keep our hair short until the fifth form; apparently then, we'd have more commonsense than to sit around all evening playing with our hair instead of studying.

"And look at your dress—it is green *paa.*" That term *paa* could be annoying too. It was always used to indicate a lot of something, like saying 'very much'.

What was this grilling for?

"Green is my favourite colour and this was my Christmas dress from last year. Esi Amanfo sewed it for me," I said almost defiantly.

"Esi Amanfo? Isn't she the woman whose husband went to Germany several years ago and hasn't even sent her a sewing needle?"

"Um, I don't know Auntie," I said, hoping the conversation would stop. I really liked Esi with her pointy bum.

"Yes, it's her. Doesn't she live behind the Methodist School near AsareMens Enterprises?"

"Yes please."

"I knew it! That husband of hers left her with many promises and yet no one has heard from him. Maybe he is happy being a *borga* and has probably married a German woman so he doesn't want to come back. Of course if it was me, I would dog him. I would demand that his family pay a fine for his deserting me. Yes, that's what I would do," she concluded determinedly.

Dogging him was slang for dumping him. I lamely nodded as she continued this tirade. I'd heard about Esi's husband being a *borga*

—one of those hustlers, who went to Hamburg, Germany and did menial jobs, jheri-curled their hair and doused it with curl activator and wore baggy jeans. They were mostly found in the industrial city of Hamburg hence the nickname 'burger', which over time had turned to *borga*. I was deep in thought wondering if listening to Auntie Jesus would net me a couple of cedis this time. Knowing that the offering had been taken already, chances were that she had very little money or none left at all. Clearly, this was not going to be a profitable exercise whereas at least in church, I could get my soul saved. I kept smiling at her until I sensed a break in the conversation.

"…that's why I say you should look after yourself properly because these days, all the good Ghanaian men are going outside to study and then they come back with white women, leaving you people with the *fianga* boys who sell cassette tapes by the roadside or look after your car by force for you at Makola market."

I chuckled knowingly and then jumped right in.

"Please Auntie, I'm going back inside."

"Ok run along now or you'll miss the best part of the service!"

Not a chance.

As I walked back into the church, I got a lecherous look from Deacon Ofei. That guy should seriously be excommunicated for the way he looks at little girls like me. And I've heard rumours.

<<>>

Almost every Sunday, after an exhausting day yelling and screaming to the Lord, we would get home to a piping hot bowl of *fufu* and peanut soup. Nana was so organized that she would

have the house help leave about an hour earlier to warm up the soup and start boiling the cassava for the *fufu*. Those maids were so afraid of her because she had a reputation for 'not standing for nonsense'—as she constantly reminded anyone who would listen. Our current house help was a boy because the last girl had gone and gotten herself pregnant with a young man from across the street. She was sent back to Asamankese with a sewing machine, one month's wages and a searing look from Nana. After her, Nana said a boy would be better so in came sixteen-year-old Johnny. He had this stupid grin perpetually plastered to his face and could calculate sums in his head but had no idea how to write his name. We liked him because he was so much fun but we heard Nana complaining constantly about him. They got him about a sixth of a plot of land to farm on, just behind Achimota Village. Sometimes, after doing his chores, he would trudge over to his farm and tend to his cassava plants. No one thought anything of it—he was allowed some free time every day because Mummy was quite liberal with her house helps. Nana kept reminding her that her kindness would not be rewarded; there seemed to be something inherently wired in house helps, she said; they just seemed to thrive on inhumane treatment. Still, Mummy was kind, allowing them to trade with her in her road side kiosk where she sold milk, sugar, flour, tiger nuts, cola, second hand denim jeans, hair dye, bread, Bob Marley song sheets and iced water!

Not too long ago, before I went to boarding school, we got back from church to hear that someone was getting a drubbing. We peeked into the living room through one of the many windows where the mosquito netting had been ripped off and there was Mummy. Her back was turned to us with a large piece of cloth tied

around her midriff, sweating profusely and gesticulating with both hands all over the place. Her scarf was half off with all the head shaking that was going on, and she had a long spatula in her hand —it still had rice on it. Johnny was standing facing her, wearing long khaki shorts and a white singlet—clothes he'd been given by Mummy since arriving in Accra less than a year before.

"And who do you think you are…eh?"

No response.

"Tell me—who do you think you are, to take the Nissan out of the garage? Do you know you are lucky to be alive?" Mummy was screaming now.

Still no defense statement from the defendant.

Council for the prosecution a.k.a Nana, stepped up from behind the shadows and stood on Mummy's side of the 'courthouse'.

"Johnny, you're the only one in your family who has a job. We brought you from the village, have paid you a decent wage every month you have been here, have clothed you and have even hired a private tutor to teach you to write your name. And then when you learned how to do that, we opened a bank account so that you could learn to save some money and use it one day when you are going to marry. Now why would you throw all that away and crash Madam's car? Is your head correct?"

That was such a Ghanaian phrase—'is your head correct'. Insanity was so feared and loathed that if you did anything that was irrational then you had to be going insane which meant you were 'not correct'.

Johnny shuffled on one foot. He was looking distraught and panicked. As we watched the drama unfold, he threw himself on the cold terrazzo floor, pleading and crying.

"Please Madam, please don't send me back. There is nothing for me to do in the village. I just wanted to see how it feels like to drive. The devil told me to do it."

"Then tell the devil that it was a bad idea," answered Nana sarcastically.

The sobbing continued.

Mummy looked very angry.

"Do you know how much it costs to repair this kind of damage? In America, they call it a write-off meaning they won't even let you fix it, let alone drive it. It's only in a place like Ghana that we drive things till they fall apart on the road. Look, you have cost me far more money than I can pay you. Get up from the floor and go and pack your things. You are going to go back to the village today."

"Please madam, what is America?" Johnny innocently asked.

Maybe he thought it was within walking distance so he could go and wreck cars there.

"Shut up you impudent boy!"

The wail that emanated from Johnny's lungs was blood curdling. He rolled on the floor, drooling and yelling and begging. Mummy was not amused. She told him that if he wasn't ready in an hour, he would have to go by public transit—the *trotro*. If he got ready soon, she would personally hire a taxi and take him back—a sort of final luxury like a death row prisoner's last meal. Turns out his brains were not affected by the crash and he wisely chose the second option. We were sad to see him go but thanks to him, we had to hitch hike to school and we hated that. After him came Kwasi, and what a different guy he was: much smarter, definitely kinder and nowhere near as annoying as Johnny!

<<>>

Mummy, and Dad when he is home on holidays from his job in London, are usually visiting church members on Sunday afternoons and will likely not make it home before I have to leave for boarding school. The afternoon is spent bumming around and relishing my last few hours of freedom before I'm thrown into the dungeon of despair otherwise known as boarding school. I also go and help out in Mummy's kiosk that is just outside our gate. Looks like the secondhand jeans are really going fast so Mummy will probably go to Tema Station to pick up some more next week. This is where all the second hand clothes that arrive from America and Europe end up and the place is chaotic. I've been there before with Mummy and its amazing how much fun it is to be haggling at the 'bend down boutique'—so called because you have to bend to sort out the clothes that are spread on large blankets on the ground. Some of my favourite clothes are from the bend down boutique.

One Sunday following a weekend spent at home, I watched as the sun slowly disappeared. I contemplated the inevitable— the packing of my bags to go back to boarding school. Yaw sneaked up behind me with a lizard he had just caught behind the house. I turned just in time to see him with an evil gleam in his eye about to drop it on my neck. I swear I would surely have peed on myself if he had ever been successful. He was so annoying sometimes, but he and I loved to sneak up on Adwoa and Stella when boys were chatting them up. That way, we always held something over their heads because they were not allowed to talk to boys. Nana explained that they could become pregnant that way and she's about to go to the ancestors so who's going to look after the babies when she's not here?

It was time to go. One part of me wished I were sick, perhaps with

malaria or some disease that doesn't kill but gives you an excuse to stay home. Mum would take me to the evil nurse that Yaw and I called Dr. Dart, the one who threw the injection needles containing chloroquine or some other malaria medication at our bottoms. He worked at 37 Military Hospital so I think he brought all that military training to administering jabs to my *gluteus maximus*—it hurt. However, since waiting in line at the godforsaken Achimota Hospital ensured that your chances of dying *not* from the disease you came in with rose by 50%, Mummy always took her chances any day with Dr. Dart. He would line us up against the wall and the force with which the needle entered the subcutaneous layer of our buttocks made it feel like he threw the needle from about 100 yards away—hence the name Dr. Dart.

I shuffled slowly out of the courtyard, threw my knapsack containing *gari*, dried fish and bottled *shito* into the trunk of the car and sat at the back. Sullen as a taxi-driver who had pulled an all nighter with nothing to show for it, I slumped in the back seat of our white minivan that has a large AMEN emblazoned on the front, and wished I could blink and be all grown up and not have to go back to boarding school. Whenever I said this though, Nana would remind me that 'there were no shortcuts to the top of the palm tree'—you had to go through each stage of life and this was just one of them. So I mustered all the strength possible, waved to my cousins, younger siblings, my parents and Nana. I tried to think good thoughts, of ripe plantains and beans as AMEN pulled out of the dusty front yard kicking a swirl of dust and no doubt some red ants, into the evening air.

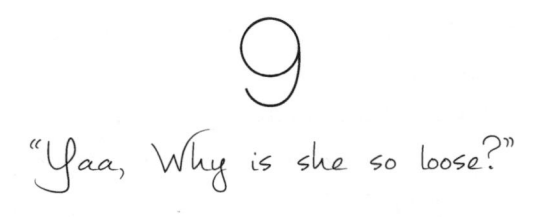

9

"Yaa, Why is she so loose?"

Nana had been married twice. First time to Sisi Yanto's Dad who as mentioned earlier, passed away while she was pregnant with the baby. When Sisi Yanto was eleven years old, Nana's brothers were approached by a family, the Aboagyes, to ask for Nana's hand in marriage. Considering that she was 'used goods'—after all she'd been married before and had a child—this was an especially good offer and Papa Kwabena as Head of the Family advised Nana she could do worse. The stigma of being without a husband was too much for Nana to bear and early one crisp *Harmattan* morning, she made the trek to New House to ask Papa Kwabena to accept the kola nuts and whiskey that the Aboagyes had brought for the *knocking ceremony*. In traditional Ghanaian households, before an offer of marriage can be entertained, the family seeking the marriage has to literally come and knock at the door of the intended. If they are allowed in to explain their mission, that's the

first hurdle overcome. If they're turned away, well, time to regroup and see if the family felt insulted by the offer of one chicken, a bowl full of kola nuts and three 250ml Hennessy Whiskey Bottles. Nana's marriage was apparently set for the end of the rainy season when Papa Kwabena would have finished all his trips down to the coast where he conducted business with various middlemen as well as Europeans. Adwoa had told me that Mr. Aboagye was still alive, obviously divorced from Nana since we never met him and he was never mentioned. Turns out Nana caught him cheating and slapped him; all 5ft of her, jumping and slapping all 6ft of him. Back in Accra, I remember asking Nana if she loved this second husband.

"Love?"

"Yes, love. Did you love him?"

"Why? Was I supposed to?" was the incredible response.

"Well," I feebly continued. "When two people marry, they are supposed to love each other so that they can have a baby together," said my romantic, teenage, Mills and Boon's mind.

"Who's been putting that nonsense in your head?"

What could I say to that? Telling her I read it in books would make her condemn books as the cause of my feeble mind. Telling her Adwoa had told me was an option that would probably get me beaten...by Adwoa. Risky behaviour does become me though.

"Well you know...Adwoa and Faithful love each other. They are always looking at each other and smiling and holding hands. Adwoa told me that this leads to marriage and can only be done when you love someone," I courageously explained.

"Look at her filling your head with nonsense. And as for that Faithful, I don't even trust him—I have to recommend he change his name although," she paused.

"... as the proverb says 'a man that does not lie shall never marry' —so maybe he's just living out the proverb!"

"Why, what has he done?"

"Not for you to know at this time. Keep quiet!"

My traitorous body ran along the back of the house, pausing to jump over a huge Agama lizard that was going in the opposite direction. Our house in Abelenkpe was square shaped and so one could run right round the perimeter without really hitting much, except a few pots and pans that the house helps had left out there. We had a winding staircase made of steel right on the left side of the house and this led up to a sitting area that was directly on top of the garage. Mum had tried to make it look like a resort, complete with lovely tables and umbrellas but if you looked further out over the rooftop, you could see the small pieces of cassava that Nana had spread out in one layer to dry under the scorching sun. Still, it was cool to go up there and look at people coming from the 'Top', which was our name for the beginning of our street. 'Down' was where the garbage dump was and the family that lived closest to it comprised a Mum who was a police officer, an older brother nicknamed Rockhead, an older sister about whom there were many rumours of sexual impropriety, and his two younger brothers Mohamed and Salifu. Yaw and John played with them most of the time and they were okay, they didn't bother me. I came out through the gate and walked towards 'down'. That was when I saw Mohamed sitting right on the ledge outside their house with his legs wide apart and tears streaming down his face.

"Why are you crying Mohamed?" I asked the ten-year-old boy.

Sobbing, he used the back of his hand to wipe the tears off his face.

"I…I…they…they…"

"They what?"

"They cut my thing off."

"What thing?" I asked.

I watched in horror as he pointed to his groin area. They cut his *willy* off?

"What do you mean, they cut if off?"

"They cut it off," and he used his hand to show a swiping motion like a matchete being used to weed grass. Okay, I thought. Either this kid was delusional or we had some serious *willy* cutters on the prowl here. Didn't they 'cut' willies at birth? Why were they cutting his now? He was ten years old for crying out loud!

"I'm sorry to hear that—we'll pray to God for you," I murmured maturely, as if I'd observed many willy-cutting episodes.

"I prayed to Allah already," he said sadly.

Well, that does it then, I thought as I skipped away. I remember when John had to have his willy cut but it wasn't the whole thing. From what I remembered, it was just the tip. Circumcision. And it was supposed to keep the willy clean. And also something about not being able to go to heaven if your willy wasn't cut. Maybe that's why Mohamed's mother had had it done even though he was so old. Poor guy.

I love being a girl. No willies to be cut.

As I walked away pondering this very serious issue, I sucked in my breath through my teeth. Interestingly, I've only heard black people do this; whether in America or in Africa, black people have that way of letting you know that someone has the nerve to step in their way—and they don't do it with words—it's with the sucking sound. I came to the large blue gate that led to the front of our house and sat on the raised ledge above the gutter.

It was almost 5:30 p.m., so many workers were going back home and our little street had turned into quite the thoroughfare. The latest female househelp, Akua was in the kiosk managing the evening customers and at this time of the evening, food was the main thing going. Mummy was really smart and picked up on these things very quickly; she'd ditched the hair products and most of the second hand clothes and was now selling mostly food. We enjoyed going with her to the port city of Tema on Sunday evenings to pick up our 'tea bread'—sometimes one hundred loaves, all packed into our van. She would get spreads such as butter, marmite, honey and eggs too, so when a customer bought a slice of bread, they got to spread for free. I loved following the train of conversation at these times.

"Oh please Madam, don't be stingy with the spread. Spread some more."

To which we'd spread some more.

Mummy always said that selling food was good business. Everyone eats. Or at least wants to.

She was now thinking seriously of opening a *chop bar,* one of those roadside restaurants that gave you food on the go and which we now call fast food restaurants. Those days, they had funny names like IF YOUR WIFE WON'T COOK CHOP BAR.

As I watched all of this activity, I couldn't help thinking that Adwoa would be coming home soon and I had to find a way to stop her from entering the house. Nana would have some choice words for her for sure and I knew I would be pummeled after she'd received her drubbing. I picked up a stick and started playing with it in the sand to disperse those pesky large ants that bite so hard your skin responds willingly to the bruising. I teased them by holding the

stick still, letting them climb on it and then shaking them off. Why did they keep coming back for more?

It wasn't till just before 6 p.m. that Adwoa's five-foot-four, 300-pound frame came slogging up the road, walking so slowly you'd think she was pregnant. She had ballooned to this size in just over a year and although at first she attracted admiring glances —turns out African men like a bit of meat on the bones of their women—she had slowly made her way past the acceptable girth. As she walked, she jiggled in places other than the buttocks—which is apparently where she must jiggle to be attractive to a black man. I decided to lay it all down, sort of, and ran to her, took her bag and escorted her home. All of which shocked her since I was not given to such acts of kindness towards cousins who were mean to me.

"*Ei*, why are you carrying my bag?"

"Why? Is it a crime?" I laughed.

"Yes, when you do it, then I know you have committed a crime."

She left it at that but I quickly added: "We haven't seen Faithful in a while," trying desperately to make small talk.

"I know, neither have I. Actually, now that you have my bag, maybe I shall just walk to his house and check up on him. It's been three whole days and each time I pop by, the boys in the house tell me he isn't home. Abi, can you take the bag inside for me and just find a way to explain to Nana that I'm on my way?"

"Yes, of course," I murmured with relief.

We parted at the front gate and Adwoa continued her walk down. Past Rockhead's house and the Secretarial School, through a mini swamp and then past the dusty road that led to Faithful's. I tiptoed gently to the room she shared with Stella, turned the handle quietly and proceeded to place her stuff on her bed.

"And where is she?"

I jumped! Turning around and pretending not to be surprised, I responded casually to my interrogator.

"Ooh, its you Nana. Um...please, Adwoa said she had to check up on something so she asked me to drop this first so you'll know she did come home."

"Is she going to Faithful's?"

Oh boy, what to say?

"She went down the road past Rockhead's but I know she has lots of friends there. Could be any of them."

Nana shuffled away, her shoulders indicating she didn't believe a word of what I'd said. Please God, don't let her follow Adwoa to Faithful's, or I will surely die a slow death. Little did I know that much more was about to unravel that evening and so I went to look for *A Pirates Love* to read. There's nothing like a trashy romantic novel to transport you to unreal worlds.

An easy hour passed and then another hour followed and then... who were those talking? I strained my ear to hear three voices deep in conversation. Mummy for sure, Nana another sure and the third? After a few minutes, I realized it was Sisi Yanto, Adwoa's mother. What was she here for? She lived about three hours away. I crept slowly behind the window of Mum's bedroom to eavesdrop and found Yaw already there—what a weasel! We scowled at one another and then realized we were missing juicy gossip by bickering with each other.

Nana: Yaa, why is she so loose?

Yanto: Is being with one man loose?

Nana: Of course it is, especially when that man cannot look after you and his tribe demands that his wife must come from his *Ewe*

village. And we are not *Ewe*.

Yanto: Nana, these days people are marrying all over the place ohhh—you can't be too picky you know?

Mummy: Ok, Ok, calm down you two. Let's try to think this through. First of all, Adwoa has found out the truth we were trying to tell her all along so this is not the time for us to start analyzing and accusing. Everyone makes mistakes—

Nana: Speak for yourself, I beg ohhh…

Pause

Mummy: As I was saying, she has made a mistake and we just have to hope that she hasn't gotten herself impregnated. We cannot afford to feed another mouth.

Nana: Oh, you don't have to worry about another mouth ohhh—his people will come and take the baby away, didn't you know? Maybe this is the time to tell you of Sisi Afia's disastrous first encounter with a man from the *Ewe* tribe. She had to leave him, and leave the children with him so don't start getting all high and mighty with me about knowing better.

Mummy: I didn't mean it like that Nana. Please forgive me. What I mean is that you never know. So, how are we going to approach it?

Yanto: We need to sit her down, have her let it all out and then we shall discuss her options. She is still a child isn't she? And do children not make mistakes?

Mummy: Yes, that's a good idea. No blaming at this point, it's a bit late for that. Nana?

Nana: Apart from wondering why his name is Faithful when he obviously can't be faithful, I have nothing to say.

Liar, I could almost hear Mummy and Sisi Yanto say. *You lie bad,* as one taxi driver so eloquently put on his rear windshield.

"Adwoa!" Mummy's voice rang out shrilly.

No response.

"Adwoa!"

Ooohhh, this was beginning to sound urgent. Still no response.

"Mary?"

"Yes Mummy," I said as I crept out from the shadows. I knew this was a moment to be ultra polite.

"Where is Adwoa?"

"I don't know, Mummy but I'll check in her room."

"Kwasi," Mum continued, throwing a glance at our house help from Ohiamatuo. "Did you throw the garbage away? You know I don't like it to pile up—the smell is really bad."

"Yes madam—I have."

"Good. Get Yaw and Esther and John ready for bed ok? See if the water is running this evening and if it is, direct them to the bath so that they can go to sleep on time."

Adwoa emerged from her den looking defeated. Her eyes were all puffy, her upper bosom was soaked in sweat or water and she wouldn't even give me eye contact. Mummy tilted her chin to look at her and told her to stop crying and then they left me in the hallway as they made their way to the master bedroom to discuss what had happened. I had no problem eavesdropping again.

"Adwoa, tell us what happened," Mummy's soothing voice asked.

Sobs, sniffles, more sobs.

"I hadn't seen him for a while so I went to visit. I've been wondering what's been going on. He never seems to be at home so I was beginning to worry that he was two-timing me. Today, I refused to turn back when the house help said he wasn't in. I used my key to open his door —yes, he had given me a key Mummy."

Through my vantage point, I craned my neck so I would have both auditory and visual memory of this event. The scene was not good.

Mummy was scowling, Sis Yanto gently shook, and Nana's face was set in stone.

"And then what happened," Sisi Yanto prodded.

"And then...and then...I saw him with another woman in the bed, doing it. I shouted at him to stop and the woman got up, picked up her cloth and walked up to me. She asked me to leave and told me I was a witch for trying to destroy her marriage."

"MARRIAGE?" shouted the three most powerful women in my world.

Deafening silence.

Then Nana begun to sing in a haunting voice that told me that this song was not a celebratory one. It had to be a song of sadness, loss, disobedience and the telling of age-old wise sayings. It seemed she was singing about young people who discard all this in our bid to become more civilized, cosmopolitan, individualistic and modern.

"Okwan tintin awareo m'enko ohh
Okwan tintin awareo m'enko
Se me nya me koh na sembi si mechi a meyehden
Se me nya me koh na sembi si mechi a meyehden
Okwan tintin awareo m'enko ohhh
Asem bi si mekyi a meh yeh den ma'ti"

"Adwoa," Nana said in the softest whisper. I had to strain really hard to hear this part.

"There is a reason why we listen to our parents and the older women in the family. Sometimes, they have gone through these things before. Other times, we know of someone very close to us to whom it has happened. I have heard it said that the white man thinks we are even more biased than they are. Maybe. Maybe not.

What I do know is that before the white man came, we had our traditions and our customs and they worked well for us. When people from another tribe wanted to marry one of our own, we forbade them because we knew that a key ingredient of marriage is unity of thought. How can you marry someone who believes that twins are evil when you don't believe it? What happens to you and your children when you happen to give birth to twins? They are humans are they not? But none of us understand why they come like that. Some—a long time ago mind you—chose to believe that having twins was a bad sign. What of the belief that descent of a person is through the matrilineal line? When someone asks you where you come from, you are supposed to mention your mother's family name but there are some tribes that think it's the patrilineal line. You may think this is not important but when a man dies, some tribes are adamant that his nephew and not his children inherit his property. I cannot tell you of countless widows who have had nowhere to turn to but to the church— to help feed and clothe their children. Now don't get me wrong, the *Ewes* are not bad people. They are just different, just as the *Ashanti* are different from the *Dagomba*. And you must know these differences before you make a lifelong commitment to one of them. One of these differences is that no matter whom he marries, he must always have a wife from his hometown. Maybe in the future that will change but for now, many practice that belief. The song I sang talks about a young girl wanting to go far away and marry. She is reconsidering because if she goes so far from home and something happens back home, will she be able to return? She realizes that marriage should be entered into with a lot of thought. With our strong family ties, we want everyone close to home to support one another. If she leaves, she will not be available to support or be

supported and this is a source of great sadness for her. You've done a stupid thing and I promised I wouldn't talk but there it is—I've said it. There are many fish in the sea so the fact that Faithful is handsome doesn't mean you won't find anyone else. Our women can survive with or without a man!"

And this was when Nana chose not to talk?

<<>>

Our driver BraTeye, who was like family to us, decided on one breezy April day to get married traditionally. A traditional marriage doesn't take place in a church; instead the two families gather at the house of the intended bride to talk business and then celebrate. Since his parents were dirt poor, he adopted ours and this dubious honour implied that Mum would 'do the engagement'; essentially meaning she'd be footing the bill. We had to leave Accra one very early morning, get inside AMEN, our trusty 7-seater van. At this time, it had been converted to a 14-seater (don't ask me how and why) and we made our way along the back roads towards a little village in the Manya Krobo traditional area. In the trunk of the car were yams, plantains, and all sorts of meat, drinks and suitcases. BraTeye was so much fun he was like an older brother to us, full of mischief and yet quite trustworthy. His only misdemeanour I remember hearing about was when he asked to use AMEN on his day off (Sunday) to go watch a soccer game with Kotoko F.C playing their arch enemies the Accra Hearts of Oak F.C at the Accra Stadium. He decked the van out in red since he was a Kotoko fan and all his drunken friends, Mr. Annan and Mr. Crentsil were all decked out in blood red outfits. They came back sounding incomprehensible and totally wasted. Kotoko had won.

Didn't want to imagine what would have happened if they'd lost! I can't remember where BraTeye and Korkor met or how, but I do remember that their ceremony was what they called a *shabo shabo* wedding, meaning we had to get it done quickly. The 'knocking' and actual engagement therefore had to be done all in one day. Yaw and I spent the better part of the 2 hour ride, using our childish brains to wrack this mystery; why would they want to get married so quickly? We wisely surmised that maybe BraTeye 'really really liked her'—there could be no other explanation. Little did we know he'd pulled a fast one and needed to pay the bride price before a baby popped out! During the *knocking ceremony*, the groom's family pays a bride price for the bride. Both the groom's side of the family and the bride's are expected to be there, along with well wishers and hangers on, the latter usually being more plentiful. Being that the typical African family is large, it is not unusual to find a family 'delegation' of a hundred people at an engagement ceremony but as I said, this was *shabo shabo* so the numbers were kept to a minimum; we hardly had more than ten from our side of the 'family'. There was a lot of food and drinks, and with the chatter and drumming, the general air was festive.

We, as the family of the groom, had to ceremoniously knock at the door of the bride's family home to be allowed in. We were kept waiting; tradition requires that we be mocked this way to indicate that we are looking for something so precious that we are prepared to humiliate ourselves outside the door. However, since BraTeye's 'family' arrived in a van from ACCRA, this waiting did not take long; girls in that village hardly got married to anyone outside the village let alone someone from ACCRA WHO DRIVES A VAN!

After a few minutes (otherwise we'd threaten to leave!), her brothers demanded an entry fee and once this was paid, we were allowed to enter. The groom's family then stated their mission, always reminding the 'audience' that the lady we sought was a beautiful one, an intelligent one, and very fecund! The bride's family agreed in principle that they had beautiful, intelligent and fecund young women in their household, but they pretended not to know who the groom's family was really asking for. One 'fake' bride was paraded before BraTeye who attested to the fact that she was not his bride-to-be. Apparently, three fake brides are the norm but being that BraTeye didn't own cows or sheep, houses or farms, (and neither did they), one fake bride was enough. The bride's family then extolled the beauty and virtue of their wonderful daughter, implying that she was too good for the groom. At which point, our family extolled BraTeye's virtues and supported all of this with gifts—a suitcase full of African fabric, lingerie, shoes, clothes and accessories for the bride, money and gifts for the parents of the bride, the siblings of the bride, the uncles of the bride, the aunties of the bride a well as the grandparents of the bride!

After the gifts were given and accepted (like they wouldn't be!), the two families essentially became one and so the drinks started to flow. Some foolish adult passed a calabash to Yaw and I, and we looked at this creamy white liquid, dancing back and forth in the calabash and drank it—after all, everyone was. It tasted wonderful! The drinks continued to flow while the music played. People got up to dance, women wiggling their bums at the men and the men laughing deep throaty laughs. The calabash kept getting filled and we kept drinking. Mum was busy hobnobbing

with the elderly women of the family so she had no idea what we were up to. A Pat Thomas song came on and everyone gave a whoop, got on their feet and started dancing so Yaw and I decided to do the same, only to find that we could hardly stand. The trees on the compound twirled round and round and my head felt like it was disconnected from my body.

We were utterly drunk, wasted beyond our wildest imagination and it felt sinfully good.

And then we started vomiting all over our nice handmade wedding outfits. All I could hear were concerned voices saying things like:

"*Buei!*"

"Give them some water ohhhhh"

"*Ei* children of today, look at them stealing drink."

"This is what happens to children in Accra. They run helter skelter, looking for big-people drink."

Hey, wait a minute, I wanted to say. We didn't go looking for 'big people drink', it came looking for us! I wouldn't have drunk alcohol if I'd known what it was so why was I being blamed? As I went through this explanatory tirade that was clearly happening only in my head, a bucket of water was poured over me and I spluttered back to life. Someone thrust a mug of cold water at me and forcefully shoved the water down my throat, causing my belly to swell to a dangerous girth. I seemed to pass out over and over again.

Can't remember much after that. I woke up in the van after it fell into a particularly large pothole, giving me what felt like the biggest headache of my life. I'd never felt so sore, weak and dazed before. Yaw's head seemed to have become bigger from the drunken experience and he wanted more. We finally got an answer from Mummy who told us we had had palm wine. Wine? We drank

wine? What an exciting revelation! Mum said that it was utterly sinful and that drinking alcohol tends to lead to poverty and eventually, death. We had to ask for forgiveness and promise never to drink again. Nana prayed over us, asking the Lord to remove the taste of

alcohol from our mouths, stomachs and minds and to replace it with the sweet spirit of God. I knew I definitely didn't want to ever get drunk again but that sweet taste of palm wine…I sure needed the spirit of God to keep me away from that!

<<>>

We got back to Accra all tired out and incredibly hungry. Instead of going home, Mummy instructed BraTeye to take us to her chop bar. *Taste and See Chop Bar* had been set up earlier that year after Mum had done her 'feasibility studies', essentially asking people who had come in to buy a slice of bread and butter whether they'd prefer fried plantains and beans. Many said yes, so Mummy decided to have a chop bar. Those were the days…you didn't need an MBA, a business plan and a consultant to determine if you were ready to open a chop bar business. Mummy moved the kiosk closer to the gas station—there was no need to get a permit since there was no government office to get it from—expanded the kiosk so that it had a sitting area with benches and tables and a kitchen area and brought in her own coal pots and pans from home. For a period of about two weeks, we just ate all our meals at the chop bar since there were no cooking utensils at home. She had a lot of traffic too—the chop bar was also situated very near to the busiest lorry and taxi station in Achimota so all the drivers came over to eat *banku, fufu, plantains, konkonte* and soup at all hours.

The chop bar attendants were busy serving customers when we got in but they hurried everything so that 'Madam' and her children could get some food. As usual Esther didn't want to eat anything that was being served. She wanted popcorn. Yaw and I wolfed our *omo tuo* and palm nut soup down and drank a large glass of water. "Why is it called *omo tuo?*" Yaw asked in between large swallows of the sticky balled rice.

"It means rice gun, silly," I responded.

"Huh?"

"Rice gun—the rice is cooked, rolled up into a ball and is so heavy that it could be used as a bullet in a gun. *Omo* is rice and *tuo* is gun, you thicko," I teased.

The whole entourage ate until belts begun to be loosened and loud burps could be heard from across the large room. There were many thanks to mom, from BraTeye's friends and family who had joined us on this momentous trip so as I lay snoozing in the back seat on the way home, I wondered what it'd be like when I got married. Would there be palm wine? Would everyone like whoever I was marrying? Would Mummy and Nana and Daddy and Papa Kwabena be there? I had it all planned out in my mind. I was going to get married on a large ship that would stop at various ports to pick up friends and family. Then we'd have lots of food — *jollof rice, fufu* and goat meat soup, some pasta—I really missed having spaghetti and meatballs—and of course there'd be buckets of ice-cream and candy floss…enough to make everyone sick—and I'd be marrying someone famous.

Of course.

10

"As a Woman, You are the Neck and the Man is Surely the Head"

There were several droughts in the mid-eighties and food prices shot up. This was not good news for mummy since she'd quit her full time teaching job to become a 'businesswoman'. It became more and more difficult to charge more than ten cedis for a chop-bar meal, so Mummy's chop bar business began faltering, and she quickly decided that she had to switch gears and sell something else. She fancied herself an entrepreneur and for the most part she was. She had great people skills, was amazing at customer service and was brimming with new ideas; she just never seemed to make a profit. The drought doused what little money she had left. One evening I heard her chatting with Nana:

Mummy: Maybe I just have to quit this buy and sell, buy and sell ohhhhh.
Nana: Why?
Mummy: I'm losing money. I can't buy plantain and cassava for

twenty cedis and sell the *fufu* I make from them for ten cedis…no business can survive that kind of economics. [Mummy although speaking in Anum, used the English word economics]

Nana: Stop speaking your big English—I don't know what that means.

Mummy: I mean that I will lose money.

Nana: Then why didn't you just say that instead of making my head ache with those big white man's words?

Silence.

Nana: What about if you dismiss one of the girls? Won't that lower your costs?

Mummy: A little bit but not much. Those girls don't cost me at all. Anyway, part of their wage is in the food I feed them….and you know some of their families come there to eat as well eh?

Nana: Maybe that's why you're losing money —feeding someone else's family is no joke *ohhhhh*.

Mummy: So what can I do? I don't want to go back to teaching.

Nana: But if that's the only way to fend for the family and support whatever your husband sends down from London…that's what you have to do.

Mummy: I hate being required to write down what I'm going to teach two weeks ahead of time, having to report by 8 a.m., not being able to ask for permission to stay home with a sick child…

Nana: *Aaaaahhhhh*…sometimes in life you have to do what you don't like…to get what you like.

The next week saw the removal of all the pots and pans, coal-pots and other cooking utensils from the chop bar. The sign outside that had read *Taste and See Chop Bar* was taken down and in its place, a new sign came up…*Emma's Own Hair Salon*. It took about

three days for the transformation to be complete and in between the drying of paint and the lettering over said paint, the sign sometimes read *Taste and Own Hair Bar*. Posters of different hairstyles were used to cover newly-painted walls and for a period of about a month, Mummy was always at the Tema Harbour taking delivery of hair dryers and salon paraphernalia that Daddy had purchased and shipped from England. It was so exciting and so much classier than saying 'My mom owns a chop bar'. Now I could say she owned a hair salon! One of the favourite hairstyles was called Chinese Way—where you'd have your hair so relaxed it was as straight as a Chinese person's hair, and then you'd be given a fringe. Amazing how many Ghanaians wanted to look Chinese.

She employed the same girls who'd previously worked in her chop bar and taught them to wash, braid, relax, colour, and style hair. I looked forward to weekends and holidays because I could spend all day in the salon, watching them and occasionally being allowed to help. When it looked like I was having way too much fun, Mummy would send me to wash the towels or go and buy some soap near the gas station from across the street.

As Mummy's confidence in me regarding hair stuff grew, I was allowed to open the salon in the mornings, lay things out and generally get everything ready for the professionals. One such morning arrived with a portent of sorts. I skipped merrily to a tune in my own head with a satchel on my back containing some chemistry books. Mummy didn't like to think that I was just going to while away my time at the salon so I had to retreat to a quiet place during the day and at least put in an hour or two of study. One Saturday morning during vacation, I got to the salon around

five thirty in the morning and started to lay things out, sweep the floor and pretty the place up. As I cleaned the sinks in the washing area, I heard a knock on the door. I ran to it and pushed the wooden door ajar. There were about ten women standing in the dim light, reeking of sweat and dirt and all talking loudly in a language I did not understand.

"Yes?" I inquired.

"Tu parles le français?"

I did, just a little bit but there was no way I could keep up with a native speaker!

"A little but I speak English better. Do you speak English?"

"Small, small," the apparent leader responded.

Then she pointed to her hair. A mass of locks that really deserved to be called locks—all tangled and woven into something that looked like rope. And it was smelly.

"We want hair. You do hair?"

I was stunned. How could I do that hair?

"No, I don't do hair. You can come back at nine o'clock and someone will be here to work on your hair."

"No, we from Chad, we go Nigeria now now. We go Mecca. We travel far. We no wait, we want now now."

Lord help me but I was about to do a very stupid thing.

"Please come in, I shall start the hair for you."

How could I let hundreds of cedis go away? Besides I thought, I could start the first one and since they wouldn't be able to leave until she was done, I would hold them there till the real hairdressers arrived to the rescue. Mummy would be so happy with the amount of money I was going to make for her.

I opened the door widely and allowed all ten women to come in.

I peered out into the daylight made possible by the rising sun and noticed a huge bus parked right in front of the kiosk with Arabic writing on the side; they did say they were going to Mecca on a pilgrimage. There were men and children sitting outside the parked bus, some eating, some playing and others just sitting there. I hurriedly prepared the perm mixture for the leader's hair the way I'd seen the hairdressers do it and started applying it to the base of her hair, making sure not to touch the scalp. I combed it through, kneaded it like it was dough and combed it out like I was making spaghetti from scratch. The stench emanating from their bodies was incredible but considering how far away Chad was, it was no wonder they smelled so badly… probably hadn't taken a shower in days or weeks even. I went back to mix some more cream since her hair was so thick and I'd barely been able to relax a quarter of her hair with the first portion of cream I mixed.

By the time the real hairdressers arrived, two pots of TCB cream hair relaxer had been used —and I was only on the first head of hair. They took over and I took a break. How come no one was congratulating me on capturing this mega business? Mummy walked in around eleven and was quickly briefed by her assistant, a beefy girl called Gertrude who had an annoying habit of picking her nose. Mummy called me outside. I couldn't wait to tell her how I had used quick thinking to capture their business:

"Can I get more pocket money?"

"Not at this rate, Mary! Their hair is a different type so the relaxers we have don't work well on their heads. We end up using an amount of relaxer on their heads that we would normally use for four people. The annoying thing is that you can't charge them four times the price."

"So, so…we won't make any money?"

"Actually, we'll lose money."

I decided at that point that I would stick to science. There was no profit or loss there, just atoms, molecules, laws of nature and calculations.

Comparatively easy stuff.

<<>>

I turned sixteen and acquired many things: a gawky boy called Akoto who I guess was my boyfriend; the permission to braid my hair; the absolute necessity of having food brought to me from the dining hall; and sitting in the back pews of the school chapel—unimaginable bliss. So funny how these things happen; now that I could eat as much as I wanted in the dining hall, I didn't want to eat anymore. I lost so much weight that my head seemed like it was dangling from my neck on a coiled spring. My Afro was to die for and there was no way I was going to cut it shorter just so it matched my thin body. I wore it to class every morning and made sure I made an entrance, even if I was learning absolutely nothing in my physics class. I thought of nothing all day except boys and told my parents that all I thought of was how to get into university. At least—I consoled myself—I was thinking of going to university. It could have been worse. Cathy's latest letter had arrived and this is what I remember it saying:

Dear Mary,

Greetings from Costa del Sol! I am here with my new husband Antonio who is so sexy I just want to eat him. Do you remember I told you about him? Well, when we turned sixteen (you forgot my birthday you bum! What kind of

best friend are you?) We decided to get married because we didn't need our parents consent. He is sooooo dishy I just die looking at him. He is also very hairy and his legs are very strong.

How can you want to go to school for that long and be a doctor? You must be barking mad! You'll be so old you will not be able to have sex. I've got a job as a shop assistant at British Home Stores and I'm in the baby section, I love it because when Antonio and I have a baby, I can get very big discounts. What do you look like now? I'm still short and I still have my freckles. Antonio is brownish with black hair all over everywhere. His chest is very hairy and sexy.

When are you coming back? I can't believe you came back when Mum and Billy and I had gone to Weston Super-Mare for the Bank Holiday. If I'd known you were coming I would have stayed behind in Chigwell. I missed you especially when Dad died. Mum is seeing a man from Mogadishu —I have no idea where that is but she says it's far away. Can you find out where Mogadishu is? He looks sort of suspicious. I wish she would find someone from the South of America like Antonio. Someone called Pedro, Juan or Carlos —that's what Antonio's brothers are called. I bet they all have hairy chests and strong legs.

I hear Antonio calling and you know why! Hahahaha. I will teach you a few things when you come back so make it quick. I love you lots —well, like girls love other girls who are their best friends —not like how I love Antonio. Don't study too hard. Remember you will grow old too fast and will not have any sex. And sex is good.

All my love,
Cathy

I still couldn't get over Cathy's dad's death and now there was this

man from Mogadishu? I thought if I said it with a squint in my eye like James Bond, it would sound really cool. 'The Man from Mogadishu'. I'd tell her in my next letter that Mogadishu was in Somalia and it was far away in Africa. I would also tell her that I was about five feet and six inches tall and I was so thin I could be mistaken for a black Twiggy. I did want to be a doctor; my ambitions and effort had just not intersected yet so I didn't feel too worried about her sex prediction…I was willing to wait. Antonio sounded interesting but scary—all that hair? And the strong legs?

Akosua, Barbara, Thelma, Afua and I planned all sorts of escapades and along with other classmates, we did stupid stuff like scale walls, visit nightclubs in really seedy neighbourhoods and stay up all night pretending to study. Club Falisa was one of the seedy jaunts we visited and I vowed never to go back because although we wanted to have fun, we didn't want it to be seedy, prostitute ridden and brimming with drunks and druggies. This was exactly how this place was but of course we had no idea. Jacob told us about it and although he was not the brightest bulb in the pack, we were bored and boredom does breed a whole lot of irrational thoughts and actions. That night, we placed pillows, clothes, or whatever in our beds to make it look like we were there and asleep, and we sneaked out by scaling the courtyard wall and jumping into cars that the boys had arranged for us.

For a brief moment, I wondered what Mummy, Nana or Daddy would say if they could see me in my mini skirt, excessive makeup and gum popping out of my mouth like I'd swallowed explosives. Who cared? I was having fun!

We drove on the Tema motorway, driving at illegal limits, dancing in the car to music that Nana would have referred to as 'of the devil' because it was about sex… 'Girl I want your body, you know I love your body…'. To top off the utter craziness, our driver didn't have a license either! We arrived at Club Falisa a little past 1 a.m. and proceeded to enter the club. Lots of neon lights increasing the tackiness of the joint, smoke everywhere, bodies contorted in various orgasmic poses. I was beginning to wonder what kind of club this was. However, no one else seemed concerned so I buried my concern and danced to '80's hits like 'Lets hear it for the Boy' and 'Mr. Groove'.

With all that jigging and twisting, it wasn't long before I needed to use the washroom. I proceeded to where the signs indicated that there were washrooms but was stopped by a group of people, blocking the entrance to both the men's and the women's washrooms. I paused, looking at the class of people —wondering if I dared have attitude. What I saw helped me make my mind up. The men and women were gyrating against one another in various crude positions that left little to the imagination. Some were slumped on the floor, possibly passed out and everyone seemed glassy eyed. The women looked cheap and tawdry and their makeup was nasty. As they carried on, they struggled to keep bra straps intact and kept trying to lean on the walls behind them to help them appear sane in their drug induced catatonic-approaching states.

Why on earth was I here? I felt very dirty and decided to hold the pee in—for how long was anyone's guess. I made my way back to the dance floor to tell my friends I wanted to get out of this place and instead, I bumped into someone jitterbugging to Bobby Brown's 'My prerogative'. He turned around to apologize and our

jaws both fell open.

"What are you doing here?" he said.

"I could ask *you* the same question – what are you doing here?" I countered.

"Nothing."

We laughed so hard.

Yaw A was my cousin—actually, my uncle—but he and I were around the same age. He was Papa Lawyer's son and we got along so well at family gatherings. He knew how strict my mum was and I knew how scary his dad was so it was quite hilarious that of all places on the planet, we two should find ourselves in the seediest club in a harbour town. I told him about what I'd just seen on the way to the washroom and he led me out by the elbow.

"Listen, what you saw was nothing—I've heard some serious stuff going down so you better get out, I'm leaving myself."

We all left just before 3 a.m. and managed to make it into our beds by 4 a.m. I missed a review class for biology as I dreamt of oceans, squids, flashing lights and police cars.

Of course all of that pays off, and by the end of my final high school year, no amount of dissecting guinea pigs gave me the confidence I would have gotten from just going to and focusing in class.

One hot afternoon as she ran after my youngest sister, Grace, bowl in hand, coaxing and begging the thin five-year-old to eat, Nana paused to talk. She had no idea that I wasn't a very effective learner but she sure had plenty to say.

"Who do you think is going to marry you when you cut animals up in pieces? Instead of watering the thorn for the sake of the rose, you are shaving off the thorns!"

I had no idea what the connection was between getting married and thorns on a rose.

She was still convinced that being a scientist was not a worthwhile career for a woman; men didn't like that. She knew of a lady who studied science and guess what? She still was unmarried at 90! I wanted to ask Nana why a woman of 90 was still looking to get married.

I told her the world was changing and just that past week, I'd done an interview for the Commonwealth Secretariat on 'Girls in science'. What I didn't tell her was that I was interviewed on campus about my challenges in science class, being one of the few girls. I told Mr. Yusuf Mohamed the correspondent, that several girls had left the A-Level Math Class because of the taunting. I also let him know that as the pre-university exams drew near, the teachers didn't make it any easier. The female teachers were nasty and the male ones were lecherous, preying on our need to pass and be accepted into the university of our choice. Why, just the other day, I was over at the Presbyterian Boys School, attending a tutoring session and getting winks from the tutor. I felt so uncomfortable and when he asked me to stay behind after the class, my thighs started to sweat from fear.

"You know I can get you to pass your exams?" he said. The beads of sweat and the saliva sticking at the corners of his mouth made me want to wretch all over his tattered second hand clothes. I continued looking at my textbook, willing him to fall through one of the many cracks I had seen on the classroom floor.

He didn't.

"Mary, are you listening to me? All you have to do is say yes and I will give you the exam papers. You do know that I'm an examiner,

right?"

I nodded and continued looking at my textbook.

"So shall I give you time to think about it? I won't hurt you. I just want to be your friend and you are a very nice girl. We can do nice things together."

I would rather die, I wanted to scream. I jumped up from my seat as he lowered his head close to mine. Our foreheads almost touched! Nasty!

I raced to the school junction and while panting hard— from running and from fear— I wondered how many sixteen-year-old girls had said yes, to lecherous older men like this tutor. Was this the price I had to pay to do well in my exams? What did the boys do to pass?

I flagged down a taxi and squeezed in beside two women, both looking like they were going home from work. I greeted them, as was the custom.

"Good afternoon."

"Good Afternoon," they both murmured.

I eased my way into the taxi, pushing as politely as I could but the two women in the backseat had bottoms large enough for four people! I wiggled my very small bottom as far inside as it could go and before I could shut the car door securely, the impatient driver had pulled out from the shoulder of the road. I stared out the window, a new fear preying on my mind, wondering how I was going to pass my exams without giving in to the tutor's advances. I knew exactly what he meant by being 'my friend' and it filled me with loathing. I reluctantly got off at the University junction, crossed over to the other side of the street to catch another ride to my school.

All the taxis and *trotros* that came by were full and my legs were beginning to ache. It was also fast becoming dark and I was worried about getting back to school before study hour was over. As I raised my hand to flag down a car for the umpteenth time, a white Fiat cruised towards me and stopped. I ran to it and noticed it was one of my secondary school teachers, Mr. Arthur. I stuck my head through the passenger side window and heaved a sigh of relief.

"Good evening Sir, are you going back to school?"

"Yes I am, hop in," he said.

I was so relieved. I slid inside the passenger side, put my book bag on my lap and slammed the door shut. He eased off the shoulder into the driving lane and started driving off past the university.

It took me all of ten minutes of the ride to notice we were not going in the right direction.

"Um…please Mr. Arthur, are we not going to school?"

He didn't answer for a full minute and then he turned to face me, smiling.

"Yes, we are. I'm just taking a short route. Sometimes there is too much traffic on the main roads." I accepted this. I had no reason not to.

However, the lack of any houses or stores or people anywhere on this road started dawning on me and the hair on my hands and legs started to stand on end. Before I could ask again about our whereabouts, he brought the car to a grinding halt.

Mr. Arthur was a decent looking guy, barely out of his thirties. He was tall, sportsmanlike and very distinguished looking, most of the time. He had a swagger that we all thought was cool and he spoke impeccable English. I sensed he was just about to do something horribly uncool.

"Listen," he said as he looked me squarely in the eye. "I have needs and I'm sure you know all about these needs because you secondary school girls are always teasing us. We can just get it over and done with here. It won't take long."

"Please Mr. Arthur I have no idea what you are talking about! You have a wife! And a child! And you're my teacher!"

"So? Having a wife is like having an old car…it doesn't mean I can't test drive a new vehicle. My child…well, she's a child, what does that have to do with my attraction for you? And as your teacher, what better relationship to build this one on? I can help you a lot, especially with the exams coming up, you will need all the help you can get—I know your current average will not get you into any of the three universities."

I started breathing heavily as panic engulfed me. You always think you'll know what to do in these circumstances but then you get into them and feel paralyzed. Shall I kick his groin, shall I bite him, shall I scream? The car was so small that kicking seemed stupid, biting meant I would touch his skin and the thought made my skin crawl and in this deserted place, screaming was the most useless idea since the pedal powered wheelchair!

As I reached for the door to run out, he got to the lock before I could pull my hand back. My book bag, which until then was sitting comfortably on my lap, slipped and fell on the floor of the car, exposing my thighs. I pulled the hem of my skirt as far down as it could go without exposing my bottom and then I calmed myself down. This war was only going to be won I thought, by appealing to whatever ounce of dignity remained in this pathetic specimen of a man.

"Mr. Arthur, don't you think this is an inappropriate place to be together? We should be more comfortable and especially for my first time, I want it to be special."

I could barely believe those words were coming out of my mouth. I sounded like a courtesan, about to lead my gentleman friend into my chamber.

He ran his hands over my left thigh with a gleam in his eye and his breathing coming very rapidly.

"Your first time? How nice. I feel so lucky. I promise I will make it worth your while. I knew you'd understand. There's so much I can do for you…you'll see. So are you saying we can go back to my place?"

"Well…yes…but isn't your wife at home?"

"Not this evening. She has gone to the village to visit her parents so we can have the house all to ourselves."

"Then what are we waiting for?" I picked up my book bag, placed it on my lap and he proceeded to re-start the car.

We sped off towards his house, which was not far from the school campus. His attitude had changed completely from the hungry lecherous tiger to the man I thought I knew. He was smiling, turned the radio on and started humming to the music. He was insane. I tried to control my breathing as the car sped along the darkening night.

Almost a half hour after I'd climbed into that Fiat from hell, we pulled up into his driveway. He jumped out, came and opened my door and held it open for me. I followed him into the house and continued standing, as if waiting to be asked to sit down.

"I would like some water please."

"Give me just one minute," he said. "I need to go and fix the bed and then I shall bring some beer. This is a cause for celebration."

I smiled coyly.

As soon as he was out of the room, I counted to ten, ran to the front door, slowly opened it and sped out into the night with my book bag annoyingly impeding my Olympic run! I dashed through the trees, across the road, past the boys' dormitories, past the chapel. I did not look back. I then made a sharp right turn into the classroom buildings thinking that if he came after me, he'd have to plough through cement!

I finally arrived at Clark House, feeling like I'd escaped a fate worse than death. I sent some Form One girls to call my friends for me and made my way to Barbara's room where we all congregated to hear my story. In Sixth Form, we were allowed to share a room with a friend so we wouldn't have to mingle with the minions beneath us.

"Doesn't surprise me," Reinette said after hearing me. She and Thelma shared a room.

"Why doesn't it surprise you?" I asked

Everyone was silent.

"Why?" I shouted.

Charlotte decided to speak for all of them.

"I think it's because we've all had these offers. We just don't talk about them."

"And why don't you? Can't we report it to someone?"

"And be blamed for destroying someone's budding career as a teacher?" Barbara piped in.

"But they shouldn't be doing that to us either. If it's a choice

between passing your final exams for admission to university or sleeping with a nasty man, which one would you choose?" I implored.

No response.

O dear God, I thought. What are we going to do? We're all so paralyzed with fear.

So in responding to Nana's questions about studying science, I told her that when the Commonwealth Secretariat sent Mr. Yusuf Mohamed to interview girls in science and he in turn assured me that things were changing and that very soon, medical schools would be filled with women, I was skeptical. But it was good enough to let Nana know that the Queen's representative believed that girls could do science.

Tschew! Nana sucked her teeth in. She knew it was lots of bull. According to her, the girls who were successfully married were those who let the boys think they were cleverer than they were.

"Listen to me. As a woman, you are the neck and the man is surely the head. But look at my head…what is moving the head around?"

"The neck."

"Of course. So let the man be the head and you can be just below him. Be the neck but be a strong neck so you can move the head around whichever way you want. You hear?"

<<>>

There were now five children in our family: myself, Yaw, Esther, John and Grace and along with all the cousins who lived with us,

it felt crowded during the holidays. The summer saw me packing a large suitcase, filled with yams and dried fish, to go and visit my father who was still working with the Commonwealth Secretariat in London. I'd had a lovely *Kaba* and long skirt sewn in the latest craze—a puffy sleeve that looked like there were pipes running across your shoulders. Of course this was quite the far cry from my 'uniform' of the year—a white top and a white skirt, accessorized with a wooden cross that hung provocatively in between what little space I had between my breasts that I could call a cleavage. Afua and I enjoyed dressing up like Madonna…she was literally an idol for us and all we kept humming to was 'Like a Virgin". We loved being virgins. But I digress…

The flight was uneventful until we arrived at Heathrow Airport where all the passengers from the Ghana Airways flight were shuffled into a separate waiting area as all the other flights were allowed to make their way to the immigration check point. I found a seat in the middle of a large room that had all the chairs back to back. We were made to wait for about an hour before someone came in to explain that there were drugs on board the flight and that they were bringing dogs in to sniff them out. I cringed. I think they're cute but I'm not really good with dogs and I really don't like the feel of a wet tongue on my ankles. I decided to look unawares and nonchalant…hopefully, the dogs would walk right past me. Within about five minutes, there were four dogs – don't even know what breed they were but they could have passed for greyhounds – sniffing, growling, drooling. I looked down and froze as one of the dogs sniffed around my ankles. I lifted my neck a bit; just enough to show I wasn't nervous and I even managed a smile at the stone- faced customs officer. After about ten minutes

of the search, a suited gentleman walked into the room and announced that we were free to go and thank you very much. I got up, picked up my bag and proceeded to the 'way out' sign, only to be impeded in my progress by two police officers.

"Ma-am, we'd like you to come with us."

I looked behind me because I didn't think they were talking to me but everyone else was being allowed to go except me. What on earth were they talking about? I put on my sweetest voice and said: 'Me?"

"Yes. Can you please come with us?"

I followed meekly. Maybe I was being discovered as a model…I'd read that Iman was discovered in some obscure place. My debut would definitely be more dramatic since I didn't know anyone who'd been 'discovered' by a drug squad at the airport. They took me to a tiny room, barely 11 by 13 and left me alone with the female officer. She produced some scissors and proceeded to cut my pipe sleeves, pulling foam out with each snip of the instrument. I couldn't help myself—the tears just seemed to pop out of my eyes as I saw shreds of my current favourite outfit falling around me like little snowflakes. The bits of foam made me sneeze and coupled with the tears, I must have made a sorry sight. The officer then led me off to another room, smaller than the first with no windows and asked me to take my clothes off. I had no fight left in me so I obeyed.

The ordeal lasted all of about two hours, during which time, Dad was apparently waiting in the arrivals lounge, watching many black people arrive and even being able to pick out the Ghana Airways passengers out…they were the ones with the striped blue and red plastic bags fondly known in Accra as 'Ghana must go'

bags. (Turns out when Nigeria threw a million Ghanaians out of their country in 1983, saying Ghana must go, they left with their belongings in that kind of bag!). I finally trudged out of immigration and customs looking like I'd had the wind sucked right out of me, dragging my carry-on luggage and trying desperately to appear decent while having flaps of fabric hanging loosely from various limbs of my body. I was a walking rag doll.

Daddy was fuming and demanded to talk to the officer who had done this to me but was coldly told that I was suspected of being a drug mule and so they'd had to do all they could to protect the 'public'. I wish I were the public. Dad had to rush back to work so he gave me the keys and we parted ways at Green Park tube station and I continued onto Holborn where I switched to the central line towards our new house in Gants Hill. I arrived and flopped on my tiny single bed feeling like I'd had the biggest sad adventure of life. One moment, I was an innocent teenager and the next moment, I was a suspected drug dealer. I took off my clothes and then decided not to put anything on. It was so hot anyway and the room was so small that the radiator made me feel like I was back in Ghana. Besides, I was the only one at home.

I walked up and down the stairs in just my underwear, taking yams down one minute, bringing a glass of fruit juice up the next. I did this trip two or three times and then remembered that Mum had warned me to make sure the peppered porridge she'd made especially for Dad had to be refrigerated. I had made my way downstairs, popped the porridge in the fridge and had just shut the fridge door when I heard the key in the front lock turning and saw a shadowy figure leaning in towards the door.

Let me describe this house for you so you get the picture. On opening the solid wood front door, there was a little foyer where we kept all our boots. Then there was another door that was made of frosted glass so you could see through it somewhat. On opening that door you would be faced with a hallway from which there was a staircase of about fifteen steps. If you were not going upstairs, you could continue straight ahead to the kitchen and then outside to the backyard. The living room and dining room were to the right side of this hallway. As the key turned in the lock, I froze. Who on earth was this and what was I going to do? I stood there, all of my nubile body on display and all I could think of was…this is it…I won't be a virgin by the end of the day. I had made it so easy for this intruder to take advantage of me by stripping already; all he needed to do was rip my underwear off.

As the key turned one final time, I cupped my breasts in the palms of my hands…yes, sadly they fit in the palms of my hands…and I waited.

It was Uncle Peter. He walked in and just about stopped dead in his tracks. I wanted to burst out laughing because he looked much more embarrassed and shocked than I felt and that relaxed me. What an awkward situation—my Dad's forty-something year old friend staring at me almost naked and all I could do was cup my breasts!

"Hi Uncle Peter," I said as I walked past him and up the stairs, taking the steps one at a time like I was in no hurry whatsoever. He couldn't speak and walked straight to the backyard to clean the shed. I got to my room, put on my clothes and sat stunned on my

bed. I had just been introduced to a man who didn't take advantage of a vulnerable young woman. How many of those exist?

That summer passed by so quickly but I do remember calling Yaw back in Ghana and telling him about our next-door neighbours. There was a man, his wife and two daughters who were as unlike as…well, one was blonde, thin and very model like and the other….mmmhhh…how shall I put it nicely? She looked like Sebastian Coe's twin. When I told Yaw, he was offended. Offended for Sebastian, since the British track athlete was the current coolest thing and it was crass to compare him to someone else, especially a girl. I quickly assured him that on the contrary, it was the girl who'd have something to complain about if she heard what I'd said about her. She was very nice though, and would always peer over the fence to say hi as I de-scaled some fish for the evening meal. She was a student at the University of London studying physics — she had plans to work at CERN. Her sister was apparently the artsy one, studying dress design at a polytechnic in the East End and she came and went in a succession of cars. Daddy had long talks in the evening with their very intellectual father—turns out they were Jewish immigrants.

Sixth form was two years long at the end of which we had to sit a mega exam called the A-Levels; the short form for Advanced Levels. The exam was worth 100% of your final mark; I failed miserably and had to resit my exams the following year during the one-year national service, which every Ghanaian student had to participate in as a condition of university entrance. I taught grade 2 at a local school, shadowing a most awesome teacher for an entire year. It

was such a rewarding experience and made me realize I wanted to be talking for the rest of my life. I just had to find someone willing to pay me to talk and for others to listen. One of my students was called Quartey and he seemed as dull as a block of wood. All the students were either on their grade level readers or had gone beyond. Quartey was still on the grade 1 reader. Mrs. Owusu Ansah, my supervising teacher discussed him with me.

"I have no idea why he can't move ahead, I've tried everything, even sending notes home but nothing happens."

We sent another note home that day, asking his mom or dad to please come to the school; it was urgent. We were not hopeful.

The following day, as other children were milling around the courtyard waiting for the morning assembly bell to ring, we saw a tall thin woman leading Quartey through the school gates.

Mrs. Owusu Ansah readied herself and she asked me to stay and observe the parent conference. Quartey's mother walked in,

greeted us and motioned for her son to come in—he was still at the door. The eight- year old walked in with eyes swollen from beatings and a cracked lip. He looked terrible. I had to hide my shock at this massacre and wondered what Mrs. Owusu Ansah was going to say.

"Madam Teacher, I am sorry that I am now coming in, but you know, Quartey never showed me the letters you wrote."

"Thank you for coming Madam but do you not check his work every night?"

"Mmmmhhhh… Teacher. I work at the seaside, I buy fish from the fishermen early in the morning, so if I am not there by 5am, I don't get any fish. After I buy it, I then come back home, smoke it and then immediately get it to market by midday. I am in the market

till late in the evening and by the time I have cleared up and gone home, Quartey has gone to sleep."

Mrs. Owusu Ansah looked sad.

"Is Quartey's father at home?"

"Father? Which father? Quartey does not know who his father is."

Oh dear, I thought. Poor Quartey had the ingredients of a troubled childhood for sure. We showed her his work but seeing what she'd done to him before she knew the extent of his lassitude, we quickly covered it up by saying we had seen some improvement. We feared she'd beat the child to death.

Reading time. Every child comes up to Mrs. Owusu Ansah or myself and reads a few pages from the leveled reader. I wearily got to Quartey's turn and motioned for him to join me at the teacher's desk. He brought his level 1 reader with him. I opened the book and started at page 1, for the umpteenth time. I prepared to begin my usual daydream, the one where I was married to this extremely rich man who didn't mind that I wanted to be a scientist. Said rich man would have no sisters or mother so I would have no bothersome female in-laws. In this daydream, I taught part-time because teaching was so rewarding and when I turned 50 I was awarded the Keys to the City of Accra for my humanitarian deeds. Today, Quartey cut short my daydream as he finished reading page 1.

And then page 2.

And then page 3.

Wait a minute, Quartey reading was not part of my daydream but it did seem like a dream, because within 5 minutes, he had finished Reader Number 1! I whisked Reader 2 from Mrs. Owusu Ansah's desk and the child ate the words alive!

Quartey read a grade 3 book that day. I struggle with the inference that the beating brought out the best in him, but there's overwhelming evidence that it had something to do with it. I wonder where he is today.

I retook my exams at the end of my one year of national service, doing a tad better. There was a double cohort that year so my grades were still not competitive enough. Dad was still working in England so I was told to pack my bags and go off to school in London. I was sad to leave. All my friends were staying behind and besides, London was cold. Everyone helped me pack and Nana sat me down before the taxi took me to the airport to give me her nuggets of wisdom.

"Study hard but remember that you must be the neck. God will never leave you, you hear? He has done so many great and mighty things for you so the moment you start doubting him, it is an indication that you are ungrateful. Before you marry—and I pray you find a good man—learn how to cook properly. Remember that you cannot eat your beauty and most of the marriages fail because some stupid girl thought cooking was not important. Things are to be tried, you know? An old lady cooked stones and they produced soup! The way to a man's heart is through his stomach and although I have told you several times, you think getting a prize for writing a test about cooking means you can cook. *Tschew,* that's not cooking; that's writing a test. Always keep family close. You will have many friends but you will only have one family. Your brothers and sisters—take care of them. There's a reason why you came first, so live up to it. Don't ever be afraid of anyone —no one should be able break your spirit. If at any time,

you feel weak, remember that it is better to be a lion for a day than a sheep for life. Don't forget where you came from you hear?"

I never saw Nana again.

11

"I don't want to leave but I must"

1989

The week before Nana died, she complained of severe stomach cramps and was rushed from our Abelenkpe house to the Achimota Hospital. The doctors were not optimistic, citing an enlarged heart and kidney failure. They didn't think she'd last even a few days, but she kept asking for Daddy. Mummy told her Daddy would be home soon, after his conference in Addis Ababa. Daddy arrived in Ghana on the 19th November and was rushed to the hospital to see her.

"Kwabena," she said softly, using his Ghanaian day name.
"Yes Nana, I'm here. Please do not leave us."
"Why not? Look at me, all skin and bones. I think I've done what I was meant to do, don't you think? You and Emma are good for

each other and Mary is now studying at one of the Queen's many universities in London. What more could I want? Just give her a message for me. Tell her I've prayed for her so that she will find a good man. Tell her to look after her brothers and sisters—even when they are being naughty. She must also remember to take a shower every day—it's not good for a woman not to bathe but you know these young people—they think they know everything. Thank you for naming Grace after me, because now I know that I will live on, if only in name…but that's okay. And that beard of yours, when are you going to cut it? It makes you look very sinister and that's not a good thing. I don't want to leave but I must."

Nana died the following day, on the November 20, 1989 while I was in my second year of university in London. Her funeral was said to be so well attended that to this day, villagers in the town of Asamankese still talk about the old lady who didn't have adequate schooling but had professors, doctors, engineers and lawyers at her funeral; a prestigious honour in that part of the world. In many Ghanaian tribes it is customary for the deceased person's favourite outfits to be put in the coffin for her to wear in the next world. When the family went into Nana's rooms to look inside her suitcases for something to send along with her, all were empty save for one. She had given away the gold and silver brocades Dad purchased for her every Christmas. She had given away the bright scarves Mummy had given to her every Sunday when Nana would confess with a sly look on her face that she couldn't find her scarves. Just one suitcase yielded some goods: two pieces of cloth, her worn out *Twi* Bible with markings everywhere, her spectacles, and a letter from seven-year-old me.

37 Northdene
Chigwell, Essex
UK
12 March 1976

Dear Nana,

We miss you so much. Will you please come to
London? There are some bad people being
bad to us and we want you to tell them to
leave us alone. Did you eat today? We have
our own TV and like to watch Batman. You
would like Batman because he takes care of
people.
We love you,
Mary, Emmanuel & Esther

PS: Mary wrote this because Emmanuel and
Esther can't spell but they agree with me.

Part 2

Sankofa

"Go back and fetch it"

12

"Do You Still Have Your Leopard Spots?"

2008

Since leaving Ghana in 1987 I'd returned only twice, going no further than Accra and staying for no more than a week. For my fortieth birthday in 2008 I summoned the courage to go not just to Accra, but to Asamankese, with the hope that in remembering Nana, that gnawing emptiness I sometimes felt would go away. I was a successful teacher, had completed my graduate degree, had three rambunctious sons and I was in a healthy relationship with a man I thought Nana would approve of. Maybe it was time to go and tell her.

Before leaving Toronto, I called Mummy to find out what to buy as gifts, since in her words 'You've forgotten everything that is

important here', meaning I have no clue that people in the village will not be amused by a Colleen McCullough book or a Spiderman DVD.

"As I was saying, it's the children who like books so don't bring any adult books—the adults are busy looking for food for their children—unless the books are about the works of the Holy Spirit of course," she reminded me for the umpteenth time.

"So what should I bring then?"

"Towels, plenty of them. And don't buy dark colors too much. I know you like brown but we don't like that color here for things."

"What's wrong with brown?" I countered.

"It's just like black."

No kidding.

"And what is wrong with black?" I nervously asked as I stood half way between my closet and the bathroom, peering into rows of black suits, black pants, black shirts, black shoes and black scarves.

"Ei, have you forgotten that we wear black when somebody dies?"

"Yes, I remember, Mom, but does that mean it can't be worn anywhere else?"

"Ok, I can see you want to argue."

No I don't. I'm just asking a question.

"Mummy please, I'm not arguing. I'm just wondering why black and brown and dark red are not popular but that's okay. I understand." There, that usually did it.

"You're forgiven," she replied.

For what?

"So as I was saying, lovely towels with plenty of 'fluffy' so it is soft against the skin, you know what I am talking about right?"

"Yes Mum, plenty of 'fluffy."

"And then sprays."

"Sprays?" I'm thinking pesticides here.

"Yes, sprays. What you call perfume but what we call sprays. Because it's so hot, people really appreciate not having a sweaty smell."

"Ah, I see. And is there any particular spray?"

"Not really but just buy decent ones—the ones still in their containers."

I resisted responding to that one. I wondered if there were any perfumes that were not in containers and if so, what would they be in?

"And, don't forget to bring some of your old clothes. You people over there are good at not wearing your clothes out, so even after several years, your clothes still look new. Somehow our sun destroys clothes I think."

What a scientific hypothesis that is begging for research, I thought. I rang off and began the packing.

<<>>

I'm in mum & dad's lovely 'summer hut' which is situated on the compound of their bungalow in Pokuase, a suburb nestled in the hills surrounding Accra about an hour from the center of the city. I've told Mummy that calling it a summer hut is a bit redundant since it's always summer in Ghana but stubbornly refuses to call it anything else. It's like when she comes to visit us in Canada and pretends she can't speak English when we're at the grocery store.

The fireflies and birds are already singing and the brooms have ushered in a new morning. I've stretched out as far as my limbs can get me and yet my body is still aching from all the tiredness;

mostly emotional and mental, I guess. Today, I have to go and visit a university and a church office to try to forge some links between them and my university back in Canada. As I start wading through all my western clothes, Mum creeps up behind me.

"Good morning, did you sleep well?" she asks.

"I did…and you?"

"Very fine thank you. Are you looking for something to wear?"

I held up a few samples of clothing I brought from Toronto: jeans, casual tops with straps, and skirts that were knee length.

"Don't you have anything decent?"

I laughed.

"If by decent, you mean 'do you have anything that covers every inch of skin' then I don't."

"Ei, but you are going to a church office and a university too. Don't you want them to respect you?"

"Yes I do Mum, but why would I be measured by my dress?"

"Mary, listen to me. Over here—in case you've forgotten—a doctor, which you are, and especially a professor—which you also are—should not take her position lightly at all! It is better not to wear the trousers to the church office, so find a decent skirt that goes down a little bit and then find a nice blouse to top it off. I hope you brought your spectacles, ohhh?"

So I chucked my jeans—clearly not a good pair of trousers—and ditched my shirt that showed a teensy bit of cleavage. Out came a camisole that I could hike up to cover every inch of my skin in and around my bust and added a very light jacket open to the front. On went my glasses that are really meant for reading and not for just walking around; I'm far-sighted. I walked over to Mum's room to get approval. She gave a quick glance and nodded.

"*Eh heh.* Yes, now you look like you could be a doctor and a professor. As for you people who've lived abroad, you don't know how to dress like your position *kraa*. You don't know how to dress at all. Sometimes, I see the white people in Accra and they are wearing shorts and short-sleeved shirts...too simple I say. And you know, maybe he is a manager of a company and he is wearing shorts."

I chuckled at the expectation that the more 'important' you were, the more you should wear 'serious' clothes, like suits, long sleeved shirts, long skirts and unrevealing blouses!
"Happy now?" I suggested gleefully.
"Of course I'm happy. My daughter will not go and disgrace me with her little dresses with the big holes in front and bottoms all short. Now you look respectable."

Glad she's happy. I've realized pleasing Mom in this way is not a big deal at all. Daddy isn't as fussy though he does give me the once over. Since retiring after spending over thirty years in diplomatic service, he's become an interesting mix of Western and Ghanaian values. That means that on any given day you can find him surfing the net—he even has a Facebook page; and yet he loves listening to indigenous highlife music, the kind filled with proverbs.

Its evening and I'm tired after a busy day. Tomorrow I go to Asamankese. I am in conflict—guilty that I've been away for so long. While I've been gone, all the old guard have died: Nana, Papa Kwabena, Papa Lawyer, Teacher Kwabena, Maa Yaa and even Sisi

Yanto. Why didn't I come earlier? I'm feeling like I need to explain myself, especially to Nana. To prove to her that I haven't lost an essential part of myself and that I'm still her granddaughter. The air is still thick with the humidity I remember from the age of ten. I can't sleep for all the apprehension trying to push its way past the air in my lungs; all because I am going back to Asamankese for the first time since I was a teenager.

What will I find there? Who is left? Probably no one will remember me. I want to listen to sounds, look at places and faces quietly and deeply. I have to sleep but I can't, so I'm up writing this and wondering if I will ever forgive myself for taking so long to come back 'home'.

First thing this morning, I donned my *kaba* and *slit* and took a seat beside Mummy in the SUV that will take us to Asamankese. We passed familiar places. Seems nothing much has changed in three decades. We made the requisite stop in Nsawam to buy "designer" bread. The street hawkers smothered us with their wares. A memory returned, of Nana bargaining for *chofi*, and I felt a pang of longing that I couldn't control. To make matters worse, Mummy was acting just like Nana did thirty years ago.

'Hey, how much is your *chofi*?" she asks.

"One cedi fifty *pesewas*." said a young girl of about fifteen.

"I'll take each one for fifty *pesewas*—give me four," she adds imperiously.

"Oh Madam, I can't give it to you for fifty, I will not make a profit," the young girl begged.

"But why is it so expensive?" Mummy asks.

Wait. Oh my. Was she going to say the oil used to fry it was from Ivory Coast? That turkey tail, fatty already with calories unheard of, was smothered in that oil and deep-fried at temperatures well over a hundred degrees Celsius. I wondered what the average cholesterol levels in this town were—let alone the rest of Ghana.

"Madam, the oil is so expensive these days. We have to buy it from China because that one is the cheapest."

But of course; clothes, military arms, anal suppositories, cell phones and now *chofi* oil? Was there anywhere on earth that *was* cheaper than China? Mummy gave in and paid one cedi for each *chofi*.

Nana would have disowned her.

Barely an hour after we left Pokuase, Mummy announced that we were approaching Asamankese. My memories of the trip to Asamankese as a child had me estimating a three-hour journey and yet, this journey was just under an hour. Maybe it was the newer road. Maybe it was the better car. Whatever. At least one thing had changed.

We got to the town limits and I stepped out of the car to take a picture of a sign that read 'Asamankese High Street'. I sat back in the car and tried to go way back in time and found that it made my stomach ache with pain. We entered the town and were assaulted by sounds and smells that jostled with other thoughts in my head. I asked Mummy to show me the bus station where we arrived on our very first trip to Asamankese in 1977. She pointed to the right where about twenty shacks, arranged in a haphazard fashion, peppered the landscape. There were about ten or so buses, all old, all dilapidated and yet still mobile, waiting at the bus station. Why did it seem so small now? It used to be so big and loud and imposing. We got to a T-junction and turned right and then

elation swept over me, coursing through my veins with such vigor that it gave me new breath. For right there at that junction was a kiosk that I remembered, a shop that I remembered and a gutter I used to jump over. And over there was Auntie Esther's shop where she used to sell colorful fabrics.

"Does Auntie Esther still sell cloth?" I asked Mummy.

"No oh. She sells cutlery now. Cloth is too expensive."

At the junction, I could have walked 'home' and what a good feeling it was—to know that I could find my way back to a place of belonging. We slowly made our way up the hill and came to a stop in front of another row of kiosks. Now, from memory, I knew that Old House was on the left but I couldn't recognize it. Oddly enough, the right side of the street hadn't changed, but the left side had.

Mummy asked the driver to go and find out if any of the aunties were home. I took the time to look around and saw children with their Bibles walking to church. They playfully chanted their Bible verses to one another; no doubt there was going to be a competition and they needed to be ready. Everyone seemed to be going about the business of getting ready for church. I wondered if the Pentecost Church was still the same?

Our driver came back to tell us that Sisi Yaa Yaabi was at home. Mum led me in between some wooden enclosures, past an unfinished brick wall and lots of dirty water and goats lapping it up, and lo and behold, there was the cave-like entrance to Old House. I walked gingerly up the stone steps, wanting to throw up due to extreme nervousness and anxiety. I wanted to see Nana again.

I was desperate to see everyone again. I entered the compound that I remembered so well and was saddened to see that it was empty. Some children I didn't know where running where I used to run,

stopping to smile and stare at my outfit; my feeble attempt to look as Ghanaian as possible. I felt oddly out of place.

I looked to the left, where Nana's rooms used to be; the large cooler that always had cold water deep within its bowels was no longer there. I looked to the north end of the compound where Maa Yaa would sit with her legs wrapped around the wooden mortar while Yaw K and Mr. Long Man pounded *fufu* that she kneaded.
It wasn't there.
There was no fire, no earthenware pot, no mortar, no pestle. Instead in their place was the beginning of a cement enclosure—a couple of extra bedrooms, Mummy explained. Over there to the right was the washroom that scared the crap out of us. It was just a deep hole with a wooden slab on it that we had to squat on. Esther was so scared she'd fall in that she didn't use the washroom at all in Asamankese! I stood in the middle of the compound house and wondered why I'd waited so long to come back. Why didn't I come back when they were all alive?

Sisi Yaa Yaabi came out of Nana's room and smothered me in kisses and oohs and aahhs and 'Look at you, you've grown'—*yah no kidding*. She ushered us into Nana's room and it had changed. There was now modern furniture where raffia chairs had stood, kettles and some modern equipment where pictures of dead relatives had had a place of honour. There were still lace curtains on every doorway and every window and albums proudly displayed on the center table.

Nana would come out soon…
I couldn't breathe. My heart was begging to cry. Somebody rescue

me please because I have to smile and laugh and say all sorts of things I am not in the mood to say. I just want everyone to leave so I can cry and cry and cry…but no one is leaving me here. They have no idea how heart-rending this is for me. Have no idea that I am purging something in this trip and I don't know what it is. Nana should be here and hugging me and telling me I'm still okay and I'm still Ghanaian and I'm going to be fine. But no one knows that I'm feeling this and I can't tell anyone because I'm not sure anyone will get it. Will anyone understand the sadness that is welling up in me aching to be let go of something I can't identify? And why am I going through this I ask myself? I'm not sure. But I do know that I have to cry but not here, not with everyone watching and laughing and happy. So the pretense continues and I am…sad.

The next stop is New House and as the car makes it way up the hill, I know where it's going. We stop at a *kenkey* seller, turn right and there it is—New House in all its old faded glory. The walls need a paint job, but every thing else is the same. There are still kids running around half-naked and people still stare at a nice car even though this is now the 21st century and Appiah John is not the only one with the car in this bustling metropolis! We get out and go inside to where we once performed a laundry-detergent commercial to the delight of my grandfather. Inside the living room, musty from disuse and sparsely decorated with plastic chairs, an old majestic memory creeps up on me, of Papa Kwabena holding court with loud music playing in the background.

I wonder why things seemed to have moved backward in this place. Why do I remember it as so much more beautiful than it is today?

There is no 13-inch television and there is no gramophone. Auntie Adjo, one of my favourite aunts who has a nervous laugh, comes out of a room; she is now grey-haired and missing an arm from an accident a couple of years ago. I hug her as if my life depends on it and she looks at me—wondering I'm sure, how Ghanaian I am. Or so I think. Paranoia has recently become a close friend.

I walk around the room, entranced with the pictures of a bygone era. There is Papa Kwabena looking the gentleman, with a suit and a parting in his hair. There is Teacher Kwaku looking like the big baby he always was. And who was that one with the smirk? Of course Papa Lawyer. Couldn't miss those bulging eyes and the self-assured attitude. The men were neatly displayed on the decaying shelf with cobwebs dancing around their edges. I wondered where the women were—Nana and Maa Yaa. Mummy pointed to one of the walls near the door and I walked slowly to look at this younger sister of Nana's. Still smiling. All with red X's on their foreheads. Where was Nana?

"Nana's picture is at Master Danso's house," Mummy replied.

I wondered why. Master Danso was the husband of Sisi Yanto, Mummy's older sister. He was in his late eighties and used to be a Head Master hence the title Master Danso, even twenty years after he received his first pension cheque.

I asked the driver to take me to Master Danso's and the mission felt like one of life and death. Somehow, it felt like if I didn't do this quickly, I wouldn't remember how she looked. We walked up to a small house, neatly landscaped with milkweed bushes and moringa plants and knocked on the door.

"*Agoo.* Hello?"

"Yes?"

A young man opened the door. We told him we were there to see Master and he took us into another musty room, heavy with curtains and thick with hot air. I thought I'd suffocate and wondered how long it'd take to get used to people not opening their windows! While waiting, I scanned the room looking for pictures and found them in the usual spots—on the floor propped up against a wall or up on a ledge about a foot above eye level. I asked the boy to take the pictures down for me. A cloud of dust sprinkled on my face and as I coughed, I gingerly carried the pictures to the verandah. I placed one in particular—the icon—on the four-foot wall and took a look at it.

Nana.

A younger Nana, but still her. She didn't have a red X on her forehead. One would think she never smiled or laughed given her austere look in this picture. But there she was, sitting resolutely in a chair some minion must have carried outside for her, wearing shoes that today would sell for $129.99 because they are retro, with her hands placed on the requisite purse. Look at her eyes. What's in them? They look tired. Worried. Frustrated. What was she thinking when she took this? Where was I when she took this? Was I alive yet? What hopes did she have for me? Would she be proud of me? I looked long and hard at the picture, willing her to talk to me. I had to capture her image digitally or I might never get the chance again. I took about six stills, came inside to say hello to Master Danso, exchanged the usual pleasantries and made my way back to New House. I didn't say anything to anyone because there didn't seem to be words that described what I was feeling. It was just as well I was here alone. What would I tell my three children who have asked me repeatedly questions about who they are?

Next stop: the gravesite but Mummy was having an anxiety attack of some sort and didn't want to go there just yet. All the emotion of the day was really beginning to tell on me also, so I didn't argue with her. My hair was all wet from sweat and I felt like hair had suddenly grown on my legs in the last few hours making me feel like I wasn't even presentable enough for such a spiritual visit.

"It hasn't been weeded for some time you know? Infact, for a few years," Mummy confessed sadly.

"Why ever not?" I asked.

"Whenever I've paid someone to weed the area and clean the gravestone, they *chop* the money. Over the years, I've come to understand that she is no longer there so I've decided to leave it until I can be here almost every week to make sure it is well looked after."

We were both quiet sitting in our car just outside New House. She abruptly turned to me and she had changed.

"Let's go to the gravesite...I think you have something to say to her don't you?"

I smiled. I had promised to visit Asamankese each time I came to Ghana. We'd purchase a marble gravestone without any words on it, just her name Nana Grace Akosua Obesebea and the date of her passing, which was the 20th November 1989.

By this time we were at the cemetery—a badly kept piece of land that had weeds all over it. I was surprised Mummy knew where it was since everything was so overgrown and many of the gravestones were missing. Mummy and I held hands and stared silently ahead. My tears tasted salty and the taste elicited more tears.

I think I now know what mourning is. I think it's that feeling that

takes over when grief starts to dissipate, if it ever does. I remembered Nana's favorite song and as I raised it softly, Mummy joined in with me....I could almost hear Nana singing with us:

"Den na min fa, min yi wa yeh
Tu mi wura, dasebre
Fa wo honhom, pa no ma yen
Na wa sem a yeh me feh
Na wo do nsenkyereni
Ni wo dom no, tra m'adwene
Tumfo ni O, Ohene kese
Ye da wa se, Yi wa yeh"

The songwriter, in awe of God's care and mercy asks what he can do to glorify Him. Towards the end, the songwriter, still in awe of God's grace, realizes it surpasses his understanding, and all he can do is say thanks. A beautiful song and so very much...a Nana song. For her, everything came from God, both good and bad. She made sure that in both circumstances, she gave thanks.

I stood silently by the small plot, trying to figure out what else I would write on her stone since nothing would do her justice. For a woman who seemed to never shut up, there were no words to describe her legacy, at least not on a tombstone. Much of who she was is in me—'the child of a lion is a lion'. I don't have to write it down. It's in my heart and spirit. And besides, knowing Nana, she'd have something to say about whatever was written on her tombstone!

Nana: Is this all you could write? No wonder our elders

admonished us to pretend we were dead so we'd see those who love us!

Me: *Ei* Nana, please oh…you're still loved. It's just that…

Nana: It's just that what? Hopefully in your old age, you are learning some wisdom! You see? I told you to learn to cook because you couldn't eat your beauty didn't I? Now look at you— you're no longer young are you?

Nana never did mince her words. She's just called me old and my North American psyche is smarting from this. I cannot be called old and I cannot be called fat. Period. Of course she doesn't stop there; Nana may be dead but I can hear her in my head asking what seem to her like important questions.

"Why did you leave the white man's land, the one flowing with milk and honey to come to Ghana to suffer?"

"Well, I'm only here for a short while but I plan to come one day and stay. I had to leave Ghana, Nana…otherwise I'd never appreciate it. What makes it even harder is that I like Canada too… and this is why I had to come back here…to make sure there was room in my heart for two places."

"And is there?" she asks.

I pause, choosing my words carefully.

"Yes. Yes there is. I'm really glad we came to Ghana when we did, as children. I think I've found that purpose I was looking for, by coming back."

"Big *Brofo!* You still speak English so well."

"Nana!!!" I said playfully. "Of course I speak English well—it's all I've spoken since leaving Ghana!"

"And that husband of yours, Joe. He is a good man."

"Yes, I know," I softly murmur, aware that Nana never had what I have—a partner I am actively sharing my life with.

"Don't forget to be a strong neck you hear?"

I smile. How can I forget that?

I keep thinking of what I've found by going back; to a sort of beginning. The Adinkra symbols of Ghana are varied representations of pieces of wisdom. One of my favorites is *Sankofa*, which translated into English means 'Go back and fetch it'. As I muse, I realise what I've done; I've gone back to fetch what was mine—a heritage that only I could have gone back to claim. I'd feared so much that I would never find it, that I'd not even know it when I found it. Childhood experiences, teenage shenanigans, college days and the immigrant life in North America had had such a profound effect on me—like rain beating down hard—that I'd forgotten that I could turn all of it around for good.

My reverie is broken by another question from her:

"So can we say that you still have your leopard spots?"

Of course she had to end with a proverb! This was one of my favorites too.

"I got them the day I was born, remember? You gave them to Mummy and she gave them to me. I'm beginning to see them in the boys too," I reply confidently.

She sighs deeply and then smiles wanly. Her nose crinkles and her eyes dance. I know she's about to say the proverb...and this time, I am listening with all my heart, my mind, my soul. And this time, I totally get it. Finally.

"Rain may fall hard on the leopard's skin, but it cannot wash out the spots. Those rains that fell on you—they didn't wash them away after all."

I nod, tears slowly dripping down my face.

"For a moment, I feared they would," she softly says.

"So did I Nana…so did I."

EPILOGUE

After teaching for several years at primary, secondary and university levels, I'm now in an administrative role as principal of a k-12 school in Mississauga, Ontario. I love my kids; the kindergarten students hug me in the hallway; the primary kids say hi; the middle schoolers pretend I don't exist and the high school students think I'm a scourge. Did I say I love my job?

My husband Joe and I have since taken our three sons to Ghana. We have built a school on a plot of land that is very close to where Papa Kwabena bequeathed me a plot of land to build a hospital. I sold the one he bequeathed in the nineties, to help pay for Teacher Kwaku's hospital bills prior to his death. We started with a junior kindergarten class (ages 4 & 5) in 2012 and are working our way up, one grade at a time. For the past four years, I've used a CIDA grant to send 2nd and 3rd year undergraduates to teach literacy to women in Asamankese. Every semester, two or three say goodbye to their Canadian families and stay in the town where I had so many experiences. There are now 12 alumni and they now eat *fufu* without gagging!

My parents, Emmanuel and Emma, are wonderfully retired in Ghana. They both went back to school: Dad at 70 to earn a doctorate and Mum at 60 to earn her diploma as a personal support worker. Daddy lectures part-time at the Pentecost University College just outside of Accra and is such a techie that we often chat on skype and he even has a Facebook page! Mum of course has started a new business; she has the salon on the side—it's called Emmaliz Salon —and she now produces locally-made shampoos and conditioners on which are plastered 'Made in USA' labels. Go figure.

Yaw (Emmanuel Jnr.) lives in Ghana and is married to his childhood sweetheart Julia and together they have five children. We tease them often about how they find the time to run their Film Production Company, Revele Films. We were thrilled when they won, together with younger brother John, an award for Best Film at the African Movie Awards—the African version of the Oscars. Their most recent movie *Elmina* ran as an art installation at the Tate Modern in London and it was also ranked as one of the top 100 iconic artworks in the last five years by www.artinfo. com.

Esther and her husband Obed have two boys and they live in Texas where Esther teaches high school Spanish and French. She enjoys writing children's stories and has completed her Master's Degree in Education. As well, she takes students on trips to Quebec and France. Just because...

John completed his master's in Oxford, England after getting married in 2008 to his physician wife Vanessa. Their wedding in London was the last time the whole family was together again

and it was an amazing time, laughing into the wee hours of the morning. He has worked with Emmanuel on several film and TV projects and was an actor and producer on *Elmina*. John has worked on community organizing in London and is currently working on film projects in Africa and Europe.

My baby sister Grace, who featured very little in this memoir because she was so young, was born when I was thirteen. Her spirit name was Nana's spirit name so she is called Obesebea. She is a business analyst and lives in Toronto with her husband Johnson and their two daughters. Grace is a mini Nana, waiting to be unleashed on an unsuspecting world…

His Majesty's Christian School, Asamankese
(2012)

This is the school Joe and I have built in the town of Asamankese. Although it's not built on the land Papa Kwabena gave me, it's not too far away—he could have walked from New House to it everyday!

Appendix 1: Map Of Ghana

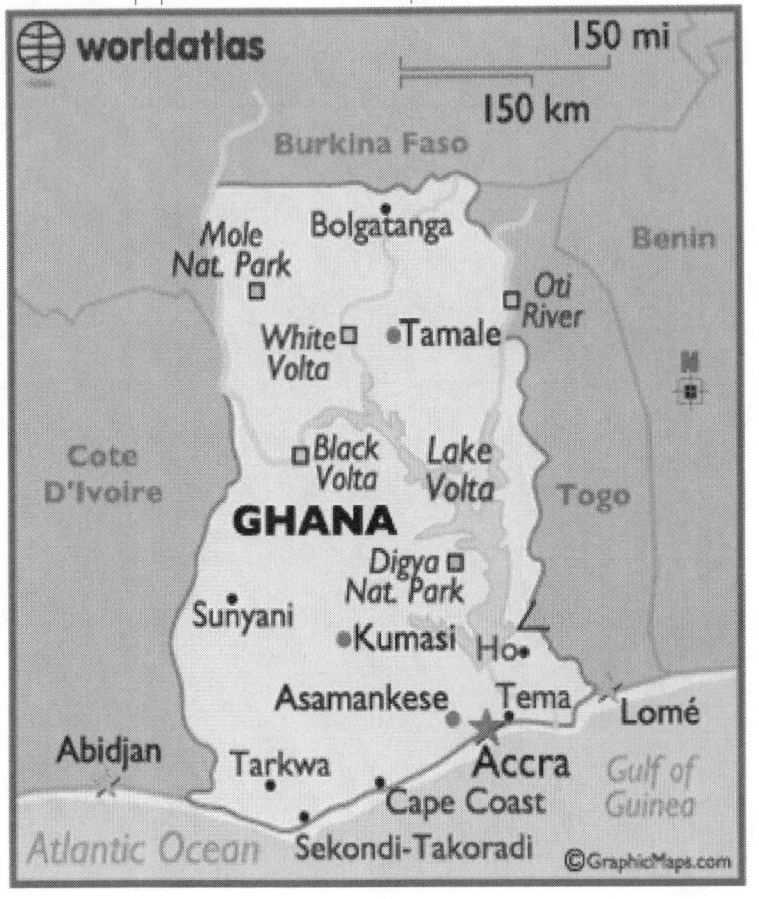

http://www.worldatlas.com/webimage/countrys/africa/gh.htm

Appendix 2:
Guide to some Ghanaian words used in the memoir.

Anum: The name of a language and a tribe in the Eastern Region

ayen: A witch (not a fun one as celebrated during Halloween in the West. This kind of witch casts evil spells, brings death and disease and is definitely NOT celebrated)

banku: A thick corn meal that is boiled and eaten with okra and meat or fish

bofrot: a bread-like snack that is deep fried.

borga: A Ghanaian immigrant who makes money abroad and comes to show off in Ghana. They usually had jehri curled hair and wore baggy jeans and spoke with an exaggerated American accent

brofo: English language

chofi: Fried turkey tail. A deadly dose of cholesterol but so yummy!

chop: Depending on the context, it can mean 'spend' e.g. that girl is going to 'chop' the boy's money. In it's simplest form, it means 'to eat'.

chopbox: The Ghanaian version of a tuckbox, where boarding students keep non-perishable items like sardines, milo, powdered milk, sugar, canned milk, gari and shito for those hungry days when the dining hall food is not enough
E-n-h? : A nasal sound that Ghanaians make that means 'Really?" It can come at the beginning of a sentence or at the end

Ewe: Pronounced 'eweh' is the name of the Eastern most tribe in Ghana.

fufu: A meal made from boiled cassava, plantain or yam pounded to make a smooth dumpling-like ball. It is eaten with soup and meat and tastes wonderful when eaten with your fingers!

gari: A grainy, white crunchy derivative of cassava that is eaten by most people in Ghana. When water is added to it, it resembles and tastes like couscous

gele: A stiff, ornate scarf folded and tied into an elaborate headdress, most common in Nigeria. In Ghana, women wear it for special occasions [definition courtesy of Mamle Wolo in *The*

Kaya Girl]

Harmattan: A dry wind that is felt during the dry season. It is akin to North America's fall weather

Hausa: A tribe that predominantly occupies northern Ghana and Nigeria

Houseboy/girl/house help(s): A (fe)male who stays with the family and does chores around the house and babysits little children as well. Often, these house help come from very poor families in the village and by living with a family in the city, they are able to make an income and even attend school

jollof rice: Rice that is cooked in stew and looks orange in color; similar to rice pilaf

kaba: The top garment of a woman's traditional dress

Kai: This is an expression that is like saying 'how disgusting!'

kalabule: Corruption

kenkey: A cornmeal meal that is boiled in corn leaves and often allowed to ferment prior to cooking

knocking ceremony: A ceremony that begins the process of requesting for a woman's hand in marriage

konkonte: A meal that looks like fufu but is made from dried

cassava. It has had a bad rap as a poor man's meal with the moniker 'face the wall' often used to describe how disgraced someone feels while eating it; they can't look you in the face...they must 'face the wall'

Kraa: An explanation of shock that means 'not at all'.

kwasia: Stupid, good for nothing wastrel

maa chio: Good morning

Maanum: A respectful term used in Anum for someone older who is not necessarily your mother. Since the extended family tends to live together, Maanum usually refers to the oldest woman in the extended family

Obosomase: A town in the Eastern Region whose name means 'underneath the god'

omo-tuo: A rice meal in which the rice is cooked and shaped into balls to be eaten with soup

paa: A word that can mean 'a lot' when used at the end of a sentence or at the beginning. It can also be said as a question, in which case it means 'Really"?

pesewas: the Ghanaian equivalent of cents. 100 pesewas make 1 Cedi just as 100 cents make 1 dollar

shabo-shabo: Very quick

"I can be changed by what happens to me, but I refuse to be reduced by it."

-Maya Angelou